D1349969

1804553150

# OFFICERS AND GENTLEMEN

*For duty, for honour, for love*

Bound by honour and family ties, three brave men fought for their lives in France…

Now, back in the drawing rooms of England, they face a new battle as three beautiful women lay siege to their scarred hearts!

**COURTED BY THE CAPTAIN**
Already available

**PROTECTED BY THE MAJOR**
Already available

**DRAWN TO LORD RAVENSCAR**
February 2014

## AUTHOR NOTE

This is the third in my latest Regency trilogy about cousins Adam Miller and Hallam and Paul Ravenscar. Both Adam and Hal have found love. Will Paul be able to put the tragedy of his brother's death behind him and find happiness for himself—or will he be forever cursed with guilt? It should all have been Mark's—the title, the estate, and most of all the girl Paul believed his brother loved…Lucy.

So here is the last of this current series about Regency star-crossed lovers. Enjoy— and tell me what you think through my website if you wish: www.lindasole.co.uk

Love to you all.

# DRAWN TO
# LORD RAVENSCAR

Anne Herries

First published in Great Britain 2014
by Mills & Boon, an imprint of Harlequin (UK) Limited,
Large Print edition 2014
Harlequin (UK) Limited, Eton House, 18-24 Paradise Road,
Richmond, Surrey TW9 1SR

© 2014 Anne Herries

ISBN: 978 0 263 23970 6

Printed and bound in Great Britain
by CPI Antony Rowe, Chippenham, Wiltshire

**Anne Herries** lives in Cambridgeshire, where she is fond of watching wildlife and spoils the birds and squirrels that are frequent visitors to her garden. Anne loves to write about the beauty of nature, and sometimes puts a little into her books, although they are mostly about love and romance. She writes for her own enjoyment, and to give pleasure to her readers. Anne is a winner of the Romantic Novelists' Association Romance Prize. She invites readers to contact her on her website: www.lindasole.co.uk

# Prologue

'**W**ell, Ravenscar,' the Duke of Wellington said. 'I regret that you must leave us. You have been invaluable these past months, one of my best aides. However, your duty is clear. Your father needs you and asks for your return; therefore, you must go.'

'I must resign my commission,' Captain Paul Ravenscar said regretfully. He straightened his shoulders, a tall lean wiry man with an upright bearing. 'My cousin Hallam has been attending to estate affairs since…the death of my brother, but he has his own duties and cannot continue indefinitely, for he is married and his wife is with child. Besides, it is my duty to care for the estate. If my father dies…'

Paul's gaze wandered about the elegant room, which was small but tastefully appointed, the doors painted cream and gold. He had become used to working here with his leader and would miss the work and the comradeship of his fellow officers.

'You are his heir,' Wellington said. 'You have my permission to leave. I vow it was easier to defeat Bonaparte on the field of battle than to settle the peace, but it is almost finished. I, too, shall return to England very soon.'

'Yes, sir. I thought it must be so... I can only thank you for giving me the chance to serve you at a time when I was near to desperation. Had I not been able to throw myself into the work...'

'No need to thank me, Ravenscar. I was glad to have you,' Wellington said brusquely. 'Get off with you then...and remember a man must always do his duty by his family, as he would his country.'

Paul clicked his heels, shook the duke's hand and walked from the office that Wellington had used these past months. So much wrangling over the peace terms and the settlement of Europe had taken place that these walls had shaken with the ferocity of the duke's anger, but it was as he said, the peace was settled now and they could all return to England.

Paul was thoughtful as he walked swiftly towards his lodgings. With luck, he would be at Calais within two days and another two should see him back at Ravenscar. He prayed that he would be in time, for Hallam's letter had spoken of his father as being very ill.

He was struck by guilt, because he knew that he ought to have stayed at home to relieve his father of the burden that his estate must place on him—for even though Hallam had done everything he could, Paul knew that his father might have been easier had his one remaining son been there to shoulder his everyday cares.

He would blame himself if his father died. Yet he'd had to get away.

Paul had felt the death of his elder brother Mark like a crushing load that had almost suffocated him. Mark was the golden one, the hero—the chosen one who should have inherited the estate and title that would one day now pass to Paul. Lord Ravenscar had always favoured his elder son, but Paul could never blame him…everyone had adored Mark from the moment he was born. A big man with strong shoulders and thighs, he was better at everything, outshining his younger brother at every turn. Paul should have hated him or been jealous, instead, he'd worshipped Mark. He had resented nothing that Mark had…except for Lucy Dawlish…

A swathe of pain made him gasp, for Paul had not been able to forget her. He had tried, God knew, he had tried to put her out of his mind these past months he'd spent in Vienna with Wellington. He had no right to think of her. She had belonged to Mark, would have been his wife had not Mark been foully murdered. She loved him—and for a time she'd suspected Paul of having killed his brother. The memory of that look in her eyes had never left him, for it lay like a dark shadow on his heart.

Lucy had loved Mark. She had grieved for him. The last thing that Paul had heard of her was that she had returned from Italy, where her mama had taken her to recover from her grief, still unattached. He had thought all these long months that she would find someone and marry him, but she had not.

She was clearly still grieving, unable to forget the man who had so cruelly been snatched from her a few weeks before her wedding.

Paul knew he must not think of her. It would be impossible to marry the girl that his brother had loved, wanted as his wife...even if Lucy would look at him. As children they had quarrelled more often than not for even then, Lucy had followed Mark as an adoring puppy. Only once...at a ball in London just before they all went down to the country to prepare for the wedding... Only briefly then had Paul felt that Lucy might like him, might return the hopeless feelings of love he'd had for her.

He was mistaken. He must have been mistaken, for she had meant to go ahead with her wedding... She had been devastated when Mark was killed.

It was useless to repine. Paul could never have taken her from his brother, even if Mark had lived, and now it was impossible. His memory would always be enshrined in Lucy's heart. She would never look at his insignificant brother.

Paul must put her out of his mind. There were enough beautiful ladies in Vienna to distract him, but apart from a brief flirtation or two with married ladies, Paul had remained indifferent to the female sex. He knew that he had aroused intense interest amongst the young women who had accompanied brothers or fathers to Vienna. Because he showed no more than polite interest in any of the gently-born young ladies, he was thought of as reserved, even cold, but that did not deter their interest. He was the heir to the Ravenscar fortune, attractive if not as devastatingly handsome as his brother had been, and personable. More than one lady of quality had tried to catch him in her net, but Paul behaved with impeccable politeness while remaining aloof…unreachable.

Paul found the attempts of some young women to compromise themselves with him vaguely amusing and took care to make sure that he was not caught behind closed doors alone with any of them. He had no desire to be married for his prospects…indeed, he had no desire to marry at all.

Paul knew that one day he would need to marry to secure the line, but for the moment he could not give serious consideration to the idea. As he shouted to his batman to pack his things, all Paul could think of was whether his father would live long enough to give him his blessing…and whether he could bear to live in the house that should have been his brother's.

# Chapter One

'It was kind of you to visit an old man,' Lord Ravenscar said and smiled as the young girl smoothed his pillows and set the glass of cold water closer to his hand. 'Your pretty face has made me feel the sunshine, Miss Dawlish, and my days have been grey long enough.'

'I wanted to visit you,' Lucy assured him, 'and Mama said that I might, as Jenny was visiting. You may remember that Adam's wife is a good friend of mine, though I had not seen her for many months.'

A look of pain flitted through the old man's eyes, for the day his nephew's wife Jenny first arrived at Ravenscar was the day his eldest and adored son Mark had been murdered, nearly eighteen months ago now. The pain was plainly still too deep and grievous to be mentioned.

'You were a long time in Italy, Miss Dawlish?'

'We spent almost a year there,' Lucy replied with a smile.

Her complexion was a little coloured by the sun, for her skin had taken on a slightly golden glow, which had not yet faded. Her hair was lighter than it had used to be, a silvery blonde and fine, making her eyes seem bluer and her mouth a delicate pink.

The room smelled of the roses she'd brought for him and was clean and sweet, for Jenny and Adam had come to stay to care for him in his last days, and the servants looked after their master, as they ought.

'We visited Paris on the way home, but Papa was feeling lonely without us and so we came home last month.'

'Yes, I dare say your father missed you. It is hard when your loved ones are far away…' There was such pain and grief in his voice that Lucy was angry with Paul Ravenscar. How could he abandon his father this way? A month or two to come to terms with his grief would have been understandable, but no loving son could have stayed away this long, knowing that his elderly father was grieving.

Lucy had once thought that she might be in love with Paul. Already promised to his brother, whom she'd hero-worshipped for years, it had come to her suddenly when dancing with Paul at a ball in London that she might have preferred to marry him. She had been anxious in her mind and considered whether she should tell Mark when he was murdered. The shock had thrown them all, for how could someone as glorious be lost so easily to a murderer's spite?

Guilt had swamped her and, for a time, she had wondered if Paul might have shot his brother in a jealous fit, but she had not truly believed it—and later, when Adam and Hallam trapped the real villain, Lucy had hoped… A little sigh rose to her lips, but she smothered it and smiled at Lord Ravenscar.

'I am sure Captain Ravenscar will return soon, sir. Hallam wrote to tell him that you were unwell.'

'He should not have done so,' the old man said testily. 'Paul was engaged on work for his country—one of Wellington's aides. Why should he come rushing home just because—?' He broke off and shook his head. 'Though I shall admit that I have missed him sorely. I think I was unfair to him, Miss Dawlish. I do not believe I ever told him…' He closed his eyes and a single tear trickled down his cheek. 'Mark was the eldest and Paul…Paul stood in his shadow. That was unfair, Miss Dawlish…damnably unfair.'

'Pray do not distress yourself, sir,' Lucy said, feelings of pity tugging at her heart. 'I am sure you will see him soon and then you may tell him yourself.' She turned as the door opened and Jenny entered the room, bearing a tray with several little bottles, a glass and a hot drink.

'Good morning, Uncle,' Jenny said. 'It is time for your medicine.'

'I shall leave you with Jenny,' Lucy said, 'for you must take your medicines, sir—but I shall ride over again the day after tomorrow.'

'Thank your mama for her calves' foot jelly,' he said. 'I am sure I shall find it most restorative.'

'Ride carefully,' Jenny said. 'It was lovely to see you again—and the silk shawl you brought me from Italy was gorgeous.'

Lucy inclined her head and then smiled at Jenny,

before leaving the room. The two young women had talked and taken tea together before Lucy came up to visit Lord Ravenscar. Seeing Jenny acting the part of the mistress of the house had brought it home to Lucy that, had Mark lived, she would have been the one to care for her father-in-law. She had known him all her life and he was as an uncle to her, a dear friend—and it hurt her to see how fragile he had become. She could only pray that he would linger long enough to see his remaining son return.

Once again, she felt angry with Paul. How could he stay away all this time when his father needed him? As far as Lucy was concerned, it was disgraceful and she would not spare him when she next saw him…

'How was dear Lord Ravenscar?' Lady Dawlish asked when Lucy entered the house. 'Was he able to speak to you, my love?'

'He is failing and very weak, but fighting it, as you would expect of such a man,' Lucy replied as she stripped off her riding gloves of York tan. She was a very pretty girl with a clear gaze, her hair wind tossed by a wayward breeze, a few springy tendrils hanging about her face where it had escaped from the fine net she wore to hold it when riding. 'I felt so distressed for him, Mama. He so much wants to see Paul and fears he will not. How can he stay away all these months when he knows his father needs him? Surely he ought to have returned months ago?'

'Do not be too critical,' her mother said with a little frown. 'You cannot know his circumstances, Lucy. The duke may have had need of him—'

'The duke might easily have found another aide to organise his work or his balls,' Lucy replied scornfully. Her mouth was hard at that moment, for in the past months since Mark's death, she had learned to hide her true feelings and to shield her heart. She had cried too many tears, both for herself and for her lost fiancé and sometimes she felt that there were none left inside her—though she had felt like weeping when she saw how fragile Lord Ravenscar had become. 'Paul is thoughtless.'

'Now, dearest, I do not like that in you,' her mother said in some distress. 'You were always such a caring girl. Not that I mean you have changed towards your father or me—but you are harsh to Paul. You must remember that he was devastated by...' Lady Dawlish faltered. 'I know you, too, suffered grievously, my dearest...'

'Yes, but some of my grief was guilt because I did not love Mark in the way I ought as his wife-to-be. He was my hero and my friend, Mama—but I was not in love with him. He swept me off my feet when he returned a hero from the wars and asked me. Had I married him we might both have been unhappy, for I do not think he was in love with me either. There were times when I sensed he wished to tell me something—but he was killed too soon.'

'Oh, Lucy dearest...' Her mother looked even more upset. 'If that is true, why are you still so affected by what happened? I hoped that you might meet someone in Italy or in Paris. There were several gentlemen who showed interest, but you gave them no encouragement. Even that charming count who paid you so many compliments. I am sure he would have asked had you given him the least encouragement.'

'I did not wish to marry any of them, Mama.'

'Your father was asking me only last evening... He worries about you, Lucy. He wants to see you married and to know you are settled. We should both like grandchildren.'

'Yes, I know,' Lucy said and there was a catch in her voice. She turned her face aside, as she said, 'I must be a sad disappointment to you, Mama. I did try to like the count and the Marquis de Sancerre was very pleasant…but I could not face the idea of being his wife. You would not wish me to marry simply for the sake of it?'

'No, certainly not, Lucy,' Lady Dawlish replied. 'I am sad and disappointed, as you say, but only for your sake. I pray that you will find someone who can make you put the past behind you and think of a new life. I should not like to think of you wasting your youth.'

'If I do meet someone who makes me feel that way, I shall tell you, Mama,' Lucy promised. 'For the moment I would prefer to live with you and Papa.'

'Very well, I shall not lecture you. You know your own mind best, Lucy—but it would make Papa and I happy to see you the way you used to be. You were always laughing, talking so fast that I could hardly keep up with you. Now you seem so serious…'

Lucy smiled, but made no further reply. She went up to her room, to change her gown and tidy her hair. Catching sight of herself in the pretty oval-shaped mirror in its frame of satinwood with painted decoration, she saw a face slightly too pale beneath the tan, which would soon wear off now that she was back in England, her eyes were large and dark, her mouth set in a hard line. Had she changed very much? As a girl she had always been ready to laugh and tease her friends—but she had carried so much pain inside her for too long.

She was concerned that her manner was causing her parents distress, but she had not been aware that they sensed the change in her. Had she become hard or uncaring? Lucy did not think so... the only person she felt anger against was Paul Ravenscar.

He had stayed away so long. Before he went away to Italy, he'd spoken of visiting her when she arrived in that country; she'd believed that once his grief had abated he would do so, but long before she set foot in Rome, he had gone back to Vienna and joined Wellington's staff. In all the long months since he had not once written to her.

He cared nothing for her! Lucy's heart and her pride had felt the blow of his indifference. Had he loved her, he would surely have made an effort to visit her. Even if he believed it was too soon for them to marry, he could have told her of his feelings…asked her to wait until he was ready. Instead, he'd ignored her and Lucy's grief over Mark's death and her feelings for Paul had turned to anger.

Why had he looked at her that way when they danced? Why touch her hair with his lips? Why hold her and look into her eyes when he helped her dismount from her horse? Why, oh, why had he engaged her feelings if he cared nothing for her? She had been a fool to care for him. Mark was worth ten of him…and yet she had not truly loved him in the way that a wife should. She believed that, had they married, neither would have been truly happy.

Perhaps she was incapable of loving anyone with all her heart. Lucy dragged a brush through her tangled hair, her throat tight with distress. If she could not fall in love, then she must look for a man who could keep her in comfort and would be kind to her.

It was not the marriage she had hoped for, because she was a romantic girl, but perhaps it would be less painful—to love someone was to suffer. Lucy had learned that lesson well these long months.

She owed it to her parents to marry, so she must put away this foolish grief. She had grieved long enough for her friend Mark, and Paul was not worth her tears. She would not continue to think of him and make herself miserable.

She would forget the past and be happy. Somehow, she would make a new life...and if a gentleman she liked asked her to wed him, she would say yes.

'How is he?' Paul asked of the butler, as he handed over his hat, gloves and riding whip. His grey eyes were anxious, his dark-brown hair ruffled as he ran his fingers through it nervously. 'Please tell me he isn't dead.'

'Lord Ravenscar is very weak,' the man replied sadly. 'However, he still lives—and will be glad to see you, sir.'

'Thank you, John. I shall go up to him at once.'

'Mrs Miller is with him, sir. She sits with him

as much as she can, but he still has a few visitors. Miss Dawlish came this morning. She left no more than an hour since—'

'Indeed? That was kind of her,' Paul said stiffly. He took the stairs two at a time, not bothering to shake off the dust of the roads in his anxiety. He knocked softly at the door of his father's bedchamber and then went in. His gaze went immediately to the bed and the shock took his breath. Lord Ravenscar had been unwell when he left home, but still a strong man—the man in the bed looked thin and fragile, close to death. Guilt raged through him, making his chest tighten. By the looks of it he was almost too late.

'Father…' he said and went forward, his throat catching with emotion. 'Forgive me for not returning sooner.'

'Paul, my boy.' The old man's hand trembled as he offered it and Paul clasped it between both his hands. Jenny smiled at him and moved away from the bed.

'I shall leave you together,' she said. 'Stay and talk to your father, Paul. We are all glad to have you back.'

'Thank you… We shall talk later.'

Jenny nodded, going out of the sickroom. Paul sat on the edge of the large double bed, looking into his father's face. 'Forgive me, sir. I should not have stayed away so long.'

'We both know why you went,' Lord Ravenscar said and his voice was stronger as he held his son's hand. 'Your brother was dear to us both. Do you think I did not know how you loved him? We were both in awe of him, Paul—yes, I, too, for he enchanted us all, did he not?'

'Yes, sir.' Paul's lean face tightened with pain. Bronzed by the sun, he had a craggy, weathered look that made him seem older than his years. 'He was all that you could ever have wished for in a son or I in a brother. I longed to be like him, but I fear I failed...'

'You did not fail in my eyes,' his father said. 'I have wanted to tell you, Paul. You were always as much my son...but you were different. I saw your mother in you, Paul. She had your hair and your eyes—Mark took after my father; he, too, was a man much larger than life and I was in awe of him.'

'I could never live up to his standards. You deserved a son who could make you proud, sir. I would willingly have exchanged my life for his.'

'No,' his father said, shaking his head. 'You make me proud, Paul. You might have gone off the rails, drinking and gambling—God knows, many would in your shoes. Instead, you buckled down to work and I know you have done well, for your commander wrote to me. He valued you, my son—and so do I.'

'Father…' Paul choked on the words, overwhelmed. 'I wish it had been me… Mark should have been here to care for you and the estate.'

'I would have given my life for him—for either of you. Mark was all that you say. But…if I speak only the truth, I believe you may be better placed to take care of the estate and our people. I have neglected them, Paul. In my grief, first for your mother and then for Mark. Oh, your cousin has done all that needed to be done, as far as it goes, but to be the lord of such an estate means more. The people need someone who cares for their welfare… I fear Mark was made for larger things.'

'I do not understand you, Father?'

'Mark would never have been happy to live here for long. He would have sought something more…

politics or the London scene. He might have been a great general or a leader of men. I do not say he would have neglected the estate, but he spoke to me the day before he died…told me that he intended to ask you to help run the estate. I believe he had some idea of importing tea or some such thing. He was too restless a spirit to stay tamely at home.'

'Mark wanted me to be his agent?'

'Yes, I believe he had it in mind. He told me that he preferred an army life and would find it hard to settle in the country. I am not sure what he meant to do, for I think he was still considering his career. I know something troubled him, though he would not speak of it.'

'I had no idea,' Paul said and frowned. 'Are you certain of this, Father?'

'Yes. I always knew he would find it hard— this house, this land, they were not large enough for him, Paul. There was something in him that needed more and I think he might have grown discontent had he been forced to devote his life to the estate.'

Paul was bewildered, for he had always loved his home and liked nothing more than to ride its fields, to talk with the tenants and entertain his neighbours. This surely was a place of beauty and content, enough to make any man feel his life well spent in caring for the land and the people who worked it.

'I am not sure what to think, sir. He said nothing of this to me—though I knew there was something on his mind. I…believed there was another woman, someone he loved, but could not marry for some reason.'

'I dare say there may have been. He spoke vaguely of being uncertain of his own mind. I do not know what might have happened had he lived, for I think… I fear he may have discovered that he had made a mistake.'

'A mistake? What can you mean?'

'I believe he asked Miss Dawlish to marry him on the spur of the moment and then realised he did not truly wish to wed her. Naturally, he could not jilt her for he was above all a gentleman—but I think he was troubled. Had he lived…'

As his father sighed, Paul's mind struggled to take in all that he had been told. It seemed that there were aspects of his brother that he had not suspected. If Mark did not particularly want to be the master of Ravenscar…if he had not truly loved Lucy…but, no, his father was mistaken. Any man fortunate to know Lucy, as Mark had, must love her.

'I can hardly credit it,' he said to his father. 'I am sorry for it, if it is true—but Mark appeared to be so pleased with the world. He spoke of the wedding and of making the estate stronger, more prosperous.'

'It was his intention to improve things, especially for our tenants,' Lord Ravenscar said. 'He spoke of pulling old cottages down and building new…and, as I said, I believe he hoped to make the money for these improvements by a venture into trade.'

'As Adam and Hallam have with their wine importing,' Paul said. 'I do not think I have such bold ideas in my head, Father. I cannot see myself investing in cargoes or selling wine or tea. I think an improvement may be made to the land by new methods of farming—and I should like to breed horses if I can afford it.'

'You are a countryman after my own heart,' his father said and smiled. 'It was my ambition to breed fine horses at one time, but I was too lazy.

If you have your mother's blood in you, you may achieve more, for she was always busy.'

'You have never gambled your fortune away, sir, as many gentlemen do. I shall have no debts to settle, as my cousins did.'

'I would have loaned them money, you know, but they were too proud to ask and in the end solved their own problems. I wish that I could have had more time with you, Paul—time to teach you things you should know, but Anders is a good man. He will help you…and Hallam knows the estate well.'

'Hallam has done his share,' Paul said. 'I shall do well enough—and I still have you to guide me, sir.'

His father's hand trembled a little on the bed. 'I fear not for much longer, my son—but I shall die in peace now that I have seen you again. All I want is for you to be happy.'

'I shall do my best to oblige you, sir. I shall make you proud of me and the estate will not suffer if I can prevent it.'

'I know you will do all I could ask, my boy,' his father said and smiled at him. 'But it is not just the estate…you must find a wife to make you comfortable and you will need at least one son—more is always better.' They were both silent, for they had ample cause to know what might happen to the rightful heir.

'Yes, Father,' Paul said, feeling a lump in his throat as his father lay back and closed his eyes. 'I shall remember. I will look about for a comfortable wife...'

No answer came and he knew that his father was sleeping. He had wanted to say so much in a short time and it had exhausted him.

Paul felt the sting of tears. He feared that his father could not live many days, for his strength was failing, but God had given them this short time together. Lord Ravenscar had given him hope, because he felt he had his blessing. Somehow, their talk had eased his grief in a way that the months of self-imposed exile had not. He should have stayed here with his father, got to know him better...but at least they'd had this time together.

Mark would always be his hero, but the feeling of having always been inadequate had lessened. His father had not thought him a failure—he trusted him to take care of the estate and its people. Paul would not let him down...and he would look for a lady to make his wife. It was his duty to his father and to the estate.

He thought fleetingly of Lucy, then dismissed her from his mind. She would not look at him, but there were other ladies almost as lovely…and perhaps one of them would be happy to be his wife and give him the sons the estate needed.

## Chapter Two

Pausing at the top of the landing that morning, as he heard the female voices in the hall below, Paul caught his breath. Surely that was Lucy's voice? She must have come to visit his father.

He took a deep breath and went down the wide staircase, with its beautifully carved mahogany banisters. As he reached the bottom he paused and she turned her head towards him, making him catch his breath. He was surprised as he looked into her face and saw a stranger. It was Lucy, but not as he remembered her—her face was thinner, older, yet in a way even more lovely—but there was something different. The Lucy Dawlish he'd known had been so open, a trusting, lovely, lively girl who had chattered heedlessly and laughed all the time… This woman had an air of reserve about her…as if she were encased in a crystal, her thoughts and feelings shielded from public gaze.

'Miss Dawlish,' he said and held out his hand in greeting. 'How pleasant to see you.'

'Captain Ravenscar,' she replied and made a slight curtsy. 'I am glad to see you home at last. Your father must be happy that you have come back, I dare say.'

He felt her censure and frowned. He knew well enough that he had neglected both his father and the estate, but he did not care to hear it from her— and it was there in her manner and her eyes.

'Yes, he is,' Paul said. 'It is good of you to en-quire. Yesterday, when I arrived, he was very tired, but today he seems better. I sat with him for an hour and we talked of estate matters. If you will excuse me, I shall leave you and Jenny to talk. I have something to do that Father most particu-larly requested.' He inclined his head to her and then glanced at Jenny. He gave Lucy a cool look, for he had retreated into that private place within him. She looked at him with eyes that saw too much and he needed to escape. 'I shall not be at home for luncheon, Jenny—but I shall certainly be back for tea.'

'Yes, of course, Paul,' she said, smiling at him. 'Adam should be home later this afternoon. I told you he had gone to London on business, but he will be so pleased to see you back where you belong.'

Paul nodded and went past them and out into the warm sunshine. It was a few moments before he felt the warmth, for he felt as if he were encased in ice. He was not sure whether he had behaved just as he ought, for it had been such a shock to see Lucy standing there looking so changed…but he hoped that he had said all that was polite to an old friend. She could never be anything more… and she was not the girl of his dreams.

What had happened to change her so? Had she grieved so deeply for his brother?

Walking swiftly towards the agent's office, he thrust his feelings to the back of his mind. His father had asked him to ride out and speak with one of their farming tenants. The house needed a substantial repair to the roof and it was needful that it should be set in hand at once. Hallam had not made a decision on it before returning to his home, but now that Paul was back at Ravenscar, it would be his decision.

He must attend to business and forget the way his heart had hammered at the first sight of the woman he had once loved. It was his duty to think of the estate and to marry a sensible woman to provide an heir for the title. This foolish yearning must be put aside. Lucy was beyond him and so he must not think of her—besides, she was not the same.

'Captain Ravenscar,' Mr Anders said, looking up from his ledgers. 'What may I do for you, sir?'

'I have it in mind to take a look at Briars Farm,' he said. 'Will you ride out with me, Anders? I should like to see the work that needs to be done for myself…and then we shall set it in train. Now that I am home I intend to see that everything is as it ought to be.'

'I shall be glad of it, sir. Major Ravenscar is a good man, but he has his own affairs and did not like to go too fast in case it was not in accordance with your wishes…and he would not trouble Lord Ravenscar more than necessary.'

'My father has put the estate in my hands, as you know.' Paul smiled, for he liked the honest cut of the man. 'You shall advise me, sir—but it is my intention to improve the estate. There are many new ideas in agriculture now and we must investigate them…and our people must be properly housed.'

'I am glad to hear it, sir,' Anders said. 'I have wanted to make changes for some time, but Lord Ravenscar was not interested in new methods. He said he was too old to change and it would be up to his sons to take up the new methods.'

'Well, now we shall begin,' Paul said. 'Walk to the stables with me—unless you are too busy?'

'Nothing that cannot wait,' his agent said and reached for his hat. 'It is a lovely day for a ride out.'

'Will you not stay and take luncheon with me?' Jenny said when Lucy came down from visiting Lord Ravenscar. 'Paul will not be back and I would much rather have your company than eat alone.'

'Yes, if you wish it,' Lucy said and looked thoughtful. 'So much has happened since you first came down here to stay with me, Jenny. You married Adam and you have your darling son. How lucky you were to fall in love with him.'

'Yes, I am fortunate,' Jenny said and studied

her anxiously. 'You look tired, Lucy. Are you not quite well?'

'I am fine, thank you,' Lucy replied, her hands curling at her sides as she fought her emotions. 'I suppose it was a shock to see Paul so much changed. Of course he has been away months and people do change. I dare say I am changed myself...'

The way he'd looked at her...not seeing her, but looking through her as if she did not exist. It had felt like a knife stabbing her to the heart. How could he look at her so coldly—as if they had never been more than mere acquaintances?

'Yes, you are a little,' Jenny agreed. 'You seem quieter, more thoughtful than you used to be, Lucy. I think you laughed and cried more easily before you left for Italy. I have not asked...was there no one that you liked? I thought you might marry.'

'Oh, I liked a great many people and I might have married,' Lucy said, 'but I think I was still grieving. However, all that is at an end. I am determined to find a husband for myself as soon as I may. Mama is anxious for me and it is my duty to marry well.'

'I am glad to hear it,' Jenny said and laughed softly. She was a pretty girl and marriage agreed with her, the light from within bringing her eyes alive. 'I should like you to be as happy as I am with Adam. You must look for someone handsome and kind…but the Season in London is sadly over for this year.'

'Mama spoke of taking me to Bath,' Lucy said. 'Papa intends to give a little dance next month. I hope that you and Adam will come? You never know, I might find a gentleman locally who would offer for me—and I should prefer to live not too far distant from my parents. I am their only child, after all.'

'I suppose that would be nice. I have no parents, of course, only an uncle and aunt. Lord Ravenscar is as dear to me as a father, for he has been so loving towards me. I shall be very sad when he leaves us.'

'Is there no hope that he will recover now that Paul is home?'

'I am not sure. The physicians say that it is only a matter of time, but I see an improvement in him. He has hung on this long because he wanted to see Paul again—and now he is home he may recover.'

'I wish he will have a little longer,' Lucy said. 'It will be heartbreaking for Paul to lose his father too soon—though he ought to have returned sooner. I cannot imagine why he stayed away so long. It was thoughtless of him.'

'I suppose that once he had accepted the commission with Wellington, he could not leave him until it was settled.' Jenny frowned. 'I believe he much regrets it now, but Lord Ravenscar is not resentful, merely pleased to have his son home.'

'Yes…' Lucy wrinkled her smooth brow. 'He told me just now how proud he was of Paul for having stuck to his duty. He says that he knows Paul has many improvements in mind for the estate.'

'Oh, yes,' Jenny said and laughed. 'He explained them to me last night in detail, but I fear that I was not truly attending. Jeffery was cutting a tooth and my mind was with him…but it all sounded very worthy and fine.'

'Poor Jenny.' Lucy laughed and her face lit up. All at once she looked beautiful again, the sorrows of the past months somehow sloughed off as her eyes danced with amusement. 'You must have missed Adam very much, for they could have talked business together.'

'Yes, indeed,' Jenny agreed. 'I like Paul very well, but farming is not my forte and I could not help listening for little Jeffrey. Nurse is very good, but he does cry so…and she will not pick him up, because she says it spoils him. I think she does not like it when I do.'

'Oh, that is unkind, but I know many nurses feel the same,' Lucy said sympathetically. 'If I had a child, I believe I should pick him up when he cried—even if his nurse did not agree with the practice.'

'Well, I do,' Jenny said. 'Nurse scolds me, but I do not care. He is my son and I shall tend him when he cries no matter what anyone says.' She offered her hand to Lucy. 'Will you come up and see him now?'

'Yes, I should love to and I shall stay to luncheon, Jenny. Mama knew that I might be more than an hour or so and will not worry.'

'I shall send your groom to tell her that you will not be home until later,' Jenny assured her. 'And you shall ride home in my carriage.'

\* \* \*

Lucy thoroughly enjoyed the time she spent with her friend, for they caught up on all the things that had happened to them in the intervening months. Their exchanges made them laugh and Lucy felt better than she had in a long time. By the time Jenny's husband walked into the salon with another gentleman, she was smiling much in her old way.

'Adam!' Jenny sprang to her feet and ran towards him, hands outstretched. 'How good it is to see you, my love. Did you have a comfortable journey?'

'Very,' he replied and kissed her lightly on the lips. 'I have brought a guest to stay for a while, Jenny. His name is George and he is the Earl of Daventry—and he was so obliging as to sell me a horse. We knew each other in the army, but have not met for…oh, more than three years… That was before George became the earl, of course.'

'Mrs Miller,' the stranger said and bowed his head to her. 'I had heard Adam had married a lovely young woman, but I could not have guessed how beautiful.'

He was an assured man, well built with dark

eyes and hair, his mouth a little thin when in repose, but nothing could have exceeded his affability.

'You flatter me, sir,' Jenny said. 'Forgive me, my lord—I must make you known to my friend, Miss Lucy Dawlish…' Lucy rose to her feet and made a little curtsy. 'Lucy, the Earl of Daventry.'

'I believe we have met once before, sir, quite briefly—in Paris.'

'Indeed, we have, Miss Dawlish,' Daventry agreed with a smile oozing with charm as he took her hand and bent his head to kiss it. 'I never forget a face…especially one as lovely as yours.'

'I think you flatter me,' Lucy said and laughed, for he was a handsome man, his manners and bearing pleasing. 'If you speak the truth, you hardly noticed me the night we were introduced. You were a little preoccupied…'

'Was I?' His dark eyes narrowed for a moment and then he laughed. 'Yes, I believe you were right—I was, in fact, a trifle the worse for drink. I had lost a fortune the previous night…but I did recall you, Miss Dawlish, upon my word I did.'

'I shall believe you, sir,' she replied and laughed up at him. He was a head taller than Adam, his build classical and elegant, in that he had the phy-sique of a Greek god and his hair was very black against his pale skin. He was dressed in a dark-blue coat that must have been made by Weston or perhaps Scott, for it had a military look, his pale breeches fitting to strong legs and encased in fine topboots. On his right hand he wore a signet on the third finger and a gold pin in his snowy cravat, but his clothes were plain in every other respect.

'I swear I would not lie,' he declared, but his eyes held a wicked gleam that made her laugh once more and shake her head.

'I must have a room prepared for you,' Jenny said, 'and then we shall have tea.'

'I asked Halstead to see to the room,' Adam said. 'Pray ring for tea, my dear. George may use my dressing room for the moment if he wishes to refresh himself.'

'I am quite content here for the moment, if the ladies will excuse me coming to their parlour with all the dirt of the road upon me?'

'Of course,' Jenny said. 'As you see, my hus-band does not scruple and I wish only to make you both comfortable after your long ride. Please take a seat, sir, and tea shall be brought, by which time your room will be ready for you.'

'I should be going, Jenny,' Lucy said. 'If you will send for the carriage…'

'You must not leave yet, enchantress,' Lord Daventry protested, his eyes giving her a look of admiration that made her blush. 'I entreat you, stay and drink a dish of tea with us.'

'Yes, you must,' Jenny agreed. 'I told your groom to inform Lady Dawlish that you would return after tea. Please do, Lucy.'

'Very well, if you wish it,' Lucy said. 'I thought only to leave you with your guest.'

'If only you also had been a guest here,' Daventry said and sighed eloquently. 'I shall hope that your home is not too far distant so that I may pay a call on your dear mama.'

'It is less than half an hour on horseback,' Lucy began just as Paul entered the large parlour. She caught her breath and could not continue as he stood just inside the door, his eyes moving over the little group, a slight frown on his brow. His was a brooding presence, his lean frame in marked contrast to the build of the earl, his features dark and graven.

'Paul…' Adam saw him and strode to greet him, offering his hand. 'I am glad you are home. You have seen your father?'

'Yes. I thank you for your care of him, Cousin,' Paul replied. 'It was good of you and Jenny to come here at such short notice.'

'Hallam asked if we could visit with Lord Ravenscar, for he was called away,' Adam replied. 'Indeed, it is Jenny who has sat with him and helped to nurse him—I have been somewhat pre-occupied with other things…but now that you are home, we shall leave in a few days.'

'I wish you will not,' Paul said. 'As you know, I have no wife and my father needs a lady to care for him if he is not to be left to the maids. Please make yourselves at home for as long as you wish.'

'We shall stay, then,' Adam said. 'I've brought a friend to visit for a few days, Paul. Daventry wishes to look at some of my horses.'

'You are welcome, sir,' Paul said and inclined his head. 'I fear there is little to entertain you here, for my father is ill and we do not invite guests—or only close friends—but any friends of Adam's are always welcome.'

Daventry went to shake hands with him, looking suitably grave.

'Adam told me the situation. I am on my way home and came to bear him company, and to look at a horse he mentioned. I do not expect to be entertained, Captain Ravenscar.'

'You know me, sir?'

'We met briefly in Vienna. You had just arrived and I was about to leave for London. I dare say you hardly saw me, for I think…you seemed much caught by your own thoughts.'

'Yes, I dare say I was at that time,' Paul said stiffly. 'Forgive me, I must visit my father. I shall have my tea with him, Jenny. I will see you at dinner—Miss Dawlish, your servant.' He nodded his head curtly and left.

Lucy sensed that he had withdrawn behind a barrier, his eyes distant, as if he hardly saw any of them…especially her.

'Paul…' she breathed, but in a voice that carried only as far as the gentleman sitting next to her.

'You must find me in the way. Perhaps I should leave in the morning…' Daventry began as Paul went out, but Adam shook his head.

'No, no, that is not at all the case. Lord Ravenscar bid me treat his house as my own and I assure you that he would not object to my inviting a guest. Paul is a little out of sorts, you understand. I insist you stay for at least two days, as we planned.'

'Well, if you insist, Adam,' Daventry said. 'I shall use my time to make the acquaintance of my new friend.' His gaze lingered on Lucy with pleasure, bringing a flush to her cheeks.

She had been enjoying his conversation, but Paul's sudden arrival, his coldness and the look he had given her had wiped the smile from her lips. Was he thinking that she had intruded by staying all day to talk with Jenny? Or did he include her as an old friend? She could not be certain and wished that she had insisted on leaving before Paul returned. She would not for the world have him think she presumed on old acquaintance.

However, she could not leave now without making a fuss. It was not easy to recover the pleasure she'd found in the company of her friends, for she had sensed Paul's resentment. This was his home and, although he had welcomed the earl and insisted that Adam and Jenny remain, he had refused to have tea with them.

Perhaps it was Lucy's presence that he resented? She felt coldness at her nape, but made a determined effort to enjoy the conversation, though she could manage no more than a tiny sandwich and a dish of tea.

After tea the gentlemen went upstairs to see about Daventry's room and Jenny sent for the carriage. She accompanied Lucy to the door and kissed her.

'I think Paul upset you,' she said. 'Please do not be hurt, Lucy. He is not as he used to be… There is a reserve about him these days, almost as if he distances himself from everyone. He has been pleasant to me, but I have felt that if it were not for his father's need, he would wish me elsewhere.'

'Surely he must be grateful for your care of Lord Ravenscar.'

'He is grateful…but he was so much more to Adam before Mark's death. They were close friends. Even with Adam there is…a barrier. If I did not know him, I should call it arrogance, but I do not believe that is the right word. I think he has shut himself off for too long and does not know how to behave with his friends.'

'Yes, perhaps you are right,' Lucy said. 'He has grieved for his brother too long. I, too, have suffered, but with you today…and before Paul came in…it was as if all the sadness had melted away and a load was lifted from my heart.'

Jenny smiled and leaned forward to kiss her cheek. 'I thought you seemed happier, dearest. I shall visit you and your mama one day before we leave Ravenscar—and you must come here again whenever you wish.'

'I am not sure that Paul would wish it,' Lucy said a little stiffly. 'It is, after all, his home and…I do not think he was happy to see me here.' Her throat caught for she felt hurt, as if by his manner he denied everything that had ever been between them.

'He is just a little awkward,' Jenny assured her. 'Paul was always your friend. I am sure another day he will seek you out and apologise. It is just awkwardness, I believe.'

'Perhaps,' Lucy said and squeezed her hand. 'Now I must go. Please come for luncheon one day, if you can manage it, Jenny.'

Jenny promised she would. They went out to the waiting carriage; the steps were let down, a footman assisted her into the carriage and she was driven away. She waved to Jenny once and then leaned back against the squabs. Her eyes closed and she felt them sting, as if the tears were close.

What had she expected of Paul? Something different to the reserve he had shown towards her.

It was all very well for Jenny to say that Paul was just feeling strange to be home again, but she had seen him twice now and on neither occasion had he seemed pleased to see her. Indeed, when he saw that she was still in his house at teatime, he had looked grim—even angry.

She had thought that he might come to her in Italy, for he had spoken of being her friend before he went away after Mark died; he had even hinted that he cared for her…as she had cared for him. Now it seemed that he had raised a barrier between them, perhaps so that she should not imagine he had tender feelings for her.

Perhaps he never had…

Whatever the truth, it was clear to Lucy that he had forgotten her. She must close her heart to him and look for someone she could like well enough to marry. There must surely be someone she could bear to live with every day in the close-ness of marriage?

For a moment the handsome, teasing face of George Daventry entered her mind. He was very charming, but Lucy suspected she was not the only lady to find herself the object of his attention.

He would flirt with her, pay her compliments and be a charming partner at a dance, but she did not imagine that he was thinking of making her an offer. Besides, she believed he had estates in the north and west of England, and she had al-ready decided that she did not wish to go so far from her family.

## Chapter Three

'Ah, here you are, my love,' Lady Dawlish greeted her with a smile as she went into the house. 'I hope you had a pleasant day?'

'Yes, indeed, Mama,' Lucy said, taking off her bonnet and shawl. Removing her gloves, she glanced up at her mother. 'Jenny begged me to have luncheon with her—and then she wanted me to stay to tea. Captain Miller returned before tea and he brought a guest with him—the Earl of Daventry.'

'Oh?' Lady Dawlish raised her eyebrows. 'I should not have thought they wished for many guests in the house at the moment.'

'Captain Ravenscar said that they would not entertain while his father is ill, but the earl said he did not wish for entertainment. He spoke of rid-

ing out with Adam to look at some horses and…
and he may decide to call on us, Mama.'

'Indeed? How charming of him,' her mother
said. 'He will be most welcome to stay for nuncheon or tea if he so wishes.'

'Yes, I thought he might like to spend a little
time here, for it is a little awkward at Ravenscar.'

'Yes, I dare say it may be,' Lady Dawlish agreed
thoughtfully. 'Captain Ravenscar must be wishing
him to the devil. Adam is his cousin, of course,
and Jenny is such a capable and kind young
woman. I dare say Lord Ravenscar would not like
to lose her. Maids are all very well, but when one
is ill it is good to have one's friends about one.'

'Lord Ravenscar seemed a little stronger when I
visited him today,' Lucy told her. 'I feel very sad
for him, Mama. Jenny says the doctor believes it
a matter of weeks. It is only because he wanted
to see Paul home that he has clung so tenaciously
to life but…I fear he may not last much longer.'
She felt her throat catch and wiped a tear from
her cheek. 'Paul will feel it so much…I think he
can hardly bear to lose his father…'

'Why did he not return months ago?' Lady
Dawlish shook her head over it. 'He might

have had so much longer with his father had he done so.'

'Perhaps he simply could not bear it,' Lucy suggested. 'It was a long time before I could bear to remember Mark…and I was apprehensive the first time I visited his father.'

'Well, we must pray that Lord Ravenscar makes a recovery. Yes, I know he is very ill, dearest, but sometimes patients do feel better—and it will cheer him having his son home,' her mother said. 'But you are feeling a little better now, I think? You look brighter, Lucy.'

'Yes, I began to feel better when I was talking with Jenny today. We were always such good friends, Mama. I have asked her to visit us if she feels she can leave Lord Ravenscar for a few hours. It must be hard for her to see him so frail… and to see Paul the way he is…so distant and reserved.'

'That does not sound like the man we knew. Well, I dare say it is grief,' Lady Dawlish said. 'But now I have some news for you, dearest. It may cheer you. Your cousin Judith is coming to stay—Judith Sparrow.'

'Uncle John's daughter,' Lucy said. 'She married Sir Michael Sparrow some years back, when she was just seventeen. I have only seen her once, at her wedding.'

Lady Dawlish nodded as she led the way into the parlour. It was a pretty room decorated in shades of green and cream, the furniture a little shabby perhaps from wear, but very comfortable. Books lay about on occasional tables and a fan of lace was lying next to an open workbox, for it was their private place where everything could be left where they wished.

'Yes, I did not approve of your cousin's marriage at the time, for Sir Michael was fifteen years her senior and I thought him too old, but she would have him and my brother approved—and now she is a widow, of course. Her husband died two years ago of a lung disorder. I know she is wealthy and may do as she likes with the fortune he left her—but she is only two and twenty and that is young to be widowed.'

'Yes, that is true,' Lucy said, her sympathy instantly aroused. 'I suffered enough and I was never married to Mark...but if she loved her husband, she must have been devastated.'

'She has not been much in company since her

husband died. My brother says she wished to live quietly while in mourning, but now she has put off her blacks and John is coming with her to stay with us. He will not stay long for he is leaving for France almost immediately, having been given a new diplomatic post. He wanted Judith to be with friends and I assured him that she would be welcome here. You will be glad of her company, I dare say?'

'Yes, of course, Mama. If she is ready to go into society again, she may attend my dance. I dare say you will give a dinner in her honour?'

'Yes, I shall—and perhaps a picnic, too. It is time we entertained again and we have several invitations to dances, dinners, card evenings and various excursions in the next few weeks. Judith could not have chosen a better time to come… and it will be better for you to have her company, dearest. I dare say you will find that most of your special friends have become engaged or married while we were away.'

'Yes, I suppose they have,' Lucy said, sadness fleeting through her eyes. She would have been married more than a year had things been otherwise. 'I shall be pleased to have my cousin to stay,

Mama. Jenny will not remain long after... Well, I dare say she misses her home. She was always my particular friend, but perhaps I shall make friends with my cousin.'

Lucy was strolling in the garden when the two gentlemen dismounted from their horses in the drive. She saw them and waved her hand, walking towards them, her parasol over her shoulder. Smiling, she greeted them warmly as they waited for her to approach.

'Adam...Lord Daventry,' she said. 'It is such a lovely day, is it not? I was tempted out by the roses; they smell so wonderful at this time of year.'

'Do you like roses, Miss Dawlish?' George Daventry said. 'We have some particularly fine ones at Daventry Hall in Devon—my gardener tells me that I have one of the best collections of old musk roses in the country.'

'How delightful,' Lucy replied. 'I think they have the best perfumes of all...some of the damask roses are gorgeous.'

'Yes, indeed they are,' he said and offered his arm as she closed her parasol. 'How lovely you look, Miss Dawlish. Yellow is certainly your colour, I think.'

'Thank you,' she replied. 'Please, you must both come in and meet Mama. I know she is hoping to see you.'

'How is your mother, Lucy?' Adam asked as he followed behind. 'Your father missed you both a great deal when you were travelling, I think.'

'Yes, indeed, poor Papa felt lonely after he left us in Italy and returned home. We ought to have come with him, but he insisted we stay until I was ready—and I was not then of a mind to return.'

'It was a terrible time for all of us. Jenny tells me you are much recovered now.'

'Yes, thank you. I only wish that I could say the same for your cousin, Adam. Paul seemed unlike himself yesterday, but I dare say he is concerned for his father.'

'He is in a better mood this morning and apologised for his abruptness yesterday. I believe he is driven to near despair by his father's illness—perhaps because he feels guilt at having left him alone for so long.'

'Is his lordship no better?'

'I thought he seemed a little better this morning,' Adam replied with a nod. 'I dare say it is having Paul home again.'

'Perhaps he will rally,' Lucy said, then turned to her companion. 'Tell me, sir, have you found a horse to suit you?'

'I am looking for a mare for my married sister as a birthday gift,' he replied. 'Adam showed me one or two and we have arranged to speak to one Major Wilson, who has several good horses for sale. We shall go there this afternoon.'

'But you will stay for some refreshment with us first,' Lucy said. 'It would be senseless to return to Ravenscar when it is but a short distance from here to Major Wilson's stud. I know Papa thinks well of his breeding lines and often buys a horse from the major... My own Silver Miss came from him.'

'Thank you, you are most kind,' Lord Daventry replied.

Lucy smiled at him, then led the way inside to her mother's parlour.

'Adam and Daventry have not returned for luncheon?' Paul said, as he entered the small dining parlour they used when just the family was at home. 'I wanted to ask Adam if he would ride out with me to look at one of the fields.'

'They went to visit Lucy and her mother—and then I think Lord Daventry wanted to look at Major Wilson's horses.'

'Ah, yes, Wilson has some decent blood mares. I think I need a new horse myself…and if I decide to breed I shall need good blood stock to begin my stud.'

'I am sure his are as good as any to be had in the district, or so Adam says—but of course the horse fair will be here in September if you do not find anything that suits you.'

Paul nodded his agreement, then frowned slightly as he said, 'I thought Miss Dawlish much changed… Did you not find her so?'

'Yes,' Jenny acknowledged. 'Lucy has grown up, I think—and her face is thinner than before, but when she laughs she looks much as she always did.'

'Oh? I have not seen her laugh…she has little to say to me,' Paul rejoined stiffly. He was standing at the buffet, his back towards Jenny.

'I dare say she feels strange with you. You have

not seen one another for an age—and you were a little abrupt when she was here, Paul.'

'Yes, I dare say I was at fault,' he said and stared broodingly at the food on the plate he'd brought to table. 'It was in my mind that she blamed me for taking Mark's place here.'

'Oh, no, how could she?' Jenny said. 'You must not feel guilty, Paul. We all know that you did not wish for this—that you would willingly have given your life for your brother's.'

'Do you?' Paul turned his gaze on her and then a reluctant smile touched his mouth. 'Thank you, Jenny. I am a fool. I should not blame Lucy for being cool to me when I had nothing but a formal greeting for her. Does it still show…my feeling of guilt?'

'Yes, to me and to Adam. We understand your grief, Paul, for Adam loved Mark, too—but can you not put the past behind you? Mark would not wish you to grieve for ever. He would be the first to tell you to move on with your life, as we have.'

'I know…' Paul sighed. 'I am trying to accept my duties here, Jenny. I have always loved the estate, its land and people—more than Mark did, I think. I believe I can accept what I must when my father… But Lucy…' He shook his head. 'No, I must not burden you with my foolish thoughts. Excuse me, I must go up to Father.' He pushed his chair back, abandoning the untouched food.

'Your father seems better, Paul. I think he may astound his doctor and live for a few more months or even longer.'

'How kind you have been to us all,' he said. 'I can never thank you enough for being here when he needed you.'

'You know I am your friend and your father's friend.'

Paul nodded and left her, running up the stairs to his father's apartments. He could only hope that Jenny was right. His father had rallied since he had returned and the doctor was pleased. Paul prayed that it meant they could have some time together. He was determined not to leave Lord Ravenscar again. They must make the most of each day granted to them and Paul would learn all he could from his father, because he wanted his people to prosper—and he wanted his father to die in peace when the time came.

A cloud passed across his face as his thoughts returned to Lucy Dawlish, as they did too often.

His first sight of her had been a shock. He had meant to be more friendly the next time they met, but she had been talking to a stranger and he had resented it—which was ridiculous. Lucy Dawlish was nothing to him or he to her, but, try as he might, he could not put her from his mind as he wished. Her face intruded into his mind without warning, particularly when he was in bed at night and sleep would not come.

His marriage was not something he could dismiss. Paul knew that he must find a young lady who would give him an heir and make his house into a home. If he were fortunate, he might find someone like Jenny. Adam was a lucky man, for not only was she a sensible, kind-hearted woman, but she had brought him a fortune.

As the heir to the Ravenscar estate, Paul did not need to marry a fortune. He could look for a young woman who made him feel happy—but where was he to find such a person? Once upon a time he'd believed he knew the lady he wished to spend his life with…but now…

Was Lucy really so much changed? She looked beautiful but seemed more reserved, cool as she looked at him, all the sparkling vitality that had made him love her gone. Had Mark's death done that to her? How much she must have loved him.

His throat tightened with sympathy for her. He knew that he had been hoping she would have put all that behind her…would look at him with laughter in her eyes and…the love he'd sometimes thought he had seen before Mark was murdered. Or had he imagined it because it was what he'd hoped for?

What would have happened if Mark had lived? Would Lucy have married him…or would she have broken her engagement because she loved someone else?

A rueful smile touched his lips. He had never been sure that Lucy cared for him, even though once or twice he had been tempted to kiss her… to beg her not to marry his brother. Loyalty and doubt had kept him from trying to seduce his brother's bride-to-be, but there had been moments when he'd seen something in her eyes and he'd hoped.

It was useless to wish that he'd spoken out when he first suspected what was in his heart, before Mark had come home in his uniform, looking like a conquering hero. Perhaps if he had…but he'd waited, not wanting to rush things, and Mark had swept Lucy off her feet. Paul wondered if she had regretted her promise to wed him, but he had never been brave enough to ask.

With a shake of his head, he dismissed his foolish thoughts and went into his father's bedchamber.

'I have enjoyed myself, meeting your mama,' Lord Daventry said and kissed Lucy's hand when she walked to the door with her guests. 'I hope to see you again soon, Miss Dawlish.'

'I believe you are leaving Ravenscar tomorrow, sir?'

'Yes, indeed, I may,' he replied with a rueful smile. 'I fear that Ravenscar's illness makes it a little awkward for me to stay as long as I'd imagined. However, I have a cousin living not too far distant and it may be that I shall pay him a little visit.'

Lucy's cheeks felt warm as she gave him a shy smile. 'Mama has invited you to my dance next month… It is under three weeks away. I should be happy if you could find the time to come, sir.'

'Oh, but I have already told your dear mama

that I shall be delighted. Even if I have to put up at a local inn, I would not miss it for the world.'

'I am sure Mama would be honoured to offer you accommodation here for a day or so, my lord.'

'I should be delighted to accept,' he said, his eyes seeming to caress her. 'But I dare say I may see you again before the dance.'

'I should like that,' Lucy replied, watching as Adam finished his conversation with her father and came out into the courtyard. 'Goodbye, Captain Miller. Give my love to Jenny.'

'Of course. She will be happy to see you any day—and if my uncle improves she may drive over to see you one day next week.'

'She must come to lunch,' Lucy said. 'We are here most days—but not, I think, Tuesday next for we have a lunch party with friends.'

Adam inclined his head. Daventry smiled at her and the two men rode off. She remained in the sunshine, watching them until they had reached the end of the drive, then turned and went into her mother's parlour.

'Well, Lucy, I like the earl very well,' Lady Dawlish said and sipped a small glass of pale sherry. 'There is nothing arrogant about him despite his lineage and his wealth. Yes, I thought him an excellent man.'

'He is very pleasant, good company,' Lucy agreed. 'He says he shall come to my dance even if he has to put up at the inn—but I told him you would be pleased to have him stay here.'

'Yes, certainly,' her mother agreed. 'I shall send a formal invitation to his home.'

'He says he may stay nearby with a relative and hopes to visit us again before the dance.'

Her mother smiled and looked pleased. 'I think the earl likes you very well, Lucy. He is perhaps a little older than I should like in a husband for you, but, if you liked him, his age would not matter.'

'He is but three and thirty,' Lucy said seriously, for she had on short acquaintance found nothing to dislike in the gentleman. 'I do not think that too old, Mama. Mark would have been eight and twenty this year, had he lived. Five more years is not so very much different in a husband—and I have grown up since then.'

'Yes, you have,' her mother agreed and nodded with approval. 'Am I to think that you would welcome an offer from the earl?'

'It is too soon to be certain,' Lucy said, wrinkling her brow. 'I like him very well. I think he would be a comfortable companion, but I am not sure I wish to marry him.'

Her mother could only agree, 'As you say, it is too early to be sure, but I am glad to see that you are beginning to think of marriage, dearest. For a while I thought you would never recover from your grief.'

'I am much better now,' Lucy told her. 'I think that if I continue to like the earl…I should be ready to marry him in a few months.'

'I am so pleased,' her mother said. 'I would not push you into a marriage you did not like, but I cannot help wanting to see you well settled—and Daventry is a perfect gentleman.'

'Yes, I believe he may be,' Lucy replied. 'I imagine he may have been a flirt in the past, but many gentlemen have their flirts… If he is looking for a wife, he will no doubt behave just as he ought. Of course, he is an accomplished flirt and his attention may mean nothing.'

Lucy left her mother to go upstairs and change her gown for the evening when the dressing gong sounded. A maid had set out a pale-grey gown for her and Lucy allowed her to help her into it, but shook her head when she looked in the mirror.

'I shall not change again this evening, Marie, but after this I wish you to put my grey gowns away. I shall wear colours all the time now. I have finished with my mourning.'

'Yes, miss. I'll have them packed away into trunks with lavender, Miss Lucy.'

'Thank you,' Lucy said. 'And I will have my hair dressed in ringlets again this evening…the way you used to do it for me.'

'I am glad, miss,' her maid said. 'I think a softer style suits you much better.'

Lucy nodded. She looked at her image in the mirror as Marie finished dressing her hair. For too long she'd worn the severe styles caught into the nape of her neck, which she'd adopted in her grief, but she knew this way of wearing her hair was prettier and suited her well.

Fastening a string of seed pearls about her throat and pearl drops to her earlobes, Lucy reflected on the time she'd spent talking to Lord Daventry. He had teased her and flattered her, paying her far too many compliments, but he had also been able to talk to her of poetry and music…and their tastes seemed much in accord. Lucy knew that she was not in love with the earl; his touch did not make her heart race, but she felt no revulsion when he kissed her hand. She liked him very well and…if she could not marry the man she still cared for… she might as well marry for comfort. Daventry would be kind to her and she would be the wife of a wealthy man…if he asked for her, of course.

Suddenly, Lucy was taken by a fit of the giggles. She had no idea whether the earl was truly interested in making her an offer. His charm might be just his natural manner with a lady and he might just be amusing himself, flirting with a pretty girl. Indeed, that was more than likely the case.

The thought caused her no pain. She would not break her heart over him if he did not come up to scratch…but if he should ask she thought she might be able to find contentment as his wife.

All the months of breaking her heart over Paul Ravenscar, all the waiting for him to come to her in Italy, seemed far away. It was as if a dark cloud had been banished. She was recovering at last, Lucy thought. Everyone believed that the change in her was due to Mark's death, and it had played its part, for she had mourned a friend…but it was Paul who had broken her heart.

She would not allow him to do it again. Lucy lifted her head, determined now that the next time they met she would do so with indifference. If he looked through her as though she did not exist, she would give as much in return.

She was not going to waste her life in regret.

## Chapter Four

'I rode over with the invitations to my dance,' Lucy said as she was shown into the elegant parlour. Jenny was sitting at a very pretty lady's writing table, made of a pale satinwood strung with ebony, preparing what appeared to be a letter. She sanded it and applied a wax wafer, impressing the Ravenscar seal. 'I hope I do not disturb you?'

'Of course not. You are always welcome,' Jenny told her and rose, approaching her with outstretched hands. 'Please do sit down. You are not disturbing me in the least. I was writing to my aunt. She asked that I visit her in London, but I do not feel able to get away and have told her she may come here for a few days if she wishes.'

'How is your patient?' Lucy asked, sitting down on an elbow chair, which was close to Jenny and by the long window that overlooked a lawn and rose beds. It was a restful room, its colours pale blue with touches of green and white in the long curtains and the light came from two aspects, making it seem bright and airy.

'He is a great deal better,' Jenny said, her face lighting up with real pleasure. 'This morning he apologised to me for giving us all a fright…but he *was* very ill. His doctor is calling it a little miracle. I think having Paul home has made all the difference—given him something to live for again.'

'How fortunate that is for you all,' Lucy said. 'You do not think of returning home now?'

'Paul has begged me to stay for a few more weeks and I have agreed. Adam left this morning and will be gone for some days. He had business to attend, as he often does—but Ravenscar is well situated for him and he does not mind living here for the time being. I can be happy anywhere that I have my family.' She reached out and rang the bell. 'We shall have some tea, Lucy. Will you stay for nuncheon today?'

'I wish that I might,' Lucy said, 'but my cousin and uncle are arriving this afternoon and I must be back in time to change and greet them.'

'Your uncle?'

'Sir John Gresham,' Lucy said. 'He is Mama's brother, of course—and his daughter is a widow. Her name is Judith Sparrow. She is older than you and I, Jenny—but only a year or two.'

'How unfortunate for her that she has lost her husband so young,' Jenny said.

'Yes, I feel for her. I wondered if you might come to tea tomorrow and meet her—if you can be spared?'

'I am certain I could spare an hour or so. I shall have someone drive me to your house, Lucy. With Adam away I sometimes feel a little at a loss.'

Lucy was about to reply when someone entered the room. Glancing towards the door, she saw that Paul was standing just inside the threshold, looking at them.

'Do I intrude?' he asked and smiled in a way that took Lucy's breath. How long was it since she'd seen that smile? For a moment it was as if he had never been away, never cut himself off from them all. 'I was told refreshments were to be served here and I came to keep you company, Jenny—but I can go away if you prefer to be alone with your friend?'

*Did he no longer think of her as his friend?* A

slashing pain cut through Lucy, but she kept her smile in place.

'Of course not,' Jenny said. 'Please come and join us. Lucy has brought invitations to her dance, which is just a few days away now. I am hoping Adam will be back in time, but I shall certainly go...and I am sure Lady Dawlish would be happy to see you, Paul.'

'Yes, I have not been to visit your mama yet, Miss Dawlish,' Paul said and sat down in a comfortable wing chair near the fireplace, stretching out his long legs. The large hearth was empty since no fire was needed in the sunny parlour that day. 'It is remiss of me, but I have been riding about the estate most days... There is much to do, for I fear my father has made no important decisions for years and some of the housing has been neglected. However, it was remiss of me. I must find time to visit my neighbours.'

'I am sure everyone will be pleased to see you. I know that both my mother and father would welcome you at any time, sir.'

'Then I must certainly come—but you understand these properties must come first.'

'Yes, I noticed that some of the houses in Little

Mallows were in poor condition as I rode by, sir. Papa always says that it is unwise to neglect one's tenants, because it causes resentment.'

'Yes, I think I agree with him,' Paul said and frowned at his own thoughts. 'However, I shall visit your mama tomorrow, Miss Dawlish—if that is convenient?' He smiled at her and for a brief moment she glimpsed the man she'd known and loved.

'I was telling Jenny that my cousin and uncle arrive later today,' Lucy said. 'She has promised to come to tea—perhaps you might escort her?'

'Yes, why not?' he replied. 'That will suit me well, for I may see to business in the morning, as usual. You will be pleased to hear that my father is much recovered, Miss Dawlish. He is sitting up in bed, reading the latest newssheet at the moment.'

'I am very glad to hear it,' Lucy said. She glanced at him again and saw a thoughtful look in his eyes; the half-smile on his lips made her wish that he would truly talk to her, laugh with her as he had when they were children. She told herself not to expect too much and by the time a maid had brought in tea and little sweet almond macaroons, she had recovered her equilibrium and was able to speak without feeling breathless. Paul was looking at her attentively, as he might a guest he had just met—but there was none of their old intimacy, the shared jests that had struck them both as being funny when others could not see it.

'How did you enjoy your trip to Italy, Miss Dawlish?'

'I found it interesting and the lakes were wonderful,' Lucy said. 'I loved the sunshine, which was more reliable than our own, for we never know here from one day to the next how it will be. In Italy, day after day passed without so much as a cloud—here we cannot have two days without a hint of rain.'

'Yes, I fear that is the truth,' he agreed. 'Though for myself I love the changing seasons and would not wish for everlasting sunshine.'

'I am sure we should all tire of it in time,' Lucy replied and sipped the tea Jenny had poured for her.

'However, I should not care for the rain if my roof leaked,' Paul went on. 'I must make sure that the inhabitants of Little Mallows do not suffer when the next downpour comes.'

'A leaking roof would be most unpleasant,' Jenny said. 'You should certainly see to it, Paul.'

'I intend to,' he replied, put down his cup and stood up. 'It has been pleasant to see you again, Miss Dawlish. Please excuse me now…'

'I, too, should be going if I am to be home in time to prepare for my cousin,' Lucy said and stood up. She made a little curtsy to Paul. 'I shall tell Mama to expect you both tomorrow—she will be so pleased. I shall see you tomorrow, dearest Jenny.'

'I shall walk with you to the door,' Paul said politely and stood back to allow her to leave the room first. He followed her into the hall. 'Do you still prefer to ride rather than use a carriage, Miss Dawlish?'

'If you recall…I was about to be given lessons when…' She faltered and looked at him. 'Forgive me, I should not have mentioned it.'

Paul stared for a moment, then inclined his head. 'I had forgotten, but it was I who promised to teach you to drive in my phaeton, was it not?'

'Yes…' Lucy blushed. 'It is not important. My father sends a carriage and groom if the weather is damp.'

'A promise should always be kept. You will be busy with your cousin visiting, but if you would like to handle a phaeton and pair I shall be happy to oblige you, Miss Dawlish. I believe we have a suitable rig and horses that are amenable to a lady's hands.'

'Thank you, sir. Perhaps when my cousin has settled in. It would be rude of me to leave her to amuse herself too soon.'

'Of course.' He bowed his head to her as they reached the door. 'Your gown is very becoming, Miss Dawlish. Yellow was always your colour— and I fancy your hair is done in its former style today.'

'Yes.' Lucy felt a tingle of pleasure as she gazed into his eyes. For a moment her breath came faster and she wished that he would give some sign that he cared for her. 'You are observant, Captain Ravenscar. I would not have expected you to notice.'

'Oh, yes, I notice everything about you,' he said gravely.

*Now what did that mean? Was it a mere pleasantry?*

'Please take care on your ride home. I've heard there may be a gang of poachers in the area.'

'I have my groom with me and Briars is always armed.' She curtsied slightly. She waited a moment longer than necessary, hoping for something more, but he gave no sign that he had more to say to her. 'Goodbye, sir.' Lucy extended her hand; he took it briefly in his own, bowing his head, but he did not hold it longer than a second nor did he attempt to kiss it.

'I shall see you tomorrow.'

Lucy smiled as best she could and left him at the door. She did not look back and was quite unaware that he waited to watch as her groom helped her to mount, going back into the house only when she rode away.

Lucy gave her attention to her horse. Head up and back straight, she trotted down the drive, fighting the foolish desire to weep.

Her heart was behaving very foolishly. Lucy had wished that Paul might kiss her hand, or at least show some sign of being affected by her nearness, but apart from some kind words about her gown he had shown none. Not that she truly knew what he said to her at the door, for her chest was tight and she'd found it difficult to breathe.

What was it he had said about noticing everything about her? Lucy had been feeling so odd that she hadn't really heard what he did say—and what did he mean by it? Why would he notice everything about her? That sounded as if he cared... but his manner was so solemn, so reserved—polite but distant, as if they scarcely knew one another. If he cared for Lucy, he must surely have shown it by a look or a touch, but his manner had been completely impersonal. Friendly enough for a neighbour, but nothing in his gestures or his voice had suggested anything more...and she would be a fool to hope for it.

She had meant to be as cool and reserved as he was, but she was very much afraid she must have shown how affected she was by his proximity as they stood at the door.

Paul went up the stairs to his own bedchamber. For a moment there he had been close to speaking out, to asking Lucy if she had missed him, but he had managed to control himself. For a moment the desire to sweep her into his arms and kiss her had been almost overwhelming, but he had banished the foolish urge. She could not wish for anything from him other than friendship. Her manner was softer that morning, her smile more like the girl he'd known, though he could still sense that she was holding back.

Well, what did he expect? She had reminded him of a promise to teach her to drive his phaeton; it had been given only the day before Mark was murdered. What might have happened had he begun the lessons he'd promised?

*Would she have withdrawn her promise and turned to him?*

For a moment he remembered the gown she'd worn that day when they met out riding—the look in her eyes as he'd teased her about driving his phaeton and the smell of her perfume. She'd worn a soft floral scent then, but now she wore something more sophisticated…with undertones of something exotic that he found sensual.

Lucy had become a sensual woman. Paul realised with a shock that the girl he'd fallen in love with had changed in a way he was not sure he liked. There was still something of the old Lucy about her at times, but she was older…different, a cool sophistication in her manner that he found difficult to accept.

What had he expected? He was not such a fool

as to imagine that she would have waited all this time for him…that she would not have changed or grown up, was he?

If he had, he was truly a fool.

Paul regretted the months he had allowed to pass without attempting to see or even write to her. When he'd left her that last time, he had meant to join her in Italy, to get to know her…perhaps to court her once they were both ready. He did not know what had made him draw into himself, throwing his heart into his work. Somehow, he'd convinced himself that she would not wish to receive his advances…that he would be betraying the brother he'd revered by making love to the girl that Mark had intended to marry.

How could he take what ought to have been his brother's? Yet she had remained in his heart and mind, taunting him with what might have been, if Mark had lived. He might then have taken her from him, for all was fair in love and war—but he could not fight a ghost.

When he'd allowed himself to think of her, he'd seen Lucy as she was before Mark died, but she had changed.

He had left it too late, Paul realised sadly. Lucy

had grown away from him, dealing with her grief without his help. He'd seen the way she responded to Daventry. Adam's friend was a man of address, sophisticated and wealthy. Lucy probably preferred someone like him to a man she'd known all her life. Paul was only eighteen months her senior and all her life she'd treated him like a brother…until that dance…

He caught his breath as the memory struck at him like the thrust of a knife. Was it too late to court her now? Perhaps she would allow him to give her lessons in driving. It would be a first step to breaking down the barrier between them…to the start of a new friendship.

Lucy was thoughtful as she rode home. For a moment as they talked, she thought she'd seen something in Paul's manner…something that showed he was not completely the cold, reserved man he seemed. Perhaps he, too, found it difficult to break down the barrier that had grown between them? Lucy wondered if it was really too late to recover the friendship they'd known. She might have read more into his manner, into a certain look she'd seen in his eyes on several occasions before everything came tumbling down. It might be that he had never truly loved her—had just been flirting with the girl his brother meant to marry.

Perhaps if she put all thought of a romance between them from her mind, she might be able to greet him as the friend that he had been for so many years. A little smile touched her lips as she remembered romping over Lord Ravenscar's estate with Paul and Mark, whenever she could escape from her governess and her mama.

Actually, they had both followed Mark like troopers falling in behind a glorious commander—and they had both looked up to him as their leader. Mark always took the blame if they were caught in some scrape, though once Paul had insisted it was his fault and been beaten for his misdemeanour. Mark had never been given more than a lecture on his inappropriate behaviour, which, when you thought about it, was a little unfair—but of course he could never be wrong in the eyes of his doting family.

Lucy and Paul had been as mesmerised as everyone else, but, when she remembered, it was Paul to whom she had confessed her childhood fears—and it was for her sake he had taken the beating.

She had been expressly forbidden to go roaming that day, for her uncle and cousin were coming to visit, but the sun had called to her and she'd sneaked off to play at pirates with her friends. During their play she'd fallen, torn her pretty gown and cut her hands and knees. Paul had driven her home in the governess's cart and when her mama scolded her, he had claimed that he had teased her into her truancy. Lady Dawlish had told his father and for that crime he had been beaten…whereas when Mark had confessed to so much worse, including putting frogs in their tutor's bed and setting the boar in with the sows, besides a hundred other tricks, he had escaped with a scolding.

How could she have been such a fool as to think herself in love with Mark when she had always loved Paul? Lucy had been blinded by the elder brother's magnificence when he returned from the wars as a hero. He was glorious and a wonderful friend, but she had never truly loved him as she had Paul. Tears stung her eyes as she realised what her mistake had cost her: her happiness.

Was it too late to show Paul that she cared for him? And what of the earl?

Lucy liked the earl and she thought that she might find a kind of content with him if Paul no longer loved her. If only she knew for sure that he had cared for her truly. Paul had spoken much with his eyes, but apart from a few emotional words before he went off to grieve alone, she had no reason to think that he had ever considered her as the lady he would like to marry.

Perhaps she had imagined the whole, which was humiliating.

Lucy felt hot all over. How could she make the first move to heal the breach between them when she did not even know if he particularly liked her? If he thought she was throwing herself at his head, she would die of embarrassment. She must give no hint of her feelings. If he cared for her, he must speak first.

Dismounting and giving her horse into the care of a stable hand, she hurried up to the house. She must change into a pretty afternoon gown to be ready for the arrival of her cousin, Judith.

'How pretty you are,' Judith said and kissed Lucy's cheek. 'It is such an age since I saw you, Cousin. When we last met you were in the schoolroom.'

'And you were about to be married,' Lucy said, and then, as she saw a flash of grief in the other's eyes. 'Forgive me, that was clumsy.'

'No, it was truthful. I was married and then I was widowed and now I have put off my mourning. Sir Michael was very good to me and I was happy as his wife, but he would not wish me to grieve for ever. I can speak of him now without hurting, Lucy.'

'I am glad. You…you look beautiful, Judith.'

Her cousin had dark hair, which was swept into a sophisticated chignon at the back of her head, a few tendrils curling about her face. Her complexion was pale, her eyes so dark that in a certain light they looked black. Her gown was crimson silk with a buttoned bodice and a deep lace collar and cuffs; rubies sparkled in her ears and in the gold brooch she wore at her throat. Anyone looking at the two girls might think them a perfect foil, the one so dark, the other so fair. Lucy had a delicate colour in her cheeks, but her lips were not as red as her cousin's and there was a sparkle in Judith's eyes—a sparkle that spoke of laughter and a joy of life.

'Thank you, Lucy,' Judith said and laughed softly. 'I would say I have more style than beauty, but I do not turn up my nose at compliments, I assure you.'

'You do have a style of your own,' Lucy said thoughtfully. 'I do not know quite what it is—but you are not like most ladies I know.'

'I am told I resemble a Greek goddess,' her cousin said, laughing. 'I think they mean statuesque... I am certainly not a wraith like you and I mean that as a compliment.'

'You mean I am thin,' Lucy said. 'Papa says I am too thin, but I cannot help it.'

'And I am nicely rounded...' her cousin twinkled '...but because I am tall I can get away with it, you see. If I were diminutive, I should be fat, but the Greeks liked their goddesses well rounded, it seems.'

'You are not in the least fat,' Lucy said and shook her head. 'You are—yes, you are statuesque, but I find that magnificent.'

'I should have visited you long ago, for you are good for my morale,' her cousin teased. 'We shall certainly be friends, Lucy dearest. I am told you have travelled to Italy and France. I should like to travel more. I was taken to Paris for a wedding trip, but unfortunately my husband became ill of a fever when we returned and was never quite well again. Our plans to visit Greece and Spain never came to anything.'

'I enjoyed my time in Italy but…' Lucy sighed. 'I was grieving and I did not wish to come home for a long time, but now I do not think I wish to travel for a while.'

'You disappoint me,' Judith said. 'Had you been eager for it we might have travelled together… but never mind, I shall not tease you. Papa says I should find myself an obliging husband, who will take me to the places I want to see, and perhaps I shall.'

'Are you looking for a husband?'

Judith seemed thoughtful, then gave an expressive shrug. 'I am not certain. He would have to be someone I could respect… A man who would be willing to indulge me and not dominate me. You see, I am quite wealthy and can afford to indulge myself. I would not risk that freedom unless…' Again she shrugged. 'The future will take care of itself. Tell me, are you thinking of marriage in the near future?'

'My parents think of it for me,' Lucy said. 'I was to have married, as you know. Since then I have not met anyone new that I liked enough. I was asked in Italy more than once, but I could not consider any of the gentlemen who were so obliging as to offer for me.'

'Well, perhaps we shall help each other to find husbands,' Judith said and her soft laughter made Lucy want to giggle. 'After Papa leaves, perhaps my aunt would take us both to Bath, if we asked her nicely.'

'I am sure she would, for she has spoken of it,' Lucy agreed and tucked her arm into Judith's. 'Tell me, Cos, do you ride or do you drive yourself?'

'I enjoy both,' Judith said. 'I have arranged for my horses to be brought down, Lucy. Do you think your father will stable them for me—or should I ask his advice as to where adequate stabling may be had?'

'How many horses do you have?'

'Three that I wish to bring with me,' Judith replied. 'Queen Mab is my mare and an excellent riding horse—but Thunder and Lightning are two of my favourites. I drive them when I go out in my phaeton—but I have others at my home. Sir Michael kept an extensive stable and I have not wanted to sell his horses, though most serve no practical purpose, other than to draw my travelling coach, because I could not handle them.'

'You should offer them to Adam Miller should you wish to sell any of them,' Lucy said. 'I think he would offer a fair price for good horses.'

'I do not know the gentleman,' Judith said. 'I would only sell to a man I could be certain would treat them well.'

'Captain Miller is a cousin of both Paul and Mark Ravenscar…Hallam, too.'

'I believe I once met Major Ravenscar,' Judith said. 'He married a lady I knew well at one time.'

'Madeline?' Lucy smiled. 'Theirs was a very romantic story, do you not think so?'

'Yes, perhaps,' Judith agreed. 'Do you drive yourself?'

'No, I have not been taught, though I once hoped to learn.'

'Then you must allow me to take you out in my phaeton. If you have an aptitude for it, I could teach you myself. I was taught a long time ago… when I was but seventeen.'

A look of such sadness passed across Judith's face that Lucy was struck by it, but in a matter of seconds it had gone. They had by this time reached the rooms Judith was to occupy and in showing her cousin into the pretty apartment, Lucy forgot that moment.

'This is quite lovely,' Judith said. She looked about her at the pretty satinwood furniture and a cabinet filled with *objets d'art*, then bent to sniff the perfume of a vase of damask roses placed on a green-leather desk top. 'What a gorgeous scent. Roses are my favourite—and green is my colour. This room might have been made for me. Thank you, Lucy, I shall be very happy here.'

'I am glad,' Lucy replied, a little shyly. 'I hope you will stay with us for some time, Judith. I never had a sister and often wished for one—now I have a cousin I like very well, which is just as good.'

'That is a pretty compliment and I believe you mean it,' Judith replied and kissed her cheek. 'I shall enjoy learning to know you, Lucy—and I meant what I said, we must contrive to find us both a handsome husband. We shall discuss all the gentlemen's faults and make all the attractive ones fall in love with us.'

'Oh, I am not sure that I know how,' Lucy said, but the comic face her cousin made at her brought laughter to her eyes. 'Well, I dare say it will be fun trying.'

'Oh, yes, that is the idea of it,' Judith teased. 'It is a lady's duty to be proposed to at least once a day—and a gentleman's duty to keep trying until she makes up her mind.'

Lucy giggled. She was a little shocked by her cousin's assertions, for Judith was certainly not the sad little widow she had imagined.

'You must show me how it is done,' she said. 'For I am sure I do not know how.'

'Do not know how to flirt?' Judith mocked her. 'My dearest Lucy, you have only to smile and crook your little finger to have them all running to do your bidding.'

Lucy shook her head and went away, leaving her cousin to tidy her gown and make herself comfortable. She had seen herself as being a comfort to her cousin, but now she saw that Judith was more likely to turn the household upside down.

As she went downstairs to the parlour, she discovered that she was humming a little tune. If only Judith was right…if only she could lift her finger and one particular gentleman would come running…

## Chapter Five

Lucy could hardly remember when she had enjoyed herself more. Certainly she had not laughed as much since before Mark's unfortunate death. Judith had brought some gifts with her, including a pretty fan and some beautiful old lace for Lucy, also a pile of fashion magazines. After dinner that evening, the cousins put their heads together on the sofa and pored over the latest fashion plates; they were in colour and beautifully drawn and the two girls enjoyed themselves, discussing the various styles.

'I love that sprigged muslin,' Lucy said, pointing out a simple but elegant gown for afternoons. 'It would look charming with a sash of yellow.'

'It looks charming with a sash of blue,' Judith said and smiled, 'for I have just such a dress in my trunk, Lucy. You must try it on and if you like it you may have it—though it would need a deal of alteration, I fear.'

'Oh, no.' Lucy shook her head. 'I would not dream of depriving you of a gown I am sure you like—but if you do not object, I should like to have one made in a similar material and style.'

'Oh, if you will not take it, you must have one made the same, but with a yellow sash, and then we shall both wear our gowns when we go out together. We shall cause a sensation.'

'Yes, that would be amusing,' Lucy agreed and her eyes lit at the idea. 'If we go to Bath, I shall have just such a gown made.'

'The seamstresses in Bath are very good,' Judith said. 'There is a Frenchwoman I have used before. She fled from the Terror in her youth and settled in England. Her sense of style is not to be beaten, I think.'

Lucy hung on her cousin's every word, for she had much to say and was more worldly than she. Because of her cousin's lively conversation, Lucy scarcely thought of Paul until just before she was falling asleep that night.

He had definitely been friendlier when she'd seen him that morning. Perhaps it was just a case of getting to know one another again. Lucy smiled just before she drifted into sleep. She thought that at last she could truly put the past behind her and begin to think of the future. Judith's teasing had made her think carefully of marriage and she realised that there would be many advantages to being the wife of a gentleman. Wealth was always welcome, for it made life more comfortable, and though Lucy did not crave a fabulous wardrobe and splendid jewels, there were things she would like to have—and one of them was a magnificent high-perch phaeton similar to the vehicle her cousin drove.

Judith had shown her the designs she'd had drawn up before commissioning her phaeton and Lucy could not wait to ride in it—and perhaps to drive it about the estate.

Before they'd parted for the evening, her cousin had suggested a drive after breakfast so that Lucy could show her the estate. They'd agreed to meet in the hall at nine the next morning and Lucy was dressed in a becoming habit of dark green when she went down to meet her cousin. However, when she saw Judith she gasped in awe and admiration.

Judith was wearing a habit of dark-crimson velvet with gold frogging on the tailored jacket, which fitted into her waist. A froth of white lace at her throat was fixed with a large ruby-and-diamond pin and the elegant shako on her head had a magnificent and very large diamond-and-ruby brooch pinned to it with a plain band of gold ribbon round the base. Her gloves were of fine leather and black to match her gleaming riding boots.

'You look wonderful,' Lucy cried. 'I have never seen such a habit; it looks like a military coat. I think you should be a Hussar.'

Judith laughed, well pleased with the compliment. 'Thank you, Cousin. My husband had it made for me...It was one of his last gifts to me, for you must know I was thoroughly spoiled. This is but the second time I have worn it, because I wore nothing but black until last month when I decided that Sir Michael would very much dislike my mourning.'

'If he liked to see you in bold colours, he could not have wanted you to wear black for ever.'

'No, he forbade me before he died, but I felt it right to mourn him, Lucy. He was a good man... and very kind to me.'

'I am sure he loved you very much.'

'Yes…' A thoughtful expression came to Judith's face. 'Perhaps one day I shall tell you the whole and then you will understand what an exceptional man my husband was…and why I felt it right to show respect for his passing.' She sighed deeply, then shook her head. 'I refuse to dwell on things that make me unhappy. Come, I want to show you my phaeton and horses.'

They walked to the stable together. When Lucy saw the matched pair of black horses and the dashing rig her cousin intended to drive, she was speechless. She eyed the horses doubtfully as they pawed the ground with their front hooves, for she knew enough to realise that these were mettlesome creatures and would take some handling. Judith must be a noted whip to be able to drive such prime cattle.

Realising that her cousin was waiting, Lucy said, 'I am in awe of you, Judith. I love your phaeton and your wonderful horses—are you not at all afraid that they might get away from you?'

'No, indeed, I was always good with horses—watch…' She went up to them and began to talk softly to the horses, stroking each in turn and showing her affection for the handsome creatures. They responded by tossing their heads a little and snorting, but the impatient pawing at the ground ceased.

'Shall we go, Lucy?' Judith asked, turning to her. 'Come and say hello to my beauties. You must get to know them and then they will be happy to let you drive them for a while.'

Lucy went to the horses and stroked their heads. 'You are magnificent,' she said and laughed, for like Judith she had no fear of them and laughed as they tossed their heads in agreement. 'Thunder and Lightning, I think I can see who is who.' A giggle escaped her as the horse with a jagged white mark on his forehead snorted at the mention of his name.

Grooms came to help the two young ladies up to the driving box of the high-perch phaeton. It was a long way from the ground and Lucy felt a thrill of nerves as she realised how precarious her seat was, for the rig had very large wheels with red trims and such vehicles might be easily overturned by reckless driving.

However, when Judith's groom stood up behind and she gave her horses the command to move off,

Lucy's slight apprehension disappeared for she could see that her cousin was in complete control. Her horses were fine beasts and mettlesome, but well trained; they responded to the lightest touch of her hand and her whip merely cracked over their heads, never once needing to touch their shining coats. She had a knack of catching her whip with the same hand, something that Lucy had seen Adam and Mark do occasionally and knew was very skilled. Any fears she might have entertained vanished like summer mist as they bowled along the country roads.

Lucy's father's estate was well tended and prosperous, but not large, so when Judith decided at the end of the tour to leave the private land and set off down the highway, Lucy did not object. She was aware that one or two gentlemen driving their vehicles towards them turned their heads to watch as Judith drove past them. Some saluted them, others, if Lucy was well known to them, waved their hand.

They had been driving for some twenty minutes or so on the road when a vehicle approached from the opposite direction. The gentleman was driving at a good pace and it was not until it drew closer that Lucy realised it was Paul in control of the horses. He seemed unaware of them until he passed them and then a startled look came to his eyes and he frowned. For a moment she thought he would halt his horses, but although he slowed his pace he did not stop, merely giving Lucy an odd stare as he drove on by.

He looked very much as if he disapproved of them, but whether it was the rig or the fact that they were driving on the highway she could not know.

Lucy's heart caught, for he had looked angry, but she dismissed the idea as her imagination. What possible reason could Paul Ravenscar have for disapproving of her driving out with her cousin?

They had reached a crossroads. Judith turned her horses neatly and drove back to the Dawlish estate. She did not offer the reins to Lucy, but after they had been helped down, she turned to her with a smile.

'My darlings were fresh today, for they had not been in harness for a while. They were driven down in short stages and have to accustom themselves to new stabling. I felt them pulling a little.

Tomorrow they will be easier with their new surroundings and then I shall begin your lessons—if you still wish for them?'

'Yes, please,' Lucy said instantly. She had seen the way the gentlemen they met on the road looked at Judith. Most had had nothing but admiration in their eyes for her—and Lucy would very much like to be as skilled as her cousin. 'I enjoyed our drive, Judith. It was exhilarating and I should like to be able to drive as well as you, though I am not certain I ever could.'

'Well, we shall see,' Judith said. 'You were not in the least nervous when I let them have their heads for a little while, so I think they will tolerate your hand on the reins.' She laughed and removed her hat as they went into the hall, placing it with her gloves on a mahogany pier table. 'The fresh air has made me hungry. Do you think your cook has more of the delicious macaroons we had for tea yesterday?'

'I think she might,' Lucy said and smiled. She was thoughtful as she removed her own gloves and hat.

Why had Paul looked so very annoyed when he saw them on the road?

\* \* \*

Lucy had changed into a pretty pale-pink afternoon gown and was seated in the drawing room with her mother, Judith, her uncle and father, when their guests were announced. Lady Benson and her son Charles had called and were shown in at the same time as Jenny and Captain Ravenscar.

Lady Benson was a close friend of Lucy mother's, and once all the greetings had been exchanged and the tea brought in, the young people were at liberty to talk, their little group having retreated to some chairs and a sofa near the window.

'Tell me, Lady Sparrow,' Charles Benson said, a gleam in his eyes. 'Am I right—was it you driving that bang-up rig this morning?'

'Yes, indeed, it was,' Judith said. 'Did we pass you on the road, sir? I was concentrating on my horses and did not notice.'

Charles was barely nineteen, still a little shy of beautiful ladies and with a tendency to blush. He looked very young as he gave her an admiring look.

'You drove those wonderful horses to an inch,' he said, clearly overwhelmed. 'I wish I might be able to handle the ribbons as well as you—and that trick with your whip was neat. Will you show me how to do it?'

'Certainly, if you wish,' Judith said and bestowed a smile on him that made his cheeks redden. 'My cousin has first call on my time, for I have promised to teach her to drive—but if you called in the afternoon I could give you lessons with the whip in the paddock.'

'Your cousin is rather different from what I expected,' Jenny murmured softly to Lucy.

'Yes, isn't she wonderful?' Lucy replied and her gaze went to Paul's face. After the first introductions he had said little, but now he put down his teacup and looked at her.

'Lady Sparrow has great skill and address,' Paul said. 'She has clearly been driving for some years. I think you might do better in a less…precarious vehicle. I am quite prepared to give you lessons in my curricle, Miss Dawlish. Lady Sparrow's rig is elegant, but a little…too bold for a lady to drive. It might be safer for you…at least until you have some experience.'

Lucy hesitated. In her heart she agreed, but his disapproval of her cousin's bold rig annoyed her.

What did he mean by telling her that he thought her unsafe to manage her cousin's horses?

'Judith handles her horses beautifully, sir. I dare say I may do so given my chance. I have known horses all my life and am not afraid of them.'

'It is not a matter of whether you are afraid...' Paul looked haughty. 'It is very well for Lady Sparrow to drive such an equipage, for she has been married and it is generally known that her husband indulged her every whim—but for you... an unmarried girl! I must tell you, Lucy, I was shocked to see you driving on the road in such a way.'

'I shall not allow you to be critical of my behaviour or my cousin's,' Lucy said, stung to defiance. 'No one else seemed to disapprove of us. Indeed, most people waved to us or saluted Judith.'

If anything, he looked more disapproving than before.

'I have told you, Lady Sparrow may do as she pleases. I am thinking of you, Lucy. Some people might think...your behaviour was fast.'

Judith turned her head to look at him, a militant sparkle in her eyes. 'Come, come, Captain Ravenscar, I cannot have you scold my cousin.

She had no idea that I intended to take my team on to the road. We went for a drive about the estate and I took a wrong turning. Lucy tried to warn me, but we were forced to drive for some time before we came to a place where we might turn—besides, my friends are used to seeing me drive myself everywhere, even in town. I do hope that does not give you a disgust of me—perhaps you find me too bold?'

Such a brilliant smile accompanied her words that Paul was silenced. He had scolded Lucy, for it had shocked him to see her like that on the road. He had spoken out, feeling that she did not understand how it might look to some other ladies. Lucy would not wish her reputation to suffer, surely—and yet now he was feeling foolish. A few high-born ladies did choose to drive themselves in town and one or two—like Letty Lade—were not above racing their vehicles.

He inclined his head a little stiffly. 'Indeed, it would be impertinent in me if I were to tell you what to do, my lady.'

'Yes, it would,' Judith agreed pleasantly. 'However, I see no reason why we should fall out over such a foolish thing. I shall be certain to keep to the estate roads whenever Lucy is driving my rig.'

'Do you not consider your horses a little too strong for teaching a beginner, my lady?' Paul arched his right eyebrow at her, his eyes a flinty grey.

Judith ignored his look, but tossed her head, a pugnacious glint in her eyes.

'Lucy does not fear them, you know, and the horses respond to a firm hand. Besides, I shall be with her. I would not let her drive alone until I was certain she could handle the horses.'

Paul inclined his head and then responded to a question from Charles Benson, but his gaze was stern as it fixed first on Lucy and then on Judith. Her laughter rang out several times and Paul could not help noticing her vibrancy and her confident manner. He had met ladies of a similar cut in Vienna and might have taken a mistress from amongst them had he been interested. None of those ladies had caught his interest, but Judith Sparrow certainly had something about her. When she saw him looking at her, she gave him an arch look, as if challenging him, and he frowned at his own thoughts.

'How does Lord Ravenscar today?' Lucy asked and he relaxed his frown.

'He seems better than when I returned, but his health will never be robust again, I fear.' Paul hesitated, then, 'I did not mean to scold you or to criticise your cousin. She has town ways and they do not always sit well in the country, that is all.'

'Judith is very brave and…magnificent,' Lucy said. 'I find her company makes me feel more alive…much better than I have felt in an age.'

'Yes, she is magnificent,' Paul said and looked at Judith as she spoke and laughed with Jenny. The widow was assured and seemed to brush off everything with a laugh or an arch of her brow. He imagined that she was not easily impressed and, piqued because she appeared to ignore him, he determined to catch her interest. 'Do you stay long in the country, Lady Sparrow? I should think you more at home in town.'

'Would you?' Her smile was deliberately provocative. Paul felt himself respond even though he'd meant to resist the challenge she threw out. 'I can be content with my horses and dogs in the country, if I have the right companions. I am not above being pleased by simple things, sir.'

'No, no, I did not mean...' Paul was on the wrong foot with her and determined to do better. 'You strike me as a woman who likes London or Paris and its pleasures.'

'If you mean would I like to travel, the answer is yes,' Judith said and suddenly smiled at him. 'It is a passion with me and I should like to indulge myself—but I must have comfortable companions about me. My father is too busy to be bothered with a widowed daughter and so I think I must look for a husband.' She laughed and looked at Lucy. 'We have been making plans to lay siege to the gentlemen of Bath next month—for we are both in need of husbands.'

'Judith!' Lucy cried and blushed as she saw Paul's eyes upon her. 'That was our secret.'

'Oh, but I do not mind sharing it with present company,' Judith said, 'for they will not be a target.'

She had thrown down the gauntlet, her eyes bright with mischief.

Paul frowned, but immediately felt the urge to make this merry widow take back her words. She was attractive and he was drawn to her. He did not know why she had got beneath his skin, but he was seized by a strong determination to make her see the error of her ways.

He began to talk about the life in Vienna, the balls the Iron Duke had given and his despair that the peace would never be settled. In this manner, he found himself the centre of attention and was bombarded with questions from the others in his little circle, including Lady Sparrow. Paul fancied she had begun to look at him with more interest and smiled. They might have started on the wrong foot, but he had succeeded in gaining ground with her.

He was well satisfied when he rose to take his leave, and did not see the odd questing look that Lucy threw at him as he bowed over her cousin's hand.

She was silent for a moment after their guests had all gone, then said she would go up to her room. Judith accompanied her, slipping an arm through hers and smiling in a satisfied way.

'I thought your Captain Ravenscar a pompous idiot at first,' she confessed, 'but then I saw there was more to him. I dare say he was merely trying to protect your reputation, Lucy—for he clearly thinks me fast and not proper company for you.'

'Oh, I doubt he truly cares what I do,' Lucy said carelessly. 'Besides, he has no right to tell me what I may or may not do.'

'He certainly has not—unless you are fond of him?'

'I like him well enough as a friend...'

'Then we shall teach the captain a little lesson,' Judith said with a naughty smile. 'I promised to show you how simple it is to bring a gentleman to heel, Lucy—and it may as well be he as any other.'

Over the next few days, Lucy and Judith drove out about the estate in the high-perch phaeton and the driving lessons were begun. Although a little nervous at the start, Lucy gave no sign and gradually she began to thoroughly enjoy driving and to feel confident, though as yet she had not mastered Judith's trick with the whip.

Charles Benson had not succeeded either, and Judith confided to Lucy that he had the worst hands she'd ever seen in a gentleman.

'I should not dream of letting him drive my horses,' she said.

'Oh, but, Judith,' Lucy cried, 'the poor man

adores you. He is here every day and stays for tea and would stay for supper if he were invited. I believe he is in love with you.'

'Oh, very likely,' Judith replied with a laugh. 'It will pass, my dear Cousin. At his age he will fall in love regularly. I do not expect his adoration to last more than a week or two.'

'Cruel…' Lucy cried, but laughed, for in truth Judith had done little to encourage her ardent adorer.

She could not think her cousin cared for him at all, but she was never unkind to her admirer and could not help it if he had fallen in love with her. She was lively and teasing and brought a sense of fun to everything she did.

Lucy had often managed to forget Paul altogether in her cousin's company, but once alone in her bed the regrets returned. She had hoped he might visit often, as he had been used to years before, but it was not until the morning of the day before her dance that he drove over.

Lucy was in the parlour, her cousin having taken her father out for a drive because he was leaving the next day.

'You will forgive me for deserting you,' she said before she left. 'I do not know how long it may be until I see Papa again and he asked if we might be alone for a time.'

'Of course you must take him,' Lucy replied. 'I shall be perfectly happy to stay at home. There are many little tasks that need doing before tomorrow.'

However, she had finished her tasks and was sitting in the parlour wondering whether to ride out with her groom when her visitor was announced. Paul strode into the room and her heart caught with both pleasure and pain as she saw how well he looked in his tight-fitting breeches and a blue riding coat with whip ends threaded through the buttonholes.

'Do I find you alone, Miss Dawlish?' His eyes travelled about the room as if searching for someone.

'Mama is still in her room,' Lucy replied. 'I fear my cousin has gone out with her father.'

'I am sorry to have missed her,' Paul said. 'Jenny wanted to assure you that she and Adam will attend your dance tomorrow. Hallam and Madeline are visiting with us, so there is no need for her to cry off—and Father seems well enough.'

'I am glad to hear it,' Lucy said. 'Are Hallam and his wife well?'

'She is with child, but otherwise very well, I think...but prefers to stay quietly at home and would not wish to attend a dance.'

'Please sit down, Captain Ravenscar,' Lucy invited. 'May I send for refreshment?'

'Nothing, thank you. I would much prefer to take you out in my curricle...if you should care for it?'

Lucy was surprised, her eyes lighting as she looked at him. Her heart missed a beat and she smiled with pleasure.

'Very much, sir—if you will let me handle the reins for a while.' A teasing light made her eyes very bright. Had she known it, she looked much as she had before the tragedy.

'Why not?' he asked, amused. 'Do you need to change?'

'No for I put on this habit in case I decided to ride out,' Lucy told him. 'My hat and gloves are here on the table. We shall go at once, for you will not wish to keep your horses standing.'

'Good.' He smiled at her and Lucy's heart caught. For a moment it was as if the years had rolled back and this was the young man she had ridden and walked with as a young girl. She felt a little breathless, her heart beating rapidly as their eyes met and held. 'I have been wondering how your lessons progressed.'

'I am not yet as accomplished as my cousin,' Lucy said as she set her hat at a jaunty angle on her fine blonde curls. 'Judith says that I have good hands and will be a notable whip in time.'

'Lady Sparrow is a very confident woman,' Paul replied, an odd smile on his lips. 'I think I set out on the wrong tack with her and must mend my ways or she will not dance with me tomorrow.'

'You are coming?' Lucy stared at him, her pleasure plain to be seen, for she had thought he might cry off.

'Hallam and Madeline will keep Father company—and I believe I ought to make some effort to renew my acquaintance with our neighbours, for I have been away a long time.'

Lucy wished that she was on the old terms with him, for once she would have hugged him in her pleasure, but things had changed and she could no longer behave like the tomboy she had once been. Instead, she inclined her head politely.

'Mama was of the same mind. We have been out to dinner twice this week, but until Judith came we had not entertained ourselves. Her arrival has been the excuse Mama needed to invite her friends once more.'

'I remember some of the evenings we had here in the past—and at home,' Paul said. 'We were good friends then, were we not, Miss Dawlish—all of us?'

'Yes, of course.' Lucy hesitated, then, 'I think we are still friends, Paul. It is just that we have fallen out of the habit of it.'

'Yes…' A smile flickered in his eyes as he looked down at her. 'I was used to call you Lucy…'

'I wish you would do so now,' she replied a little shyly as they went outside. Paul's groom was standing at the head of his pair of matched greys. Paul helped her up and then climbed up beside her.

'I shall,' he said. 'Jake, you may wait here until I return.'

'Go to the kitchen for a glass of ale,' Lucy said kindly.

She watched as Paul flicked his reins and his horses moved forward at a walk, which increased to a trot once they were clear of the drive. He waited until they were upon one of the estate roads, before turning to Lucy with a question in his eyes.

'Do you feel you can handle them?'

'Yes, of course,' Lucy said. She had noticed that the horses were a little more inclined to shy and toss their heads than Judith's pair, but as Paul was beside her, she felt no fear in accepting the reins from his hand. Immediately she felt the horses pull as if they thought they could get away from this new hand, but she gave a light tug and they responded immediately.

'They are beautifully trained,' she said. 'I think they have soft mouths, for it needed only the slightest indication to hold them back.'

'Horses will always test a new hand, but these are well trained. Had I brought my chestnuts I should not have been so inclined to allow you to handle them…though you are doing well. Your cousin is right, you do have good hands. I remember that you always rode well.'

'I should, for you and Mark taught me,' Lucy

said. 'Do you recall that pony with the wild eyes? Papa bought it for my tenth birthday without seeing it and when it came it was so wilful…always kicking the grooms and trying to throw me off.'

'It succeeded more than once,' Paul said and laughed. 'Had your father known he would have sold it immediately.'

'But I loved Treacle,' Lucy said. 'I should have hated it if Papa had sold him—even though he did not like to be ridden. Besides, you told me that I should get back in the saddle and not sniffle. What choice did I have?'

'You were very brave,' Paul said, laughing. 'I always admired you for that, Lucy. Between us, Mark and I managed to train the wretched animal and I think you had no more falls after he was broken.'

'Only one, which was my own fault. I put Treacle at the hedge at Long Mile Bottom and he refused. I went sailing over his head and knocked the breath out of myself.'

'I am not surprise he refused,' Paul said. 'That was a foolish thing to do, Lucy. You deserved to be thrown…but, no, I should not have said it. You might have been badly hurt.'

'If I had it would have been my fault,' Lucy said and laughed. 'We got into some terrible scrapes together, did we not? I remember how cross Mama was the day my best dress was torn...'

'And my father took his stick to me for tempting you out when your mama had forbidden it...'

'It was not truly your fault, for I sneaked out to join you...'

'But I had dared you to...do you not recall?'

'Ah, yes...' Lucy laughed. She felt a surge of happiness, for this was the first time they had talked properly since he returned. 'We had such fun, all...three of us.'

'Yes, we did,' Paul replied and for a moment the smile died from his eyes. 'I worshipped him, Lucy, as I know you did.'

'Yes...' She could not take her eyes from the road. 'He was a hero, Paul...larger than life and that was before he won honours on the battlefield.'

'Yes, he was always the golden one,' Paul said and a soft laugh escaped him. 'I do not know why, but I can think of him now and remember the good times...it no longer hurts as desperately as it did.'

'I know,' Lucy agreed, a little nerve flicking

in her throat. She, too, had felt the ice that had formed about her heart begin to melt away since her homecoming. 'We all loved him, Paul, but we cannot grieve for ever. Mark would not wish us to.'

'He would think it ridiculous,' Paul said, a harsh choking sound in his throat. 'He told me once that if he should die I was to mourn him for a week and then get on with my life.'

'Yes, I imagine he would say that,' Lucy said. 'I think it was the manner of his death...so cruel when he had returned from the war unscathed.'

'Yes, that seemed most unfair,' Paul agreed. He glanced at her and for a brief second she met his eyes, but could not read their message. 'Are you tired? Let me take the reins again. You have done well, but these horses are strong and take some holding.'

'I am not tired,' Lucy said, but relinquished the reins into his hands. She wanted to look at his profile, which she could not while driving the pair. 'I think they are fine horses, Paul—but less used to the touch of a lady's hand than Judith's team.'

'I dare say, for they have not been used to it, but

they will learn—if you will allow me to take you driving sometimes?'

'Oh, yes, when I can, thank you,' she said and her heart caught as she saw the little nerve flicking at his temple. 'We go down to Bath at the end of next week, you know.'

'Ah, then I must wait until you return, for I may not be able to come often in the next few days.'

'Oh...' Lucy felt a pang of disappointment, for she had thought they were progressing so well.

'I have business for the estate. I have set some improvements in hand and they may keep me busy for a time, but I shall come one morning if I can... perhaps on Sunday, after you return from church?'

'You must stay for nuncheon, then, and we might drive in the afternoon,' Lucy said. 'I shall see you tomorrow, of course.'

'Yes...' He looked thoughtful. 'Perhaps you will be engaged when you return from Bath.'

Lucy's heart drummed, the sound filling her ears as she said with a laugh, 'You are thinking of what Judith said...it was mere nonsense. She likes to tease.'

How could he think she wished to marry anyone else?

'Yes, she is a clever and beautiful woman, full of vitality and life.'

'She is,' Lucy agreed, feeling a pang of what she suspected might be jealousy, and a most unworthy sentiment. 'I dare say she may find a husband, for it is what she wants…a companion who will take her travelling and indulge her whims.'

'I imagine any man would be happy to indulge a woman like Lady Sparrow.' His tone was casual, but his words had more force than if he had shouted them, for they showed how deep was his admiration for her cousin.

'Yes, of course.'

Lucy felt her throat catch and the tears were close, though she fought them back. Such praise from Paul for her cousin hurt her, though she agreed with every word. Judith was beautiful, bold and magnificent. Lucy already knew that she drew gentlemen to her like a moth to a flame, for Charles Benson was not the only gentleman to call at Dawlish in the hope of seeing her.

As they arrived at the courtyard at the back of Dawlish House, Lucy noticed that a travelling chaise had pulled up. She saw a figure get down and turn to look at her. It was the Earl of Daventry and he was smiling in a way that told her he was very pleased to see her. He came forward to help her down, before Paul could give the reins to his horses and do so himself.

'Miss Lucy, I am charmed to see you,' he said. 'I had hoped to return before this, but was unable to do so, yet I was determined not to miss your dance—and here you see me.'

'Lord Daventry, I am delighted to see you,' Lucy said and gave him her hand to kiss. 'Captain Ravenscar has been giving me a driving lesson— but I am glad we were back in time to greet you.'

In the flurry of greetings, she felt that she had left things unspoken and would have wished to take a private leave of Paul, for she needed to be certain that she had not read more into his words of praise for Judith than was intended. However, Daventry was determined to claim her attention for himself.

'I wrote, but perhaps my letter did not arrive, for I was not sure until the day before yesterday what day I should come. I can stay at the inn, for

I would not wish to put your dear mama to any trouble.'

'Your room is prepared, for you were expected any day,' Lucy said, smiling at him. She turned to Paul, her brows raised. He had not dismounted and was looking at her oddly. She felt that he disapproved of her greeting the earl in such a friendly fashion. 'Will you come in and take luncheon with us, sir?'

'I thank you, Miss Dawlish,' Paul replied and the distant look she dreaded was back in his eyes. 'I am expected at home. I shall see you tomorrow—your servant, Daventry.'

'I hope all is well with you, sir—your father?' the earl enquired.

'As well as can be hoped for,' Paul replied, inclining his head in a cool nod. 'Good day to you, sir...Miss Dawlish...'

The exchange between them had been friendly enough, but Lucy sensed an undercurrent—of dislike, she thought. They were both gentlemen, but they certainly had no liking for each other.

Lucy's heart sank as she watched Paul drive away, his groom beside him. For a time that morning she had thought they were back on their old footing, but now it seemed that the barrier was in place once more. She felt hurt by his coldness. Why was he angry—and if he disliked the earl's attention to her, why had he not stayed to luncheon and paid her some attention himself?

Surely Paul was not jealous of the earl? No, he had no reason to be.

Her throat caught as she recalled their conversation concerning her cousin. Paul clearly admired Judith very much. He had acknowledged his long-standing friendship with Lucy, but it seemed he saw her as just a friend. It was Judith that had aroused warmer feelings in his heart.

He might have stayed if Judith had asked.

Forcing the slashing pain to a distant corner of her heart, Lucy took the earl's arm and walked into the house with him. He was as charming as always and very attentive. She had thought he might have forgotten her, but his absence was soon explained; a cousin had died after he left them and he had been busy seeing to family affairs.

'I was determined to put it all to rest before I came here,' he said. 'I am now at your disposal,

Miss Lucy. I hope that we shall become good friends in the next few days…or weeks.'

'We go down to Bath at the end of next week, sir.'

'Ah, yes, I seem to recall that I have reason to visit that excellent place.' George smiled down at her. His eyes seemed to caress her and she felt some of her hurt melt in the warmth of his smile. 'You see, Miss Lucy, I am determined not to be parted from you again too soon.'

Lucy laughed, letting go of his arm to walk ahead as the butler relieved the earl of his hat, gloves and capped greatcoat. His banter was just foolishness, but it was pleasant after the coldness she'd seen in Paul's eyes before he drove away. She gave her mind to making her guest welcome and put away all thought of the man who had been entertaining her all morning.

How could he remind her of their childhood friendship, laughing as if he had not a care in the world—and then revert to the cold, reserved man she'd first seen at Ravenscar after he came home?

What had changed him so swiftly?

Her mother had just come into the hall to greet their visitor. Lucy went on into the parlour where she found Judith sitting perusing a magazine for ladies. It had been delivered to her with some letters forwarded from London and she had her writing case on the small mahogany wine table beside her.

'Did you enjoy your drive?' Judith asked. 'How fortunate that you were not out with me, Lucy.'

'Captain Ravenscar enquired after you,' Lucy said. 'I believe it was you he came to ask, but finding me alone took pity on me.'

Judith's eyes sparkled. 'I hope he allowed you to drive his horses?'

'Yes, for a time. They are very strong and more restive than yours.'

'My darlings are well trained, but can be restive if they do not get enough exercise,' she said. 'Captain Ravenscar rides more often than he drives, I think.'

'Perhaps,' Lucy said. 'He is to come to the dance tomorrow…and we have a visitor.'

Judith arched her brows in question, but before Lucy could answer her mother came into the room with the earl behind her.

'Judith my dear,' she said with a smile. 'May

I present you to our guest the…the Earl of Daventry.'

Lucy was looking at her cousin and saw that her face was very pale as she rose to her feet and made a slight curtsy.

'Sir…' she murmured.

'Lady Sparrow,' George Daventry said and his eyes narrowed. 'No need for introductions, Lady Dawlish. Lady Sparrow and I met years ago…before her marriage to Sir Michael.'

'We met briefly,' Judith said. 'In the country, I think, sir. I trust you are well?'

Judith had recovered herself, but Lucy noticed that her mouth had thinned and one hand clenched at her side.

'Oh, come,' George said with his charming smile. 'It was a little more than that, I believe… but we shall say no more since you have forgot me. I dare say you had more important things to think of.'

Judith inclined her head, but did not speak. Lucy had the distinct suspicion that she was either nervous or very angry.

Paul gave his horses into the care of his groom before dismounting in the courtyard. He had driven all the way home in silence and merely nodded to the man as he strode into the house. His mood had descended on him as he witnessed the delight with which Lucy Dawlish had greeted the Earl of Daventry.

Damn the fellow for intruding where he was not wanted! Paul had believed that she had opened herself to him as they drove. In recalling their childhood misdemeanours the barriers had tumbled for a time. He had even thought for one moment as she looked at him that she might have stronger feelings towards him than mere friendship…but then something had happened and she had withdrawn again.

What had he said? He could not for the life of him think of anything that should have upset her.

And then she'd been in raptures when that damned fellow turned up!

Paul ground his teeth as he walked up the stairs to change. Women were a mystery. He was damned if he understood them…and at the moment, he wasn't sure he wished to!

Yet, later, when he was in bed and sleep did not come, he could not help remembering how pleasant their ride had been. For a short time it had been as if nothing had ever happened to spoil their friendship. Perhaps it could be that way again, if he could put his guilt and sorrow behind him.

# Chapter Six

'Do you have reason to dislike the earl?' Lucy asked her cousin later that evening when they were alone for a few moments.

'I do not dislike him,' Judith replied calmly, though there was a little pulse beating at her temple. 'What made you think it?'

'Oh…it was just a look in your eyes when he entered the parlour and…and I thought you were angry?'

Judith paused, then, 'Before Daventry inherited his uncle's title he visited us often at home. His father's small estate was close to ours. At one time he paid me some attention but…we had a disagreement and he left the area. I had not seen him since then and feared there might be some awkwardness, but there was not and so it is all very well.'

Lucy looked at her doubtfully. 'I am sorry if his being here makes you uncomfortable, Judith.'

She laughed and shook her head. 'Not at all, Lucy. Daventry is interested only in you and will not bother me at all…unless he means you harm, in which case he may find I have something to say.'

Lucy was astonished. 'Means me harm, Cousin? What harm could he possibly mean?'

'None, I dare say,' Judith replied, but her expression was serious. 'He is a rake, Lucy. You must have realised that he flirts outrageously with all the ladies…and I believe he has had a great many affairs of a clandestine nature.'

'Yes, I can well imagine a gentleman of his address…' Lucy's cheeks, burned for it was a delicate subject. 'But you could not imagine… He would not try to seduce me, I think.'

'No, no, he dare not,' Judith agreed quickly. 'You have family to protect you and he would not think of it… It was only that I thought he might trifle with your affections and break your heart.'

'He may attempt it if he wishes,' Lucy said and smiled. 'I like him well enough and if he were to make me an offer…well, I suppose he would do as well as any other. They do say that a reformed rake makes a good husband, I believe.'

'Yes, I've heard it said, if his heart is engaged. I merely thought to warn you, Cousin, but I see I need not have troubled.'

'I do not think I am in danger of having my heart broken,' Lucy assured her. 'As yet I have not made up my mind to marry...but we must see what the future brings.'

'Yes, indeed.' Judith nodded her agreement. 'In Bath I dare say we shall both find we have a surfeit of suitors. I have received an offer of marriage since I came to stay with you, but I shall not take it—I do not care to be nursemaid to Major Barton's brood of five noisy children...'

'Oh, has he asked you?' Lucy said and laughed softly. 'I vow I pity him for he has asked most of the single ladies in the district. He is desperate to find a mother for his children and I fear no one will have him.'

'Then he must employ nursemaids and a housekeeper.'

'He already has several nursemaids and a housekeeper, but still his children run wild,' Lucy said. 'He hopes that a new mother would content his unruly brood, but I fear she would have to have nerves of steel.'

'They would not bother me if I found the father attractive,' Judith replied with a twist of her mouth. 'But I look higher—and I want, if not love, at least mutual affection.'

'Yes, of course.' Lucy agreed with her. 'Marriage would not be comfortable if one did not at least like one's husband.'

Yet many young girls of their class had no say in the matter, for their marriage was arranged for them, sometimes without their consent. Lucy knew that she was fortunate in having parents who would not dream of forcing her into marriage, though they hoped for it, of course.

The cousins parted in mutual agreement and it was not until Lucy was in bed that she wondered at some of Judith's remarks concerning the earl. Had Daventry trifled with her and then broken her heart? Judith had not said as much, but she would not have warned Lucy had she not thought him a little dangerous.

If she imagined that such remarks would daunt Lucy, she was mistaken. It had done Daventry no harm in Lucy's eyes to know that he was a rake, for she had suspected it from the start. She felt herself in no danger of being seduced. Indeed, had a certain gentleman given her reason to hope, she would not even consider the earl as a possible husband. However, Paul seemed as if he had forgotten he ever cared for her—and Lucy had begun to doubt her memory. Perhaps she had made too much of the looks Paul had given her, the touch of his hand at her waist as they waltzed and his breath against her hair when he'd held her too long after helping her to dismount from her horse.

These things had set her flesh tingling and made her feel so vital, so alive, and she'd believed that he cared for her deeply, even though he had not spoken. Yet how could he when he believed her to love his brother?

Had she imagined that emotional farewell before Paul left her to travel to Italy and then to Vienna? Lucy thought they had parted with hope of something more than friendship in the future— but, again, perhaps she had read too much into his words? Perhaps he'd seen her feelings too plainly and, not returning them, had decided to stay away in the hope that she would marry elsewhere.

This last thought caused her cheeks to burn,

because she was afraid it might be the case. She had imagined that Paul returned her feelings, but she had deceived herself. Oh, how foolish! How foolish!

It was so embarrassing. For a few moments Lucy felt as if she wanted to sink through the floor. How could she have been so mistaken? It was humiliating for her to think that Paul had believed she was throwing her cap at him. She saw it must have been in his mind, for why else had he warned her that he was interested in her cousin rather than herself?

His praise for Judith had been warm indeed. Indeed, he was quite possibly falling in love with her.

Lucy welled up with a mixture of conflicting emotions. She had longed for Paul to come to her in Italy, but believed it was his grief for Mark that had kept him away. Now her eyes were opened and she realised that she had been a complete fool. Paul had merely been flirting a little with his brother's wife-to-be. He had never loved her. Indeed, if he admired anyone it was Judith.

Hot tears stung her eyes and trickled down her

cheeks. She could not believe that she had been so very misguided.

After perhaps twenty minutes or so the tears ceased. Pride came to Lucy's rescue. It was as well that she had said nothing to remind Paul of what she'd thought was his promise to return to her when they had both healed. Lucy could not bear to see rejection of her love in his eyes.

She would give him no cause to think that she was expecting an offer. She would be friendly, of course, because to be anything else with a man she'd known all her life would be ridiculous—but she would be cool.

Her hurt pride eased a little in the reflection that she had one admirer, even if he was a rake—and in Bath she would no doubt meet several gentlemen she could like.

With that thought in mind, she fell into a troubled sleep.

Lucy woke at her usual time, feeling less than refreshed.

However, it was the day of her dance and she could not be miserable on such a day, for flowers and small gifts from friends began to arrive before she had been served her breakfast in bed. Lucy normally rose and went out riding or walking, but today she had been ordered to remain in bed until midmorning.

A maid brought up her breakfast tray of honey and rolls and a pot of dark chocolate, and another girl brought several posies, cards and small tributes. She discovered that one posy of roses was from Paul Ravenscar, but refused to let herself believe the tribute was more than mere politeness.

George Daventry had sent her a jewelled posy holder with his tribute of fragrant flowers, which were freesias and very delicate. Since they were a pale-lilac colour they would go very well with the gown of delphinium blue that Lucy had chosen for her dance. All the other posies would be left in her room in little vases, but she would acknowledge every one with a thank-you card after the dance.

Her mother came in while she was still looking at some cards and small gifts. Lady Dawlish was bearing a velvet box, which she gave Lucy with an affectionate kiss.

'These are some earrings, which I thought would go well with your pearls, my love.'

'Thank you, Mama,' Lucy said.

'Who has sent you flowers, dearest?'

'These are from the earl,' Lucy said, showing her the freesias in their holder. 'Paul sent me the white roses and...oh, there are cards and posies from most of our guests. People are amazingly kind, Mama.'

'Yes, my love. I expect they feel pleased to see you ready to dance and be happy again. Paul sent Judith some pink roses—was that not kind of him? She has had three posies, I think, but it is your dance and so you have many more.'

Lucy felt the pain strike at her heart. Paul had sent roses to Judith, too. Had she needed more proof of his feelings for her cousin, she had it now. She had fallen asleep after making up her mind to forget that she had ever cared for him, but that did not stop the crushing pain in her breast. However, she pushed it away and smiled at her mother.

No one must know that she was breaking her heart for a man who did not love her. Forcing a smile, she changed the subject.

'Did you know that Major Barton had asked Judith to marry him? She said no, of course.'

'How foolish of him,' Lady Dawlish said. 'To

be sure, I thought she might be grateful for any husband before she came to stay with us and was determined to help her—but she is an independent and stylish lady. I am sure there will be many offers for her hand once it is known that she is no longer in mourning.'

'Yes, she is…beautiful,' Lucy said, choking back the unworthy feeling that she knew was jealousy. Even her mama thought that Judith was exceptional. It was no wonder that Paul's interest should have been aroused. 'I know she looks for a husband, but I am certain she will choose someone who will indulge her by taking her travelling for a while.'

'She might travel with a chaperon and a trustworthy manservant if she chose,' Lady Dawlish said. 'Yet I know it is more comfortable to have a gentleman with one. We missed your papa when he left us in Italy to return home, did we not?'

'Yes, Mama. It was foolish of me to want to stay there as long as I did. I should have returned sooner.' She looked down at her flowers, picked up a posy at random and sniffed it. 'I am feeling better and I have quite decided to marry, Mama.

If I meet a gentleman I like and he asks for me, I shall accept him.'

'Shall you, Lucy?' her mother asked, frowning a little. 'I suppose there is no one in particular?'

'At the moment, no,' Lucy said. 'At least…if he were to ask…but he has not as yet and Judith tells me he is a rake.'

'You speak of the earl?' Lady Dawlish looked thoughtful. 'He does have a certain reputation, dearest, but I believe… I am certain that if he married a young lady he loved that would end.'

'Do you approve of George Daventry, Mama?'

'I like him very well, my love. Both your father and I…we could not help noticing his attentions to you. If you did take him, I should be content, but only if you are happy, my love.'

'Thank you, Mama,' Lucy said and leaned forward to kiss her. 'You and Father have been so kind to me. I know most fathers and mothers would expect to arrange a suitable marriage for their daughters—but you have not pushed me at all. You did know that I received several offers in Italy?'

'Certainly. You are my only daughter,' Lady Dawlish replied. 'I have been in no hurry to part from you, my love. All I want is that you should be happy with your choice.'

'I am very fortunate,' Lucy said. 'I hope that very soon I shall make you proud of me by contracting a respectable alliance.'

Lady Dawlish smiled, rose to her feet and left her to continue her breakfast. Lucy picked up the roses from Paul and held them to her nose, her eyes sparkling with unshed tears, which she blinked away.

It was ridiculous to waste her life in regret. She would accept the first man she felt truly at ease with, if he should ask her to wed him.

She would not cry for Paul Ravenscar again.

The dance was in full swing by the time the party from Ravenscar arrived. Lucy had been dancing with various young men from the beginning and her card was filled apart from two dances, which she had kept back for latecomers. She saw Jenny and Adam just as a dance was ending and prevailed upon her partner to take her to greet them.

'I had almost given you up, dearest Jenny,' Lucy said. 'Did something delay you?'

'There was an incident upon the road,' Jenny said. 'A chaise had overturned and Paul helped to push it off the road so that we could pass. He will be here shortly, but wanted to make sure that the occupants were not harmed and that help was sent to them. I believe he returned to Ravenscar to send our grooms to assist them.'

'Will he come at all?' Lucy asked, smothering her disappointment. It was obvious that he did not particularly wish to dance with her, for he would rather dance attendance on strangers than come to her ball.

'Yes, I am sure he will,' Adam said. 'He may wish to change, for he must have soiled his clothes helping push that chaise off the road.' He smiled at her. 'I hope you have a dance left for me, Lucy?'

'Yes,' she replied. 'You may have the dance before supper.'

Adam scrawled his name in the space, which meant she had but one left.

Lucy's hopes of seeing Paul that evening had faded and it was not until two dances before supper that she saw him enter the room. He spoke to Jenny and Adam, and then looked round the room.

She thought that he meant to come to her, but at that moment her partner claimed her and she was swept into a throng of merry dancers performing to a country air. When she looked over her partner's shoulder a few moments later, she saw that Paul was dancing with Judith and laughing, seemingly enjoying himself very much.

Adam claimed her for the next dance, which was a waltz. She could not but wish that Paul had been her partner, but the other dance she'd reserved had been and gone and she'd used the time to tidy her gown. Some of the excitement of her special evening had been lost because she knew her chance to dance with Paul was lost.

She had looked forward to it, hoping that perhaps the magic of that dance in London would return and that this time Paul would speak…but of course that was ridiculous. He had hardly looked her way since he arrived.

However, he and Jenny joined her and Adam after the last dance before supper and they all went in together. Daventry and Judith came to sit at the large table and the gentlemen went off to order supper for them all.

'Are you enjoying your dance?' Jenny asked

when the ladies were left for a short time. 'You look beautiful. I love the colour of your dress— and that posy goes so well with it.'

'This was a gift from the Earl of Daventry,' Lucy said. She glanced at Judith and saw that she was wearing pink roses pinned to her gown by a diamond clip. 'You look lovely in green, Jenny. It has always suited you.'

Judith's gown was white silk with pink-tulle frills to the skirt and little puffed sleeves; she wore a pale-pink stole over her arms. Paul's roses complemented the gown beautifully. Lucy had thought her cousin meant to wear yellow and was surprised at her choice of gown since the prim-rose silk was new. Had she changed her mind on which gown to wear because of Paul's roses?

When the gentlemen returned, bearing cham-pagne buckets and followed by two footmen with large trays of delicious trifles, Lucy could not help noticing that Paul chose a seat between Judith and Jenny. She felt hurt, as if he were de-liberately snubbing her, but in another moment she had forgot him as the earl applied himself to serving her with some of the delicious little pas-tries and jellies.

Lucy smiled up at him, giving a very good impression of being well pleased with his attention.

The conversation was general for a time. Daventry was truly the soul of the party, making them all laugh with his gossip and his wit. He told stories of the Prince Regent and of other people he knew well. Lucy laughed at his stories, some of which were a little *risqué* and brought colour to her cheeks.

Raising his glass, George Daventry said, 'To Miss Lucy Dawlish—the belle of the evening.'

'To Lucy,' everyone said and raised their glasses.

Lucy blushed and glanced at Paul. He seemed to glare at her, but in the next moment he was saying something in a quiet voice to Judith and they laughed together. Lucy's skin prickled, for she felt they were laughing at her, and she turned to the earl, asking him to tell her about something the Regent had said at a party and listening intently as he obliged.

She peeped at Paul again and saw that he was once more frowning at her. It was almost as if he disapproved of her for being pleasant with the earl.

As people began to leave the supper room, Lucy

excused herself. She went upstairs to make herself comfortable before the dancing began again. As she returned to the ballroom, she saw Paul standing alone in the hall looking thoughtful.

'I hope the people you rescued were not harmed by their accident,' she said.

He turned to look at her, his eyes narrowed. 'The ladies were elderly and much shaken, but I fetched one of our carriages to them and gave them a little brandy and they were able to continue. I fear it made me too late to secure a dance with you, Miss Dawlish.'

'I saved one for you earlier, but my card is full, sir. In fact, I must not keep my next partner waiting for I think the music is about to start.'

As she went to pass him, Paul clasped her wrist. The touch of his strong fingers sent little thrills down her spine. She caught her breath, her heart beating wildly.

'Daventry is charming, I know, but be careful of him, Lucy. His reputation is not all it might be.'

'I thank you, sir,' Lucy said, made uneasy by his touch. She resented his advice, for it was unnecessary and impertinent. 'But I do not stand in any danger. I believe the earl knows better than to try to seduce me.'

'It was not of seduction that I meant to warn you. The fellow would lead you a pretty dance if you wed him, Lucy. He would never be faithful to you. I should not like to see you unhappy.'

'Indeed?' She arched her brow, feeling angry. 'It appears to me that you should keep your opinions to yourself. I do not see that it is any affair of yours, sir.'

'Damn it, I thought we were friends,' Paul said. 'It was merely a friendly warning from an old friend. There is no need to put on that look with me.'

'I do not know what you mean,' Lucy said, bristling. 'I do not believe I am in any danger from the earl, sir.'

She wrenched away from his hold and he let her go. Her head high, she walked into the ballroom, refusing to look back even though she felt that he was watching her.

How dare he warn her against the earl when he had been flirting with her cousin ever since he had arrived? Why, he was no better than the man he had chosen to vilify.

Lucy's throat was tight, though she wasn't sure whether it was from anger or hurt that Paul could speak to her that way. He had trifled with her and broken her heart when he left her after his brother's unfortunate death. Who was he to criticise her or her admirers?

Anger banished the tears. He was arrogant, careless and impossible!

She discovered her next partner waiting for her and was swept into a lively country dance. After that came a waltz and, as George Daventry claimed her for it, she saw that Paul was dancing with Judith once more. Her cousin's laughter floated above the music and Lucy could not but be aware that Judith was showing every pleasure in encouraging Paul's attention. She herself had danced with the earl twice that evening, but when she saw her cousin dance with Paul yet again as the dance ended, she felt as if her heart was breaking again.

He had danced with Judith three times. It was a mark of special attention; he must be planning to make her an offer. Lucy's throat tightened and she felt the tears build.

No, she would not let it spoil her evening. Refusing to heed the tears that pricked her eyes, Lucy began to say goodnight to the guests who had come for her dance and were now leaving. A few, like the earl, were staying for the night and lingered with a glass of wine, but those who lived locally were sending for their carriages and Lucy went to each in turn to wish them a safe journey home.

She was congratulated on the dance, which had been much enjoyed by all, and more than one lady of her acquaintance gave her a knowing look and commented on the Earl of Daventry's pleasant manners.

'You must be happy and excited to have had such a successful evening,' Mrs Morrison said archly. 'I dare say we may look to hear some good news soon...'

Lucy's cheeks felt warm. She knew that she had laughed at the earl's jests and that he had been most attentive to her all evening—also she had chosen to wear his posy. It was obvious that her mama's friends were putting two and two together and making five.

'I have enjoyed myself very much,' Lucy said. 'People have been kind to me.'

'And one particular gentleman more kind than any other, perhaps?' the lady said and smiled as she left.

Lucy felt her cheeks flame. One or two of her mother's friends also made gentle hints, but none as obvious as Mrs Morrison. Lucy did not think she had been more particular in her manner to the earl than to any of her other guests, although she had danced with him twice and only once with most of the other gentlemen.

She had not danced even once with Paul and that was a disappointment to her, for she had hoped that she might feel as she had once before in his arms…that he might look at her with love…but there was no sense in repining. Paul preferred her cousin.

Jenny and Adam had come to say goodnight to her.

'I may not see you again before you go to Bath,' Jenny told her. 'Hal and his wife leave in the morning and I shall be busy. I hope you have a lovely time—and that you will have news for us when you return.'

She smiled and kissed Lucy.

Lucy swallowed hard and managed a smile,

but made no answer. It seemed that even Jenny thought she'd made up her mind to have the earl and she wondered what she had done to give that impression. She had not intended it, but perhaps in her hurt over Paul's behaviour she had laughed a little too much.

Paul was taking his leave of Judith. She saw him kiss her hand and it took all her time to keep her smile in place as he came to her.

'Goodnight, Miss Dawlish,' he said. 'I hope you will have a pleasant stay in Bath.'

'I dare say we shall. Judith wishes to buy new gowns and I dare say we shall attend the assemblies and the theatre.'

'I am sure you will be engaged every evening,' he replied and smiled in an odd way. 'If my father continues well, I may come down for a couple of days. Lady Sparrow wishes for my advice on a matter concerning some horses and I promised to come if I could.'

'Oh…is my cousin desirous of buying a new horse?' Lucy asked, her nails turning into the palms of her hands as she struggled to keep the pain from her voice.

He would come to Bath for Judith's sake, but he

had not even bothered to come in time to secure a dance with her this evening! She needed nothing more to convince her of where his interest lay.

'I believe Lady Sparrow intends to look for a house in Bath, but wants to make sure that there is sufficient stabling for her horses should she wish to live there for a part of the year.'

Lucy was surprised. Judith had said nothing to her of purchasing a house in Bath. She had assumed that she would make her home with them until she married.

'I see...' she said and swallowed hard. 'We shall expect you in Bath then, sir.'

'If my father's health remains stable,' he said and bowed over her hand. 'I hope you enjoyed your evening, Lucy—and that you shall not regret any decision you made.'

'I am sure I do not know what you mean,' she said, but could not meet his eyes, for she knew exactly what he was referring to. She had ignored his advice concerning the earl. 'I hope Lord Ravenscar goes on well, sir. I am fond of him— we all are.'

'Yes, I dare say. He thinks of you as a daughter.'

'Thank you.' Lucy swallowed miserably. Why

must they always quarrel, when all she wanted was to see approval in his eyes? She lifted her head proudly. 'Goodnight, sir.'

'Lucy—' Paul began, but was interrupted as some more guests came into the hall. For a moment he seemed to hesitate and she was surprised by the look in his eyes, as if he would have said something important, but then he nodded his head. 'Goodnight. I wish you happy…'

She stood blinking as he went out. Her heart was aching. At times he could be so like his old self that she was reminded sharply of everything that had gone before—and yet at other times that look of reserve was in his eyes.

Paul had changed. He was not the carefree, young man she'd known before his brother's death.

She would be a fool to pine for something she could never have. Lifting her head, she went to say goodnight to more guests.

Lucy was kept busy for another thirty minutes saying goodnight to her friends and neighbours. When she returned to the ballroom to find it all but empty, she saw that Daventry was having a glass of wine with her father and Judith was standing with her mother.

'I think I shall go up now,' Lucy said. 'It was a lovely evening, Mama. I thank you and Papa for arranging it for me.' She smiled brightly at George Daventry. 'Goodnight, sir. I shall see you in the morning. Are you ready to go up, Judith?'

'I am just coming. Goodnight, everyone,' Judith said and then came to take Lucy's arm. They walked from the room together. 'Well, that all went as it ought, I think. You did not sit down once, dearest—and I also only had one dance without a partner.'

'I am sure you would not have had that had Captain Ravenscar not been delayed.'

Judith laughed, a look of mischief in her face. 'He is trying to arouse my interest, because we got off on the wrong foot,' she said. 'He did not care for my indifference at the start and is piqued. I allowed him three dances this evening, but when he comes to Bath I shall see… I have not yet made up my mind to have him, though I find him good company and he is attractive.'

'Captain Ravenscar will inherit the title and his father's estate. Ravenscar is quite a large estate.'

Lucy wondered why she was singing his praises. Did she wish her cousin to marry him?

'Yes, I know he is wealthy, but I have money of my own,' Judith reminded her. 'I should require more than mere wealth. I am not sure of his ambition. A man with ideals or a voice in the world is probably what would suit me. If Ravenscar would take his seat in the House one day...I think a role as a political hostess in London would suit me well.'

'I thought you wished to travel?'

'Yes, that is my intention, but not for ever. One day I shall hope to return to London—and I enjoy entertaining. Sir Michael had some embassy experience and we had a varied acquaintance.'

'P—Captain Ravenscar said you thought of buying a house in Bath?'

'I have thought of it,' Judith replied. 'I am as yet unsure where my future lies.'

Lucy stared at her, not sure if she approved. She had thought her cousin amusing, beautiful and clever...but if she merely intended to use Paul until something better came along...that was not kind in her.

Lucy felt distressed at the thought that he might

discover the truth too late and spend the rest of his life regretting his marriage.

*Why should she care how he felt? He did not care that he had hurt her feelings.*

'You seemed to enjoy yourself dancing with Daventry,' Judith said and gave her a thoughtful look. 'I believe he means to make you an offer, Lucy—shall you take him?'

'I…I don't know,' Lucy replied. 'I like him but…' She sighed and shook her head. 'As yet I am not sure of the earl's intentions. He has not hinted that he is serious.'

'Oh, I am certain of it,' Judith murmured, a glint in her eyes. 'Yes, I believe he will speak to you soon, my dear Cousin—and you should be ready with your answer, for he will not take kindly to being asked to wait, I assure you.'

'Oh…' Lucy caught her breath. She had enjoyed the earl's attentions that night, but a part of her knew that the reason she had laughed so much in his company was because she'd wanted to show Paul that she did not care if he preferred her cousin.

But she did…she did…

# Chapter Seven

Lucy rode over to take her leave of Jenny and Lord Ravenscar the day before she was due to go to Bath. Judith had engaged herself to drive with Charles Benson and her groom and George Daventry accompanied Lucy to Ravenscar.

'I would like to see Lord Ravenscar for a little while,' Lucy said when they arrived at the house. 'Perhaps you would keep Mrs Miller company, sir.'

'Of course. You must do whatever you please, Miss Lucy. I am your servant, as ever.'

'Thank you,' Lucy said. He helped her down from her horse but did not hold her in his arms longer than necessary.

When they went into the house, they discovered that Jenny was busy, but both Adam and Paul were at home. Lucy greeted them with a smile and then the housekeeper took her upstairs to Lord Ravenscar's apartments.

She was delighted to find that he was sitting in a chair fully dressed with a light rug over his knees and went to him with a cry of pleasure.

'You look much better, sir,' she said. 'I am so glad that you have recovered.'

'I feel better than I did,' he replied. 'Your pretty face must always cheer me, my dear. How are you now?' He studied her face. 'You seem less unhappy than you were. I should be glad to think that you had recovered from your grief. Mark would not have wished you to be unhappy, Lucy. You have shown your respect for him and now you must think of your own life.'

'I know it,' she agreed. 'I did miss him so terribly, as we all did—but I am happier now. Mama is taking my cousin and me to Bath and Lord Daventry is to escort us. We shall have many friends there for the London Season is well over and everyone will go to Bath.'

'Yes, I dare say. You young things are forever here and there...' He smiled and patted her hand.

Lucy talked to him for a few minutes longer and then went downstairs to the parlour. The sound of Jenny's voice told her that her friend had returned from her errand and she went in, pausing on the threshold.

'May I join you?' she asked shyly.

'Of course, Lucy. We were waiting for you to come down.' Jenny came to her at once and kissed her cheek.

'I am glad you came to say goodbye before you left,' she said. 'I wanted to tell you what has been decided. Paul will join you in Bath for a few days and when he returns we shall go home for a while.'

'Then I am glad I came indeed,' Lucy said. 'I hope I shall see you again before too long.'

'I dare say we shall visit here again in a few months,' Jenny said. 'But by then you may be married…'

Lucy felt her cheeks heat and hoped that the earl was not looking at her. Her eyes sought Paul and she saw that his were narrowed, his mouth pulled into a tight line. Why? Did he care if she married someone else?

'Who knows what may happen?' Lucy managed to reply with a laugh. 'I know Mama would be pleased, but she does not push me into it, you know. I dare say my cousin may marry before me. I believe she desires her own establishments in London and Bath so that she can set up her salon…and she desires a companion to travel with her when she wishes for it.'

Lucy saw Paul's quick frown and wondered at it. Had he been ignorant of her cousin's plans for the future? Did he imagine that Judith would be happy to settle here at Ravenscar for months at a time? Lucy did not think it would suit Judith to be in the country for long.

'Your cousin has been married before,' Jenny said. 'I have been hearing that she was well known as a hostess in London when her husband lived. She enjoyed inviting poets and writers, as well as singers and men of intellect, to her soirées.'

'Yes, I believe so,' Lucy said. 'I had no idea of it and thought her to be a sad and lonely widow when my uncle asked us to take her in for a time.'

'I dare say she had been living in isolation for some months after her husband died,' Jenny said. 'She told me she had every intention of entertaining on a grand scale once she was in the position to do so. I suppose she looks for a husband of some importance on the social scale.'

'I do not know,' Lucy replied, feeling a little

guilty at having been drawn into a discussion of her cousin in her absence. Paul was watching her and she sensed disapproval in him—but was not sure what had caused it.

She happened to glance at George Daventry and found him looking thoughtful, but as refreshments were brought in then she had no time to ask him what lay behind that expression of speculation.

She had chosen a seat near the window, but Jenny had moved closer to the centre of the room to dispense tea and comfits, also wine to those who preferred it. Lucy was therefore alone when Paul brought his cup and came to sit beside her on the small sofa.

'Your cousin did not care to visit with you today?' he asked as he stretched out his long legs, his gleaming boots crossed one over the other.

He looked so handsome that Lucy caught her breath, picking up the clean scent of his linen and some light fragrance that wafted about him.

'Judith had an engagement to drive out with Charles Benson,' she replied as casually as she could. 'She asked me to say all that was proper and hopes to see you in Bath next week.'

'At the moment I see no reason why I should

not come down for a day or two,' Paul replied. 'My father, as you have discovered for yourself, seems very well. Adam and Jenny stay here until I return. This is their home as much as mine and they spend a great deal of time here—but Adam and Jenny have things they must do at their own estate.'

'You must be glad of their company,' Lucy said. 'A house like this is too big for two people.'

'Yes, indeed it is,' Paul said. 'I know my father's wishes upon that matter and I must attempt to oblige him sooner rather than later—perhaps I shall do so before too long.'

*He was thinking of offering for Judith.*

Lucy's heart contracted with pain. He must truly love her if he was thinking of offering for her, because he must know that Judith preferred to live in town. Indeed, she would hardly be content here for longer than a few weeks. Would Paul be happy with a wife who spent most of her time in London entertaining her friends?

'I must wish you success, then,' she said and saw his quick frown. 'I should like to see this house filled with company, as it used to be. I remember the balls and the grand picnics in the gardens when your father entertained.'

'Yes, it was a happy place then,' Paul replied and again she saw a thoughtful look in his eyes. 'The right woman could make it a home again—Jenny does very well for us, but we have not entertained much for a long time, and she has her own home. If Father continues well, I shall begin to ask a few friends to dine soon.'

'Yes, you should…' Lucy looked up as George Daventry came to sit on a chair close to them. 'Captain Ravenscar was speaking of opening the house up again soon. It would be pleasant to have a ball here as we used to do, I think.'

'Yes, indeed, for it is a magnificent house, sir,' George agreed. 'You like to dance, Miss Lucy—and it suits you. I dare say we shall be invited to some private dances in Bath, but a ball here would indeed be a pleasure.'

'Yes…' Lucy put down her cup and stood up, aware of an undercurrent of tension between the two gentlemen, though she did not understand it. 'I think we ought to return, sir. Mama will be concerned if we are too long, for she does not want me to be tired tomorrow. I am so glad to have seen you all before I left.'

'You must write to me when you return to Dawlish after your stay in Bath,' Jenny said. 'If you have no other arrangements, you might care to come to us for a week or two?'

'I should very much like that…if Mama has no other plans,' Lucy said, though she knew it was her own plans that Jenny meant—for she, like others, was expecting news of a wedding before too long.

Lucy's heart skidded in her breast as she saw the expression in Paul's eyes. He had taken Jenny's meaning and the censure was plain to see.

Jenny thought that Lucy might be engaged when she returned from Bath. She was aware of a fluttering in her stomach. Had she given her friends reason to think it was settled with the earl? If she had done so, she wished that she had been more discreet. Lucy had thought that her mind was made up, but suddenly she was unsure again. Would she be wise to marry without love?

Could that bring anything but unhappiness in the long run? The thought of living with a man she only moderately liked as her husband brought Lucy to the reality of her thoughts.

Was she truly ready to give up all thought of love?

Jenny walked out to the door with them as their horses were brought round from the stables. Jenny's groom held her horse, but it was George Daventry who helped her to mount before going to mount his own horse. Sitting tall in the saddle, Lucy looked at Paul standing just outside the house and found his eyes intent on her. Her heart jerked and she hoped for a smile, but he remained grave and thoughtful, as she waved to her friends and then moved off with the earl and her groom following.

Just what was in Paul's mind when he spoke of his future marriage? On the night of her ball, he had seemed to be courting Judith, but something in his voice…in his look that morning…

Lucy kept her sigh inside her. It was ridiculous to let herself hope again, for she had made up her mind never to think of Paul in that way. She had been sure that it was her cousin he preferred… though Lucy was certain that Judith would not make him happy…

Lucy felt a pang of despair. It was all such a tangle. A man she liked very well but did not love was courting her—and the man she did love seemed to go from liking her to indifference and back.

What was she to make of it all?

Paul watched as the earl lifted Lucy into the saddle. He clenched his fists at his sides, an unreasonable anger striking through him. What right had that rogue to touch her? Damn him! He was not good enough to kiss her feet.

Paul had hoped that his hints about marriage would arouse some reaction in her, but instead she'd seemed to withdraw. Had he left it all too late? He felt regret swathe through him, for he must take a wife in time—but no other woman would truly content him.

'I think Lucy looks much better this morning,' Jenny said, recalling his thoughts. 'When she first came to visit us after her return from Italy she seemed too quiet, a different girl, but she laughs more now and I think she is over her distress at last.'

'She grieved for Mark a long time,' Paul said as they turned and walked back into the house.

'If it was grief for Mark...' Jenny said. 'I had thought there might be something more to her distress, someone else she cared for—but of course she has not told me anything. Whatever it was, I think she is over it now.'

Paul murmured something appropriate, but he was thoughtful as he went up the stairs to his bedchamber. Was it possible that Lucy had felt something towards him...as he'd half-believed before Mark died?

His mind was reeling from Jenny's casual statement. It had taken him a long time to come to terms with his own feelings of guilt, but recently he'd begun to realise that he need not have tortured himself as he had.

If the letter he'd found in Mark's things meant what he suspected, then he would not be stealing his brother's intended bride. He needed to investigate further to be sure...but what if his suspicions were proved true?

He was not sure that Lucy felt more than friendship for him now, though for a moment during their drive, as they laughed over old times, he thought there might be more…but her mood had changed suddenly.

Why? What had he done or said to upset her? He could think of nothing, but he had not been mistaken in her withdrawal.

And she had been so pleased to see Daventry. She had danced with him twice at the ball and seemed to laugh at everything he said to her. Was she considering taking him if he asked? He could not help thinking she would regret it, for he knew something of Daventry's past—something unpleasant that would distress Lucy if she should learn of it. Of course, it would be a dishonourable act to tell her with the deliberate intention of making her distrust the earl—but perhaps he ought. She had seemed enchanted with the man at her dance…

It occurred to Paul that he had danced with Lady Sparrow three times. She, of course, was not an innocent young lady, but a widow with experience of the world and there was no question of his arousing hopes in her breast, for she had told him she looked for a comfortable husband.

Lady Sparrow was not looking for love. She had money and she wanted a husband to be a companion and accompany her on her trips overseas. She also planned to have a salon in London and entertain a great deal, but she could, if she wished, hold her dinners and balls at Ravenscar when the Season was over. If they should marry…

Paul had discovered that he liked the merry widow. She had a sense of adventure and liked to laugh, ignoring the strictures that governed ladies of her class, at least in the smaller things. He thought she would make a pleasant companion—and if he must marry…

Could he bring himself to forget the dreams he'd carried so long? A stormy look touched his face. If Lucy Dawlish married the Earl of Daventry he would have no choice but to find a woman who would make few demands on him.

He imagined that Judith Sparrow would do her duty in the matter of heirs for Ravenscar. After that, they could live their own lives.

If that was all he could expect of life, then so be it.

Judith asked Lucy if all was well at Ravenscar and nodded when told that Paul expected to visit them in Bath the following week.

'I wished I might have come with you this morning,' she said, 'but I had promised Charles that he might drive me out one last time before we leave for Bath. He says that he shall come down, but I hope he will not. He is devoted to me, but just a boy. In time, such devotion becomes a little wearying. He would not suit me as a husband at all—I need a man, not a lapdog.'

'That is unkind,' Lucy said, feeling out of patience with her. 'It might have been kinder not to encourage him so much.'

'Are you cross with me, dearest?' Judith asked in surprise. 'I assure you I have never encouraged Charles. Indeed, I have been frank with him and I behave to him as I might a younger brother—but it makes no difference. Indeed, I believe he feels safe flirting with me, because he knows I would never marry him.'

'Oh...' Lucy blushed and felt foolish. She knew that her cross feelings towards her cousin had nothing to do with Charles Benson and everything to do with Paul Ravenscar.

'Do you encourage Captain Ravenscar?' she asked, her cheeks hot. 'He was speaking of his marriage this morning. I believe he means to marry because he needs an heir. I do not know if he has hopes of you, Cousin?'

'He may have,' Judith admitted. 'I find him interesting…though, at the beginning, I admit I was determined to teach him a lesson. He seemed arrogant the first time we met, but I have discovered that he is not so at all…it was rather a distance in him. I dare say it may have something to do with the death of his brother.'

'Yes, I expect so,' Lucy agreed. She'd thought Paul cold and reserved at first, but gradually he had become more like the man she'd known… though older, of course. Everyone had changed over the years.

Perhaps she expected too much in thinking he ought to be the lively, carefree man she'd once known.

'I think he might make a pleasant husband for the right person,' Judith went on. 'However, I am not certain he would suit me, for I do not want to be buried in the country. I should need an assurance that he did not expect me to live at Ravenscar the whole time.'

'Paul is determined to make his father's estate prosper. I dare say he would be happy to visit London for the Season and an occasional visit to Bath or—' She saw Judith's expression. 'You should not marry him if that is not your wish, Cousin.'

'Perhaps I shall not,' Judith replied, shrugging her shoulders. 'As I said earlier, I have not yet decided. I may meet someone in Bath I like better...perhaps an older man. Captain Ravenscar is quite young.'

'Yes, not much older than I am,' Lucy said thoughtfully. 'Yet he seems older...'

'Yes, he has an air of distinction,' Judith said. 'It is his experience in the war and as one of Wellington's aides, I dare say.'

'Yes, perhaps,' Lucy said, though she believed it was the terrible murder of his brother that had changed him from the daredevil prankster he'd been as a boy and a young man. He was certainly a man of the world now and must be admired wherever he went.

'Well, I must see to my packing,' Judith said. 'I shall not take all my things with me. Some may remain here and be sent on when I decide where to reside. I shall buy new clothes in Bath, though I hope to visit Paris before too long.'

'Will you take a companion?'

'Only if I cannot find the right husband,' Judith said and laughed. 'Where is Lord Daventry? I thought he escorted you this morning?'

'Yes, he did—but he went off to speak to Papa about something.' Lucy arched her brow. 'Did you wish to speak with him?'

'Oh, no…nothing that will not keep,' Judith said. 'Excuse me, I must decide what I need to take with me.'

Lucy was a little puzzled by her cousin's manner. She had quite thought Judith meant to have Paul if he asked her, but now she was not sure. Her cousin seemed to think that love mattered very little in the arrangement of a marriage, for if she loved Paul surely nothing else ought to matter.

If only Lucy could be as practical about her own marriage. She had thought she could when she spoke to her mother but now she had her doubts.

Lucy had finished sorting through her gowns and left the packing to her maid when she came back downstairs later that afternoon. She decided to sit in the garden for a while and went into the back parlour. The French windows were open and she could feel the warmth of the sunshine filtering into the house.

Stepping outside to the terrace, she made her way across the lawns towards the rose arbour. When she heard voices she stopped, listening. That was Judith's voice and...yes, Lord Daventry. Their voices were raised, as if they were quarrelling.

'Can you not forgive me for what happened so long ago?' George was asking in an angry voice. 'Had I known how you felt, I should never have left you so abruptly...you made me angry, Judith.'

'We quarrelled,' Judith replied. 'You deserted me. I wept bitterly, but you did not write, nor did you return...and I had no choice but to marry Sir Michael. My father demanded it.'

'His fortune was more than I could ever expect to enjoy at that time. I dare say it was not such a sacrifice for you...'

Even as Lucy hesitated she heard a cry of anger and then what sounded like a slap. Feeling guilty and embarrassed, she turned away and walked quickly to another part of the garden. She ought not to have listened to a private conversation. Yet had they kept their voices lower she would not have heard.

She frowned as she thought of what she *had* heard.

Judith had been quarrelling with Lord Daventry and it seemed it was not for the first time. Lucy was not sure what it all meant—had there been something more than a flirtation between her cousin and the earl in the past? Had Judith been in love with him?

Lucy was stunned, for she did not know what to think. Judith had said their past acquaintance had been slight, but it had not sounded that way to Lucy. Why would they be arguing in such a heated manner if they had not been more than friends?

She felt a little sick in her stomach, for if there was something between them…why had Judith not made it plain to her from the start?

Why would Daventry pay so much attention to Lucy if there were a long-standing affair between them? It could not but reflect badly on him and was surely reckless. She could see no reason for it—unless he wished to arouse Judith's jealousy?

The thought stung Lucy, humiliating her and

making her feel hot. She had been imagining that Daventry was thinking of making her an offer, but now it seemed that she had merely been his tool in making Judith notice him.

She felt angry and embarrassed, but not, she realised, broken-hearted. Her pride had received a knock, but her heart had always been protected.

Lucy wandered away deep into the garden. She was shivering, though the afternoon was very warm.

Why had Judith accused the earl of deserting her? It sounded like a serious matter and Lucy was shocked. Ought she to ask Judith what her feelings were towards the earl? She had warned Lucy of him, because she said he was a rake— had she good cause for her warning?

Lucy would have spoken to Judith that same evening, but there was never a chance to be alone with her, and, when the time came to retire, she had found herself quite unable to raise the subject.

'Goodnight, Cousin. Sleep well. The day after tomorrow we shall be in Bath.'

'Yes, are you excited?'

'I think so…a little.'

'You should be, for I am certain you will make a stir,' Judith said. 'You will find yourself much admired, I believe. If I were you, Cousin, I should keep an open mind for a while.'

She was warning Lucy against Daventry!

Lucy thanked her and wished her goodnight again, for there was no way that she could ask her about her feelings for the earl after that. If something had happened before Judith's marriage, it belonged in the past...and the confidence must come from Judith herself.

Lucy was thoughtful as she undressed. It seemed she'd been wrong in imagining that the earl's attentions to her were more than mere flattery.

She had believed that he would make her an offer before too long had passed, but perhaps she had read too much into his compliments—and she was not the only one to do so.

He had been very particular in his attentions at her dance. Surely he would not have acted in such a way if it were her cousin he wanted? Lucy was puzzled by his behaviour—unless he hoped to torment Judith into breaking her silence? Lucy had noticed the reserve in her when the earl was present and he might have been driven to flirting with Lucy just to distress her cousin.

If that was the case, he was despicable! Yet he could be so charming and perhaps she was wrong to suspect him of such deceit.

Lucy sat at her window, looking out long after her maid had left her. She had no desire to sleep and felt more confused than ever. Perhaps the earl had come to her home with the intention of offering for her, but had met Judith and remembered that he had once cared for her. If that were the case, his behaviour might be excusable, though had Lucy fallen in love with him she must have been hurt.

However, Lucy would not wish him to feel that he must make her an offer. In fairness, she had only considered the idea because Paul had shown her that he no longer loved her—if he ever had.

She had thought the earl might suit her if she could not have the man she truly loved, but now made up her mind to draw back a little. In Bath she would meet many new friends and perhaps she might meet a gentleman who made her swoon with love for him. Otherwise, she might find herself upon the shelf, for she had met no one in Italy and there was certainly no one living close to her home she would wish to marry…other than Paul Ravenscar.

Paul, it seemed, was in need of a wife and Lucy was sure he was considering her cousin. Judith did not love him. Supposing he married her only to find that she did not care for him? Lucy found the idea distressing and her throat caught with tears. Paul had suffered enough; he deserved to be happy.

It was all such a muddle. Why did no one speak openly about their feelings?

Her heart told her that she still had deep feelings for Paul, but he appeared to like Judith more than he liked Lucy. Oh, yes, he was her friend and they had a long history of happy times in their childhood—but men looked elsewhere when they thought of marriage. Paul seemed to think the kind of marriage Judith wanted might suit him… for the sake of some heirs.

Lucy was aware of a curious pain about her heart. She wanted Paul to be happy when he married and she could have borne it had he married Judith, if she cared for him…but if she still had a feeling for Daventry…

Oh, it was all supposition and mystery! Lucy went to bed, wishing that she had not overheard those raised voices in the garden.

The journey to Bath was uneventful. Lucy could see nothing in George Daventry's manner to show that he had changed his allegiance from her to Judith. He was scrupulously polite to them both, charming to everyone and especially to Lucy's mama, making sure at every stop that all the ladies were comfortable.

Lord Dawlish had been glad to relinquish the chore of escorting his family to Bath, for he preferred a quiet life in the country. Lady Dawlish was grateful for the earl's care of them and forever remarking to Lucy what beautiful manners he had and how considerate he was.

'It is so comfortable to travel with a man of address,' she told her travelling companions. 'A servant will do what he can, but a man of the earl's consequence can secure the best rooms with just a lift of his brow. What an admirable husband he will make some fortunate young lady.'

'Yes, it has been a comfortable journey, Aunt,'

Judith said, looking thoughtful. 'We have reason to be thankful to Daventry.'

The earl had chosen to ride beside their carriage, leaving more room for the ladies to sit as they wished. A heavy travelling coach lumbered behind with their baggage and maids, and Daventry's groom was driving his chaise with his valet for company. They made an impressive show as they arrived at the various inns to change horses, choosing to spend the night in a large and busy one where the food was excellent. The ladies all had rooms in the quieter side of the house and were able to sleep tolerably well.

Because of the ease with which everything had been arranged they arrived in good time at the house Lord Dawlish had secured for them. A large end-of-terrace dwelling, it had several good bedrooms. The ladies had rooms on the first floor and the earl was given his choice of rooms on the top floor. Once all the baggage had been brought up to the various bedchambers, the arrivals were able to tidy themselves before taking refreshments in a large elegant parlour at the back of the house.

Daventry excused himself almost at once. 'I shall make an exploration of the town,' he said to them with his charming smile. 'I wish to discover whether we have acquaintances in Bath and put our names down at the Assembly Hall so that the master of ceremonies expects us at the next ball.'

'We shall not go to an assembly for three days,' Lady Dawlish told him. 'We must all have new gowns and accustom ourselves to our surroundings first—but we might go to the theatre tomorrow evening.'

'I shall secure a box,' Daventry promised and went off, leaving the ladies to explore the house, and the two younger ones to take the opportunity for a walk after nuncheon while Lady Dawlish had a little rest on her bed.

'How pleasant it is to be in Bath again,' Judith said as they strolled away from the Crescent. 'I think if one were forced to live alone with a companion, it might be the very place.'

'But you do not truly consider it?' Lucy asked.

'I shall marry if the right offer comes my way,' Judith replied, her eyes sparkling. She nodded to a matronly lady and her daughter as they passed. 'The Standish family is here then. I knew them well once...'

'Tell me…' Lucy took a deep breath. 'What does Lord Daventry mean to you, Cousin?'

'Why do you ask?' Judith said, her manner suddenly alert. 'Has he said something to you?'

'Nothing… I heard you speaking with him in the garden the day before we left home. I thought you seemed angry, though I heard only a few words.'

'Well, I had best be plain with you, Cousin,' Judith said. 'I have reason to be angry with him. I was barely seventeen when we met and…I lost my heart to him for he flirted with me outrageously. I had not then been out in society and I thought he cared for me…that he meant to offer for me…but then he left me without even a word to say where he meant to go.'

'Oh…I am sorry he mistreated you,' Lucy said. 'It was cruel of him. Do you still feel something for him?'

'No, nothing,' Judith replied. 'I married Sir Michael and forgot him. What you heard was a quarrel between us. I fear I demanded to know if he intended to behave properly towards you and he asked me what business it was of mine. It led to recriminations…but then he apologised and we made up our quarrel.'

'I see…' Lucy saw that it had cost her cousin to speak calmly. 'Were you much hurt when he deserted you?'

'More than I can tell you,' Judith said. 'Indeed, he did me a wrong, Lucy, for we had been seen kissing and there was gossip, which led to some loss of reputation for me…but he has explained to me why he left without a word and I think it best forgot.'

'I am glad if he was able to explain things to your satisfaction, but I still think him careless to abandon you, especially if he had exposed you to gossip. He should not have aroused expectations in your mind if he did not intend—' Lucy broke off and blushed. 'Forgive me. It is not my affair.'

'You have a right to know, for you think of him as a possible husband,' Judith said seriously. 'Apparently, he was called away to his uncle's side. He left a letter for me, but I did not receive it. I think my father might have destroyed it. Papa did not approve of George Staples, as he was then. He had not then become the earl, you see, and if his cousin had not died of a fever, still unwed, before his father died, he would not have inherited the estate.'

'He was not wealthy, then?'

'No. He had very little but a career as a professional soldier.'

'Your father wished you to be secure?'

'Sir Michael had asked for me and, because he was rich, my father persuaded me to accept him.' Judith's face was pale, her hands trembling a little. 'He was kind to me and I did not regret my decision, although I never loved him. We were happy enough in our way and I mourned him sincerely when he died.'

'But you are free now… Would you not wish to marry the earl if he asked you?'

'I am not sure that I should. I have changed,' Judith said. 'When I first saw him again my first thought was to warn you—but it was unfair of me if he cares for you. If you are satisfied to be his wife, you should accept his offer.'

'Daventry is charming and thoughtful,' Lucy replied. 'Yet I cannot but think it was wrong of him to desert you—but if he claims to have left you a letter… Are you certain he does not still care for you?'

'I do not think he cares for me, though I dare say he likes my fortune—' Judith broke off with a conscious look. 'Perhaps I wrong him… Ah, here comes a gentleman I know.' She smiled as a gentleman came up to them and bowed.

'Lady Sparrow, how charming to meet you in Bath. I was thinking the company very dull, but now all is changed.'

'Mr Bertram, you flatter me, as always,' she said and laughed. 'Sir, may I present you to Miss Lucy Dawlish, my cousin. Lucy—this is Mr Bertram. We have known each other for an age, for his estate marches with my father's in Dorset.'

'Sir…' Lucy bobbed a curtsy to him and smiled. He had fair hair and blue eyes and wore a blue coat that must have come from Weston, his long legs encased in perfect pale-cream breeches and riding boots that shone like a mirror.

'Miss Dawlish, your servant. I shall call tomorrow,' he said and bowed over her hand. 'Where may I find two such divine creatures residing? In an enchanted palace?'

'Foolish,' Judith said, but laughed. 'You will find us in the Crescent, of course…the last house at the end.'

Lucy looked at her as he bowed once more and

walked on. 'Do you have many friends like that, Cousin?'

'Quite a few,' Judith said, amused by her look. 'I disregard such fribbles, I assure you. Charming, but a flirt and no money, of course. I dare say his father left him nothing but debts.'

'Is marriage always a question of money?'

'In many cases. It must be either money or a title that means something for me this time,' Judith replied. 'I have money, of course, so perhaps I should look for consequence this time round.'

'And what of love?' Lucy asked her curiously.

'I thought love was important to me once,' her cousin said. 'I was wrong... Look, Lucy, there is a delightful milliner's shop. Shall we go inside and try on some of the hats?'

Paul looked at the young lady's letter. If her claims were true, it would appear that his brother was not quite the demi-god they had all believed him to be.

Why had Mark proposed to a respectable young woman if his heart was not engaged?

Paul was disturbed by the information the letter contained, which was more serious than he had imagined. Ought he to tell his father that he had a grandchild, though born without benefit of marriage—or should he keep the whole thing secret?

He must arrange to see the young woman himself, for if she was coarse or common, there could be no question of a meeting between her and Lord Ravenscar. He would take a slight detour and do so on his way down to Bath.

And there were Lucy's feelings to be thought of.

What would she feel if she knew that Mark had fathered an illegitimate child?

He would have to find a way of telling her, but it would not be easy.

Yet it meant that he was now free of guilt, free to follow his heart. Paul felt his spirits lift. He was young and strong and perhaps it was not too late after all to find the happiness he had once hoped for. He would find a way to tell Lucy the truth and then he would speak to her—tell her that he loved her. Only if she no longer cared for him would he consider making a marriage of convenience.

It was not until Lucy was alone in her room after supper that evening that she had time to think of what her cousin had revealed to her on their walk.

Judith denied thinking love important and was determined to make a marriage of convenience and consequence.

She had been in love with George Daventry, but he'd left her and she had married a man she did not truly love. Lucy felt that she must have been very unhappy for a time, though she appeared to be quite over it now. She had greeted George that evening with a nod and exchanged pleasantries with him across the supper table, for they had dined at home.

'We shall be out most evenings in future, unless we entertain here,' Lady Dawlish had told them. 'A quiet evening will suit me very well after the travelling.'

George had excused himself after supper, having engaged himself to play cards with some friends. He had, however, secured a box at the theatre for the following evening and they were to see a farce by Sheridan and a recital by an opera singer.

The ladies were left to amuse themselves and, after playing a game of cards, found themselves yawning over the teacups and very soon went to bed.

Lucy sat brushing her hair before the mirror for a long time before taking a book to her bed. She could not help wondering if her cousin still felt something for the earl, despite her denials…and that took her thoughts to Paul.

It would hurt Lucy to think of him married to a lady who did not love him. She thought that Judith was a little selfish to encourage his advances if she had no intention of marrying him…and hoped that he would see her cousin for what she was.

Oh dear, was she jealous? Lucy thought she might be, and soon came to realise that she might be accused of being as heartless as her cousin. She had encouraged George Daventry and, because he was accepted into her family now, it was almost expected that he would offer for her. If she said no…then she was as careless of his feelings as Judith seemed of Paul's.

How had it happened? She had never intended to become so embroiled, but Paul had hurt her by showing that he admired her cousin so much more than he admired her. Had he not made his feelings clear—and then arrived far too late at her dance—this would never have happened.

Yet, if her suspicions were correct, it was she

who had been used by Daventry. For she was certain there was more to their quarrel than Judith had told her—and why had she spoken so oddly just before they met one of her friends?

Had she been hinting that Daventry was interested in rekindling their affair only because she had a very large fortune at her disposal? That would be despicable indeed! To use Lucy to make Judith jealous in the hope that she would quarrel with him—and then perhaps show feelings of love towards him…

Could the earl be that callous? She would not have thought it for his manners were so good and he could be very charming. Perhaps it was merely because he'd let Judith down once that she suspected him.

Tears stung Lucy's eyes and she felt confused and bewildered.

Why could things not be simpler? If Judith had not been staying with them, perhaps Paul would have taken her driving more often and he might… he might have discovered that he still liked her very well. She might even now be promised to him.

Her throat was tight with emotion as she snuggled down into the warmth of her bed. She felt as if she had become enmeshed in silken bonds, which tightened about her each time she moved.

It was all too difficult and Lucy needed to sleep.

The next day was spent visiting silk merchants, dressmakers, milliners and various other establishments that sold the trifles ladies found so necessary for their comfort. In the evening they attended the theatre and a stream of gentlemen visited the earl's box. The earl introduced each in turn to the ladies, a smile on his face as they showered both Judith and Lucy with pretty compliments. Glancing at him as the tenth gentleman asked to be presented, Lucy saw amusement and then a flicker of annoyance in his eyes. She wondered at it, particularly as the young man, who had been introduced as the Marquis of Elver, paid particular attention to Judith.

When the footlights went down and the curtains were drawn back, George Daventry sat at Lucy's side. She turned her head to look at him, seeing that he was still deep in thought.

'You would seem to have many friends in Bath, sir?' she said playing with her pretty fan.

'Yes, indeed, I had not thought myself so popular,' he said. 'I dare say I can find the reason easily enough.'

'Do you not mind that they did their best to charm Lady Sparrow…and me? We are, after all, your guests.'

'Beauty brings the bees as to the honey,' he said. 'Why should I mind, Miss Lucy? Lady Sparrow informed me that the purpose of her visit was to find a husband who would oblige her by giving her the lifestyle she desires.'

A frown creased her brow, as she caught something in his tone. 'Do you think she means it—or is she merely funning?'

'I believe she is in earnest,' he replied. 'But Lady Sparrow is free to do whatever she wishes with her life—I have no right or interest in advising her. You must know that, Miss Lucy?'

Lucy's cheeks fired and she could not look at him as she said, 'But I believe there was an understanding between you once.'

'Where had you that from?' he enquired and she sensed annoyance or perhaps tension in him.

'I was given to understand that it was some years ago—before my cousin's marriage.'

A glimmer of anger showed in his eyes then. 'I should be sorry to think something of this nature should give you a dislike of me, Miss Lucy.'

'A dislike, no,' Lucy said honestly. 'Pause for thought, yes. My cousin is dear to me, sir. Anyone who hurts her…well, they would not be a friend to me.'

'Ah, then I understand,' he replied and she saw his hand clench. 'I had wondered… There has been a slight distance in you since we visited Ravenscar last. I thought…but if Lady Sparrow has raised doubts in your mind…'

'No, no, it was nothing Judith said,' she denied, wishing to protect her. Lucy took a deep breath, then, 'I am fond of my cousin, sir, and would never do anything to disoblige her—but my mind was never made up, you know. I must consider carefully.'

He inclined his head and said no more during the play, though Lucy was aware of his displeasure and wondered if she had spoken too openly. She was not certain why she had decided against him, but something inside her had made her draw back before it was too late. Although the earl did not show his anger, she felt that she had perhaps lost a friend and was regretful, for though she now knew that she could never have married him, he was still a charming man.

After the play was finished, he assisted the ladies to their carriage with every care and then bowed and begged their pardon.

'I shall not return with you this evening,' he said. 'I have something of importance to do, Lady Dawlish. I fear that tomorrow may be my last day as your guest. I must leave Bath for a few days on business.'

'Oh, that is disappointing,' Lucy's mother said, surprised. 'I had hoped you would be our guest for the whole of our stay.'

'I shall return to Bath in time to escort you home, perhaps a day or so before your journey,' he promised and inclined his head. 'And now I bid you goodnight.'

Lady Dawlish frowned as the carriage drove off. She said nothing of her disappointment until they were back at the house and she was alone with Lucy in her bedroom.

'Have you quarrelled with Lord Daventry, Lucy?'

'No, Mama. We are friends as always.'

'I was quite certain he meant to make you an offer—but he has not, I think?'

'No, he has not, Mama,' Lucy said, but felt guilty for she knew that it was her fault. She had spoken out and clearly offended him. 'Perhaps he changed his mind.'

'How do you feel, dearest?' her mother asked, looking anxious. 'Is this a great disappointment to you?'

'No, not at all. I had not decided on my answer, Mama. Had he asked me, I should have requested time to think. He is charming, but marriage is a serious affair.'

'Well, I suppose you have not known him long,' her mother said. 'He has promised to return to escort us home…so perhaps he will ask you then. We must just make the most of our time in Bath…'

# Chapter Eight

The next few days brought a stream of visitors to their house and a flood of invitations. They attended their first public assembly and Lady Dawlish was to be seen in the Pump Room most mornings, where she attempted a sip or two of the water. However, Lucy and Judith were more often out walking, shopping or driving. Between them they had more than twenty admirers, all of whom found excuses to call or to walk in the gardens when the ladies took the air.

'It is vastly amusing, is it not?' Judith said to Lucy when they were preparing for yet another evening party. 'I am not sure who is the most ardent of your suitors, Cousin. Would you say it was Lord Brough or Sir Arden?'

'I really do not think that any of them mean anything by it,' Lucy said, for she thought most of the young men that flocked about them idle and so wealthy that they needed constant amusement to prevent them from boredom. 'Perhaps Mr Havers might be more serious than his friends…'

'James Havers is the very one for you, though I would not have picked him out,' Judith said. 'He is extremely rich, you know, though he has no title and will not—unless his two male cousins were to die.'

'How shocking if they should,' Lucy said. If she had not believed her cousin to be teasing, she would have found her words truly shameful indeed. 'I do not know that he likes me above any other lady of his acquaintance.'

'That is nothing to the point,' Judith cried, her eyes bright with mockery. 'If you thought he would suit, we could devise a way to bring him up to scratch. It is easy enough, for we need only contrive to lock him in a room with you and then discover you in his arms.'

'Cousin! You go too far,' Lucy reproved. 'I am in no hurry to marry—it is you who has set your mind to it. Have you discovered anyone who would suit you?'

'Oh, I do not know,' Judith said and for a moment the light of laughter had left her eyes. 'This husband-hunting is not as amusing as I had thought…though I suppose Elver would do. He is in earnest, I believe, and he has both title and fortune…but I think he might be a little too kind and I should hurt him.'

'You do not care for him?' Judith shook her head. There was something in her eyes then—a secret sorrow that made Lucy frown. Now she thought of it, her cousin had not been quite her usual self for days…since the earl left them.

Lucy had thought when they were at Dawlish that her cousin meant to have Paul Ravenscar, but Judith had not mentioned him once since they had come to Bath. She had, on the other hand, asked several times if Lucy thought the earl would return sooner rather than later.

'I like him very well. I dare say he would be a comfortable husband,' Judith said and sighed. 'In truth, I do not know my own heart, Lucy. I think I may be more vulnerable than I imagined.'

'Is there someone you would rather marry… someone who is not here?'

'No, if you mean Ravenscar,' Judith replied and now she was smiling again. 'I did consider him, but he would not suit me at all, Besides, I do not mean to be buried in the country. I intend to live in London when I am not travelling.'

'No, I wasn't thinking of Paul,' Lucy said, though it hurt her to hear Judith dismiss him as if his feelings counted for nothing. 'Forgive me if I intrude, Cousin, but I thought…perhaps you still cared for Daventry?'

'Daventry!' Judith's colour waned and then returned. 'How could you think I care for him? He has eyes only for you, Lucy—and I can only think you quarrelled with him or he would never have left Bath so suddenly.'

'We did not quarrel,' Lucy replied. 'However, I gave him to understand that I was not certain of my mind.'

'So that was it. He would not like that, Lucy, for he is very proud.' Judith's gaze narrowed. 'My aunt told me that you meant to accept if he offered. It was the reason I—' She broke off and turned her face away. 'It does not surprise me that he left us if you refused him.'

'He did not ask in so many words,' Lucy said. 'He gave me to understand that he admired me and I… believe I made him angry, though he was perfectly polite.'

'He would be,' Judith said and looked thoughtful. 'Daventry keeps his own counsel. It is difficult to know what is truly in his mind. Do you really not want him, Lucy?'

Lucy smiled at her. 'I thought he might do for a time, though I never loved him,' she confessed, 'but then…'

'There is someone else, is there not?' Judith's eyes were intent on her face. 'Is it Paul Ravenscar, Cousin?'

Lucy felt her cheeks heat. 'I have loved him for years, but I think…I am sure he likes you better.'

'Oh, no, he is not in love with me,' Judith told her. 'I should not have tried to bring him to heel had I known you cared for him, Lucy.' She laughed. 'What a coil! We have been at cross purposes, Cousin.'

'Yes, perhaps,' Lucy said, her throat tight as she added, 'I had thought he might have come before this…'

'I dare say something delayed him,' Judith said. 'Well, I shall not stand in your way, dearest Lucy.

I am determined to marry soon…it may as well be Elver as any, I dare say.'

'Judith, do not throw yourself away if you do not love him,' Lucy begged her. 'I admire you and I know what you want of life, but surely…would it not be better to wait until your heart is involved?'

'I gave my heart once, only to have it broken,' Judith replied with a little shrug. 'I shall not do so again.' She glanced at the pretty gold watch pinned to her pelisse with a gold bow. 'We should go home, Lucy. It is time to prepare for Lady Marling's ball and I am engaged to the marquis for the first waltz.'

Lucy watched her cousin doubtfully. Judith was dancing with Elver for the second time. She was undoubtedly the belle of the evening, surrounded by at least fifteen young men who vied for the favour of dancing with her or fetching her a glass of iced champagne or the fruit cup. Judith's laughter rang out several times and it was evident that something was exciting the noisy group.

Lucy's partner escorted her to her mother's side and left her as he went in search of another young lady to whom he was engaged for the next dance.

In another moment Lucy's partner came to her and she took his hand. Since she could see that her cousin was still talking rather than dancing, she asked Captain Hanson what was causing so much laughter in the group he had just left.

'It is the most famous thing,' Hanson told her, his blue eyes alight with amusement. 'Lady Sparrow has challenged Major Carter to a road race in her phaeton. Harry had been boasting that no one can beat his blacks and Lady Sparrow told him that she would bet five hundred that her team would show him the way. They are arranging the details and laying odds against each other.'

Lucy gasped, for she could hardly believe her ears. She had thought it shocking enough that Judith should drive her own horses on the road, but to race a gentleman she knew only slightly and on the road…to allow the other gentlemen to lay bets on the outcome…was outrageous.

'Are you certain you have that right?' Lucy asked her partner. 'I cannot quite credit that my cousin is engaged to race Major Carter. Where, pray tell me, is the race to happen?'

'Why, beyond Bath…over a distance of some ten or fifteen miles, I believe. They were still settling the details when I came to claim my dance with you, Miss Dawlish.'

'I am…surprised,' Lucy said. She would have said shocked, but did not wish to be openly disapproving. Her cousin was still surrounded by a large group of admiring gentlemen when the dance finished.

She thanked her partner and left him to approach the group around her cousin. Judith saw her come and greeted her with an excited laugh.

'Lucy, my love, it is the most famous sport. Have you heard that I am to race Major Carter the day after tomorrow? We leave from Bath and the race begins at the fork in the road and ends at the Nag's Head, which is upon the London road and some fifteen miles or so…just a nice little dash for my darlings.'

'Judith…' Lucy breathed. 'I think you very brave, but…'

'Do not tell me you think it too dangerous, for I assure you it is not the first race I have taken part in—though that was on Lord Broughton's estate, I grant you. I raced Lord Ackrington then and was an easy winner, but I think I have more of a match this time. As I was saying just now, it is not only the horses, but the hands that guide them that matter.'

'I am sure you are right,' Lucy said, her smile a little forced. She had noticed one or two of the older ladies looking their way in a manner that told her they were stunned by her cousin's behaviour. The news of the race must have spread and many ladies would think it shocking.

She was relieved when Mr Havers touched her arm and reminded her that it was their dance, going with him willingly.

'Thank you, sir,' she said and smiled up at him. 'I was a little uncomfortable. I believe my cousin must…must have been funning, do you not think so?'

'I wish that I might reassure you,' Mr Havers said, looking anxious. 'I fear that Lady Sparrow has a reputation for being reckless on occasion. When her husband was alive he sometimes restrained her, but she has no one to advise her now. We must hope that Lady Dawlish may be able to bring her to reconsider the idea.'

'I do not think Mama… Indeed, I shall hope that my mother does not discover what is afoot, for she would not like it.'

'I do not wonder that you feel it unwise,' her partner said. 'I have seen Lady Sparrow drive very skilfully and I witnessed the race on Lord Broughton's estate, but a race on the high road...'

'I wish she would reconsider,' Lucy said anxiously. 'I am not prudish, Mr Havers, but apart from the danger...I would not wish my cousin to lose her credit with society. I know some ladies would think this...highly improper...though I do not wish to criticise her myself.'

'You are very loyal to your cousin,' Mr Havers said. 'I would offer to speak to her myself, but I fear she would think it impertinent, for I have no right. Perhaps Elver...'

'I think she would be angry if any of us spoke to her,' Lucy said. 'My cousin...is truly independent and would not listen to advice that ran contrary to her wishes.'

'Then we must hope for her sake—and your family's—that she sees the error of her ways and calls this infamous wager off.'

Lucy could only agree, but she was doubtful and felt that a shadow had been cast over the evening. Although she herself was never without a partner and the ladies of her acquaintance continued to smile on her, she could not help noticing that one or two of the sticklers had avoided Judith. There was no shortage of gentlemen to partner her cousin, for she was already much admired for her boldness and this could do her no harm in the eyes of the racier set. However, Lucy felt that within the best circles, this kind of behaviour could not be overlooked—it might be that the wife of a marquis could get away with such madness, but the widow of a mere baronet would surely find herself shunned the next time she went to a ball. She might find herself excluded from the more exclusive circles of society if this got about, as it was sure to.

Unknown to Lucy, Judith had already been made aware of the Marquis of Elver's disapproval. He had taken the first opportunity of dancing with her and had asked her to give up the idea, but finding that his pleas fell on deaf ears, had excused himself at the end of the dance and left the ballroom almost immediately.

Judith's vivacity had not wavered while the dancing continued, but when the three of them left in Lady Dawlish's carriage at the end of the evening, she seemed a little quiet.

Lady Dawlish made no comment on the evening until after they were home, when she requested to speak to Judith before she retired.

'You may go up, Lucy,' her mother said in a voice that she had never heard from her before. 'Judith, a word in my boudoir, if you please.'

Lucy shot a look of sympathy at her cousin and went to her own room.

It was quite half an hour later when Lucy was ready for bed and had sent her maid away that Judith knocked on the door and entered. She looked pale and Lucy could only feel sympathy for her.

'Did Mama give you a scold?'

'My aunt was good enough to point out that she thought my behaviour was immodest and brought shame upon all of us...which I think ridiculous.' Her eyes glinted with defiance. 'I am sorry if my wager has distressed your mama—and I should not like to think I had brought shame on you, Lucy—but this is ridiculous. I am not a milk-and-water miss. I have been married and must be allowed some freedoms.'

'I would not wish to tell you what you ought to do,' Lucy said. 'Mama meant only to point out that some ladies might…might cut you if you behave in a way—' She broke off as she saw the look on her cousin's face. 'I do not think you would care to be cut by some of the important hostesses, Judith. You had such plans for your salon…'

'As if I care for the mealy-mouthed gossiping cats,' Judith burst out angrily. 'My aunt could not see it—but surely you must, Lucy. It was a wager and I cannot…shall not draw back.'

'I do see that it would be embarrassing,' Lucy agreed. 'What made you agree to it, Judith?'

'Oh, I do not know…I was bored, miserable,' Judith said. 'I have been out of sorts for a while. I needed something to make me feel life was worth living again. I did not think it was so very bad. It is merely a race between friends with a little wager—where can the harm be in that?'

'It is not what many people would think proper,' Lucy said and saw her cousin's eyes narrow again. 'I think it amusing if it were on private land…but I do not wish to censure you, Cousin. I am sorry if you think me a prude, but I feel you ought to withdraw.'

'Well, I shall not,' Judith said militantly. 'I have told my aunt that I will leave her house if she wishes, but I shall not give up my race. It would make me look a coward and foolish.'

'What will the marquis think? Does he not mind that people will think you fast or immodest?'

Judith shrugged. 'If he cares for such foolishness, I am sure I do not care. He may give his allegiance to another. What does it matter? I have enough admirers...'

Lucy thought that most of the gentlemen who flocked about Judith were foolish young men drawn to her by her bold manners and her sparkling eyes. Whether those same men would be as eager to offer for her hand once her reputation had suffered the reverse it must, Lucy could not say. All she knew was that she found it distressing. Judith was her cousin and she would have liked to see her happy; she could not think this race would bring anything but disaster.

'I shall go to bed,' Judith told her and yawned. 'I've told your mama that I shall think carefully about what she has asked, but I have no intention of calling it off. Naturally, I shall have to leave after the race so I shall say goodbye to you now,

Lucy. I wish you every happiness…and I hope you marry the man you want.'

'Judith…please reconsider this madness. I would not have you leave us in disgrace.'

'Goodnight, Lucy,' her cousin said and went out. She had her face turned and despite her defiance, Lucy thought she was close to tears.

Lucy sat on the edge of her bed. If Judith continued with this foolish race of hers, she might ruin herself. She made up her mind to speak with her mother in the morning. Judith was headstrong and there was no way of preventing her taking part in the race, but surely it would be better if she remained with them? To ask her to leave their house would be to compound the disgrace and to appear to judge her unworthy. She must then be ruined indeed.

Feeling anxious and uncertain, Lucy went to bed, though she lay wakeful for some hours before she finally slept.

In the morning Lucy went downstairs to discover that her cousin had already gone out. She was alone in the parlour and about to go in search of her mama when a visitor was announced. At the sound of his voice greeting her, she sprang up and ran to him, holding out her hands. He took them and held them, looking into her face, one eyebrow raised.

'You are pleased to see me?'

'Oh, thank goodness you are come, Paul,' she said. 'It is so awful. Judith has got herself into a scrape and I do not know how to get her out of it, for she says she will not withdraw…and if she does not I fear Mama will send her away and she will be ruined.'

'Lucy,' Paul said in the greatest astonishment, 'what are you gabbling about? If you wish me to understand, you must speak more slowly.'

'Forgive me, I was just so glad to see you, for there is no one else who can help us,' Lucy said and gave a little sob. 'Judith has wagered that her horses will beat Major Carter's in a road race— and everyone has wagered on the outcome. Mama heard of it…indeed, everyone at the ball last night heard of this infamous wager. Mama was angry and told Judith that she would shame us. She asked her to withdraw, but my cousin is stubborn and proud and will not. She says she will go away afterwards, but that will just make things worse.'

'Infinitely,' Paul said, thoughtful but serious. 'You must both support her or she is ruined indeed.'

'I cannot like the idea of this race, yet I understand it is a matter of pride with her—but I do not want her to be ruined, Paul. I care for her—even if she does go too far at times. I know she likes to flirt, but indeed…I think it is because she is unhappy. I believe her heart was broken as a young girl and she pretends not to care…but she does.'

'How wise you are, Lucy,' Paul said and then, surprising her and perhaps himself, he touched his lips lightly to hers. She felt a shooting thrill of pleasure and it was all she could do not to lean her head on his shoulder. 'It does you credit to seek to protect your cousin, Lucy. I shall do what I may to bring her off safely, though at the moment I am not sure how much I can do. Some damage has already been done.'

'Oh…' Lucy smiled at him, because his kiss, although light, had been sweet and comforted her. This was the man she'd known and loved restored to her, as if all the pain and doubt had never been, and her heart swelled with love as she looked into his face. 'If she could be brought to cry off…'

'No, I do not think that will serve,' Paul said. 'It would only prove the gossips right. We must think of some other way to bring her off. The race must go ahead, but we shall support her.'

'Do you think so?' Lucy was uncertain, but he seemed so sure and his very presence had a calming effect on her. 'I am so glad you are here, Paul.'

'I am glad to be of service to your family, Lucy.' His eyes were warm, a little amused. 'Do you remember that I scolded Judith for merely driving on the road and that put her on her mettle? To forbid her would be to push her into worse. No, do not fear, Lucy, I shall contrive to make this affair more respectable.'

'She has gone out this morning. Mrs Hickson said that she was wearing a carriage gown, so I imagine she means to drive out in Bath—to show people she does not care, I dare say.'

'She could not do better,' Paul said. 'We must make it appear that she is used to driving herself everywhere and perhaps it will not then seem quite so strange.'

'I am grateful for whatever you can do,' Lucy said. She was about to say more when they heard the door and then Hickson came to the door of the parlour and announced that the Marquis of Elver had called. 'Oh…he has been most attentive to Judith.'

'Good,' Paul said and turned to greet the marquis with a smile and an outstretched hand. 'Elver—I fancy we met in Vienna?'

'Yes, I recall it,' the marquis said and gravely shook his hand. 'I came to ask if Lady Sparrow will see me.'

'Unfortunately, she has gone driving,' Lucy said. 'She will be sorry to have missed you.'

'I shall call this afternoon. It is important that I speak to her…she cannot realise…' He stopped, embarrassed. 'I had hoped I might ease the scandal…my estate is not ten miles from Bath…'

'Ah, I see, just the thing,' Paul said and looked at him with approval. 'Yes, if we rearranged the race to take place on private land…and put it about that it was always meant to be there…'

'I thought I might arrange a picnic in the grounds, invite people who are inclined to oblige me…we may bring it off. You see, I know Lady Sparrow will not withdraw.'

'Yet if her race were one of several it would not be so remarkable. You might give a trophy,

Elver—and some of us might compete—a time trial rather than a race, perhaps?'

'An excellent idea,' the marquis said and frowned. 'If only Lady Sparrow can be brought to agree.'

'I think she will,' Paul said. 'Pray arrange your picnic, invite your friends. I shall engage to race against...' He turned to Lucy. 'Will you try your hand against me if we can find a team to suit you?'

'And my sister Hetty against me,' the marquis said.

'Me?' Lucy was astonished and then excited. She laughed and tossed her head. 'Yes, I see how much better that would be—it is to be a party of friends and these races are no more than sport one may find at any picnic.'

'Well, not quite,' Paul said, but gave her a look of approval. 'Bravo, Lucy. If Elver does his work and you play your part, we can scotch most of the gossip. Judith may still find herself ostracised by some of the old tabbies, but—'

'She will not if she will oblige me by accepting my offer of marriage,' the marquis said, looking proud. 'I care for Lady Sparrow, you see, and though I did not like to see her so reckless last night, I shall not desert her.'

'Oh, generous,' Lucy cried. 'How good you are, sir. My cousin could not do better than to marry you.'

A rueful smile touched his lips. 'I wish that she might be brought to see it,' he said. 'I thank you for your kind words, Miss Dawlish—but I love her, you see.'

'Then she would be a fool to turn you down,' Paul said. 'I shall hope for your success, sir—and, if Lucy will excuse us both, I shall help spread the word that these races were always to take place at Elver Towers.'

'Oh, please do go,' Lucy said. 'We dine alone this evening, Paul—shall you come?'

'Yes, certainly. Please tell your mama what we have arranged and beg her not to desert your cousin. Elver and I will bring her off safe, I give you my word. But your mother must not throw her off.'

'Mama was angry last night—I have seldom seen her so,' Lucy admitted. 'But I am sure she will have thought it through by now and will be only too relieved if you can bring this off.'

The gentlemen took their leave. Lucy went up to her mother's bedchamber and, after asking prettily, was admitted. Lady Dawlish, looking fetching in a white shawl, lace nightgown and cap, was sitting up against the pillows, looking upset.

'What are we to do about all this?' she asked Lucy. 'I told Judith she must go if she insisted on racing, but the poor child would be ruined and my brother would never forgive me.'

'She must not leave us, Mama,' Lucy said. 'Captain Ravenscar has arrived this morning and the Marquis of Elver called—they have fixed it between them. There may be some gossip, but it cannot be too bad...'

'What can you mean, child? I do not see how it can be fixed, for Judith is too stubborn.'

'The marquis means to give a picnic, Mama. There will be several races held, not just Judith's, all on private land. They will be more in the nature of time trials, though, a gentleman against a lady. I am to pit my skill against Paul's.'

'Lucy! I forbid it.' Her mama was scandalised. 'How could you think of it?'

'I would not be upon a public road, Mama—but

such things often happen at a gentleman's estate, you know they do—and it will help to take the sting from the whole affair. You will be there and lots of the marquis's friends. I dare say he may prevail upon his sister to time trial her horses against his own.' Lucy reached forward to take her mother's hand. 'Do you not see, dearest? It would then make the whole thing commonplace and Judith would not be ruined.'

Lady Dawlish was silent for a few moments, then inclined her head reluctantly. 'Yes, I do see it, my love. I cannot quite like it, but if Lady Hetty also takes part...she is above censure. Yes, it might scotch most of the spite, but...will Judith see the sense of it? You know how stubborn she is about these things.'

'Yes, she is stubborn,' Lucy said, 'but I think she may realise her mistake and be glad of a way to scotch the worst of the scandal. Besides, the marquis means to ask her to marry him.'

'Judith to be his wife?' Lady Dawlish sat up with a look of relief. 'How wonderful that would be... Yes, I see now that this plan is the very thing. If the marquis's sister is to race, then I see no reason why you should not, my love. And against an old friend…for you have known Paul Ravenscar all your life.'

Paul was thoughtful as he left Lucy that morning. He had meant to speak to her at once, to ask her if there was a chance for him, but when she'd told him of her troubles he'd known that he must wait. Lucy was naturally anxious for her cousin. He must do all in his power to pull Judith off safe and then…perhaps then the way would at last be clear for him to speak of what was in his heart… if only it were not too late.

# Chapter Nine

'How dare they interfere in my affairs?' Judith cried when Lucy spoke to her on her return to the house later that day. 'No, it shall not be—I shall not give in so tamely.'

'You are not withdrawing,' Lucy said. 'The wagers may stand and you may race against Major Carter—but it will be on private land and others will also race. Do you not see that it then becomes respectable?'

'Why should I wish to be respectable?' Judith asked, but Lucy could see that she was thoughtful.

'Because you wish to set up your own salon in London. Do you think all those you wish to entertain would come if you blacken your name with this foolish nonsense?'

Judith glared at her, turning away to look out of her bedroom window. There was some dampness in the air, though there had been no rain to speak of. For a moment or two she did not speak, then, without turning to look, she said, 'Who else would race tomorrow?'

'I am to race against Paul and Elver against his sister Lady Hetty—it is more in the nature of a time trial, but you may race Major Carter and I shall do my best to beat Captain Ravenscar.'

Judith turned at that and she was smiling. 'I have good friends,' she said and swiftly crossed the space between them to kiss her cheek. 'I was in such a mood last night, but as soon as the words were spoken I knew I had been a fool. A race on private land is one thing, on the road another— and I should have found myself on the edge of society, unless I married very well.'

'You must thank Paul and the marquis,' Lucy told her. 'Elver came up with the idea and Paul thought of making it a time trial with others taking part. I think I shall enjoy myself, though I cannot believe I shall beat anyone's time.'

'Remember what I taught you and I do not see why not,' Judith said and laughed, then her smile faded. 'What does my aunt think of this scheme?'

'She sees that it is a good plan—and she will

be one of the guests at the picnic. Her presence and that of other friends of Elver's must make it respectable.'

Judith sighed. 'Do you never tire of being respectable, Cousin? I vow I do sometimes. I suppose it was that that made me take the wretched wager. Yet I am glad to have it settled and I shall thank both Captain Ravenscar and Elver when I see them.'

'I am happy that you agree to their proposals,' Lucy said and caught her hand. 'And I hope you win your race, I truly do.'

'You are a good friend to me,' Judith said. She hesitated for a moment, then, 'I do not think you would take him, Lucy—but I shall warn you again to be careful of Daventry. He made love to me for three months and gained my love—and then he deserted me. I would not have him break your heart, dearest Lucy.'

'I do not think he could, even if he tried,' Lucy told her with a smile. 'I love Paul…and I think, I believe he quite likes me. He felt guilty because his brother died, you see…but perhaps now he can see me not as Mark's betrothed, but as a girl he was used to like very well.'

'I shall not stand in your way,' Judith said. 'Had I known you cared for him I should never have flirted with him, Lucy.'

'Do you think of taking Elver? I believe he truly cares for you.'

'Yes, perhaps he does,' Judith replied. 'I am not yet sure…' A sigh escaped her. 'I should be a fool to turn him down in favour of another…but I cannot forget…'

'I have thought you still care for Daventry.'

'Yes, for my sins I feel something. I ought to loathe him and at times I do. I know if I married him he would never be faithful to me—and he might break my heart. I should put him from my mind…besides, I think it is you he wants, Lucy.'

'No, no, I am sure he does not. Besides, I have decided that I should refuse him if he asked,' Lucy said. 'I liked him, for he can be charming—but I know my heart now. If Paul cannot bring himself to wed me, I shall not marry—at least for years.'

'That would be a waste,' Judith said and laughed. 'Perhaps I should give him a nudge in the right direction?'

'I wish you will not,' Lucy said and blushed. 'I have confessed my secret to you, Judith—but I pray you keep it to yourself.'

'I should not dream of disclosing it to anyone,' Judith said. 'Besides, I rather fancy that Captain Ravenscar is a man who knows his own mind. When he has made it up he will not be swayed from his path. It was that about him that made me realise we should not suit. I need someone to spoil me and give me my own way…to rescue me when I have been too reckless.'

'Yes, you do,' Lucy said and smiled at her. 'I can think of someone who would do just that… but I shall not tease you.'

'I must change for tea,' Judith said. 'I shall ring for my maid—and you must too, Lucy, or we shall keep my aunt waiting and she is not best pleased with me.'

'I think she forgave you soon after she scolded you,' Lucy said and walked to the door. Looking back, she said, 'Captain Ravenscar is coming to dinner this evening.'

'I am glad that he has come to Bath,' Judith said. 'I was afraid you might take Daventry and that I am sure would have been a mistake.'

* * *

At dinner that evening Lady Dawlish was everything that was kind to her niece. She wanted an end to any discord between them and was pleased to find Judith her charming self, inclined to oblige her aunt in any way possible. They spoke little of the picnic the following day, but when they had all retired to the drawing room, Paul sat next to Lucy on a little sofa and told her that it was all arranged.

'Elver was so casual that I almost believed him myself,' Paul told her. 'He explained that in the heat of the moment they had all misunderstood the wager and that it was always to have been on his estate. Indeed, he has given a silver salver as the prize and several other gentlemen and their sisters or female friends have entered the contest.'

'Oh, how clever it is,' Lucy said, looking at him admiringly. 'You said you would bring her off and you have done it.'

'With Elver's help,' Paul said modestly. 'I had something of the kind in mind, but I was relieved when he came to us with the idea. I should not like to have seen your cousin in such trouble, for I like her despite her foolish, stubborn ways.'

'I like her, too,' Lucy said and looked a little shy. 'I thought for a while that you might…but, no, it is not my affair.'

'I did consider your cousin as a suitable wife, for I must marry for the sake of my father and the estate,' Paul admitted, looking grave, 'but I soon came to my senses.' He hesitated, then, 'I have something to tell you concerning Mark, Lucy… something that has changed things for me a little. I believe you should know—but this is not the time.' He glanced about him at the company. 'We should be private when I tell you what I must.'

'I do not understand you,' Lucy said with a frown, but the tea tray had been brought in and her mother was calling her to help pass the cups.

She left Paul and went to her mother, noticing that Judith got up and went over to him for a moment, before returning to her seat. Paul drank a dish of tea with them and then took his leave, promising to pick Lady Dawlish and Lucy up the next day. Judith was to drive herself to the picnic, with only her groom to accompany her.

There was no more time for private conversation and the ladies retired soon after Paul left them. Lady Dawlish had invited him to stay with them, for there were enough bedchambers, but he had politely refused her invitation, saying that he was settled in good lodgings and quite comfortable.

Lucy said goodnight to her mama and Judith came to her room with her. 'I gave him to understand that I was looking elsewhere,' she said. 'Captain Ravenscar said that he quite understood and had not considered either of us bound to the other.'

Lucy did not reply, because she already knew that Paul did not consider himself committed to her cousin.

'I shall think about taking Elver seriously,' Judith said and kissed her cheek. 'Sleep well, Cousin. You must not be tired tomorrow, for you will wish to win your race.'

'Yes, perhaps,' Lucy said. She would like to at least keep up with Paul when they drove against one another in the time trial, but for her it was only important to drive well and to see Judith's reputation restored.

She went to bed and, after a few minutes during which she wondered what Paul could possibly have to tell her that concerned Mark, drifted into a deep sleep and did not wake until her maid came in to draw the curtains.

Lucy and Lady Dawlish were helped into the curricle that Paul was driving the next morning. He told her that she was to drive his horses and phaeton at the picnic, because she had driven them before, while he had arranged to borrow a rig from a friend.

'Havers's horses have less tender mouths than mine,' he told her. 'He offered them to me when he understood the plan. I believe he is a friend of yours, Lucy?'

'Yes, I like him well,' Lucy agreed. 'We have met several pleasant friends here in Bath, but Mr Havers is very pleasant.'

'I understand that Daventry left Bath more than a week ago,' Paul said, arching his brows. 'I had imagined he meant to stay with you for the length of your visit here?'

'He had intended it, I think,' Lucy said, a faint flush in her cheeks. 'I believe he discovered he had business elsewhere. I dare say he is a busy man.'

'Yes...' Paul looked at her intently and she could

not meet his eyes. 'Well, I think this little affair should be amusing—do you not agree?'

'Yes, I believe so,' Lucy said. 'I only hope that I shall not disgrace myself.'

'Oh, I do not think it,' Paul replied with a smile. 'You are not yet as skilled as you will be in time— for it was my intention to continue our lessons when we have the leisure. However, I think you will find that you make good speed if you let my horses have their head.'

'All I care is that she conducts herself with discretion and does not hurt herself,' Lady Dawlish said, glancing over her shoulder. 'I cannot see Judith behind us. Do you think she is all right? I hardly like to think of her driving herself alone.'

'She has her groom, Mama,' Lucy said. 'I am sure there is no need to worry.' She looked round and caught sight of Judith's phaeton some distance behind them. 'She must have been delayed, but she is coming now.'

'Good,' Lady Dawlish said in tones of long suffering. 'I pray that all goes well today, for my nerves will not stand much more.'

'You must not fret, Mama. Judith is a good driver.'

Lucy was well aware that her mother was not speaking of her cousin's driving ability, but there was no point in dwelling on the scandal that had been neatly averted by the marquis and Paul's contriving.

The marquis's estate was large and well managed, his house a sprawling, early Georgian manor that had been enlarged over the years, but retained its elegance. Ahead of them was a queue of carriages of all kinds, several of them sporting rigs. Lucy judged that there would be many more entrants for this infamous race than even Paul and the marquis had bargained for. Several light rigs were being driven by ladies, always accompanied by a gentleman or a groom. It seemed that Judith was not the only female that liked to drive herself.

When first Lady Dawlish and then Lucy were helped down, before a groom took the vehicle away, Judith had caught up with them and she saw with a little shock that Daventry was with her.

He came up to them as Judith's phaeton was led away.

'What a famous idea,' he said and bowed over first Lady Dawlish's hand and then Lucy's. 'It seems that I returned just in time, for I should not have liked to miss the fun. Had I known previously, I should have brought my phaeton and joined the challenge.'

'I believe the race may be oversubscribed already,' Lucy said, looking doubtfully about her. 'I do not know how many of these people intend to enter...'

Paul turned to look and frowned as he saw her speaking with the earl. He came up to them, holding out his hand to Lucy in a manner she could only think imperious. However, instead of feeling annoyed, she was grateful to take it and looked up at him in a pleased way.

'Come, Lucy,' he said. 'We must join the other competitors. How do you do, Daventry. I did not expect to see you here today.'

'I went away to attend to some business and make up my mind about something,' the earl said. 'I returned as soon as I could—as I told Miss Lucy I should.'

There was something challenging in his manner as he spoke. Lucy frowned, for he was not telling the whole truth and seemed to imply something that was not true, but she could hardly tell him so in front of company.

There were so many people milling around that she was glad when Paul moved them along to where the picnic itself was being held. She saw that two long tables had been set out with plates of delicious foods: small pastries, cold meats, relishes, new potatoes in melted butter, peas, little pies and quiches. Also a variety of little cakes, sugared almonds and plums, and marchpane for the ladies. Footmen in livery were circulating with trays bearing hot canapés and iced champagne, and set on the table was a silver salver and a blue-and-silver scent flask, also a silver hand mirror and a case for cheroots. Prizes for ladies and gentlemen, it seemed.

Apart from the ladies and gentlemen, a quartet of musicians was playing and some children were toying with a hoop and a ball a little further off. Lucy thought the marquis had done very well to turn it into a pleasant social occasion for all, though she was not sure he had intended so many people to turn up for the event.

When the marquis announced that there were to be ten races, each to start ten minutes apart, and each consisting of one lady driving against a gentleman and judged by time, rather than who came in first, there was some cheering. Lucy was a little surprised that so many ladies should have wanted to test their skill, but so it was and she heard some very excited voices on all sides as people picked their chosen candidate for the winner.

'How well it has turned out,' Paul said, looking down at her. 'And it seems the weather will keep fine for us.'

'Yes, indeed.' Lucy laughed softly. 'It is just like it used to be at home, Paul…do you not think so?'

'Yes, I believe it may be,' he said. 'Shall we make a private wager ourselves?'

'Yes, if you wish it?'

'If I win, you must pay me a forfeit—and if you win, I shall give you a light rig you can drive yourself, and a pair of horses.'

'That is a large bet,' Lucy said, feeling overwhelmed. 'What is it you wish from me?'

'Shall we say a kiss?'

Lucy's heart hammered wildly in her breast, her cheeks flaming as she inclined her head. She sensed that Paul intended to say more, but the marquis had begun to explain the rules of the race and they were forced to listen.

There was to be a prize for the winning time by a gentleman, another for a winning time by a lady and an overall prize for the fastest time of all.

Lucy felt a flutter of excitement herself. She ate a small pastry and sipped her flute of champagne, but was too busy looking and listening as she heard laughing voices taking wagers on who would win the various prizes.

*What had Paul been going to say to her? And why did he wish to kiss her?*

The marquis and his sister were to drive first since they were the hosts of the picnic and wanted their own challenge out of the way so that they could attend to the needs of their guests. One of the marquis's own grooms was to ride with each contestant to direct them on the route so that it would be fair to all.

Lucy stood under the shade of a tree on a crest, for it afforded an excellent view of the route, though at one point it disappeared into some trees and then emerged again a little distance from the spot where the picnic was held. The start-and-finish line was where all the guests could see and cheer their favourite on.

The marquis achieved a creditable time of twenty minutes and fifteen seconds, his sister Hetty did rather better since she came in on twenty minutes exactly.

Not certain of the route, Lucy thought their times could hardly be beaten, but then another pair took their chances and the gentleman was back in just under twenty minutes, the lady taking almost five and twenty. And so the contest went on. Lucy found that she was to drive second from last and Judith was to follow her.

Judith came up to her just before the eighth couple started out. 'There is a steep bend to the right soon after you start,' she said, 'and another to the left when you return. Good luck Cousin. I am certain you will do as well as any lady here.'

No lady had so far beaten Lady Hetty's time. When Lucy's rig was brought up, she discovered that it was lighter than the one she had driven before and realised that Paul had after all given her the borrowed vehicle, perhaps because it would be easier for a lady.

He came to assist her to the driving box. 'The horses are mine and you will manage them easily—the rig is Lady Hetty's own. She has kindly lent it to you.'

'How kind of her,' Lucy said and smiled. 'Good luck, Paul. I shall try to beat you.'

'Yes, of course,' he said and kissed his fingers to her. 'Good luck, Lucy.'

She set off first, as was the rule with the other contestants. Only one gentleman had overtaken his opponent, for it was time that counted, but the young coxcomb had wanted to prove his mettle and come in at nineteen minutes and twenty seconds after overtaking so dangerously that the marquis ruled he was disqualified for almost oversetting the lady's rig. He'd scowled over it, but so far no one had beaten the time he'd set.

Lucy set out with Paul a few seconds behind her. She had felt nervous for a start, but the horses responded so beautifully that she gave them their head and let them take her round. They went at such a spanking pace that she knew there was a respectable distance between Paul's rig and her own. He made up a little ground towards the end, but remembering Judith's warning, Lucy brought her horses to the finish and she fancied Paul had not quite caught her.

Their times were given as nineteen minutes and fifty-five seconds each and so it was called a draw between them. Lucy was laughing as he came to help her down, her cheeks pink from the excitement and a light breeze.

'Did you let me keep ahead?' she asked him as he set her down and the horses were led away.

'No such thing,' he said, his hands about her waist as he looked down into her eyes. Her breath caught in her throat and her heart thudded. Something in his eyes seemed to say that he liked her very well indeed. 'You handled them with style, Lucy. I fancy I might have gone faster with them, but I am glad to have equalled your skill.'

Since three other gentlemen had gone faster, Lucy knew that he was not in the running for the prize, but she was the quickest of the ladies and was greeted with applause as she rejoined the party.

However, it was now time for Judith and Major Carter to race and everyone was crowding to see what would happen. Judith looked magnificent as she set off at a cracking pace and the major set out after her. It was obvious as he urged his pair on that he meant to catch and overtake her if he could and a feeling of tension seemed to spread through the spectators. The other races had been watched with an air of pleasure or amusement, but this was the race everyone had been waiting for, because, despite all that had been done to avoid scandal, no one quite believed in the picnic. Most of the company had bet on the outcome, which was not the case with many of the other contestants.

When the horses approached the bend that took them behind the trees, it looked as if Major Carter was about to catch up with his beautiful opponent. There was a collective sigh as both rigs disappeared from view and everyone waited, then a cheer went up as the first rig was seen to come round the bend on the return…and it was Judith. She was fairly flying down the road, her horses at full stretch. As Lucy watched she looped her whip and caught it again as the major came after her. His horses were lathered, because he had pushed them hard on the first part of the course; he was still pushing them, but it was clear that they were blown and would not catch Judith.

'By God, she's done it in eighteen minutes and

fifty seconds,' someone cried as Judith brought her horses to a stop. 'Carter is fifty seconds behind her...'

Cheering broke out on all sides and Judith was clapped as she climbed down from her rig and handed her reins to a groom. She was announced the winner, but Major Carter had driven fastest of the gentlemen and was awarded a prize. He accepted it with good grace, though looked a little sick, because the prize was a mere trinket while he was known to have bet more than a thousand guineas on himself.

'You won,' Lucy said, going to her cousin to kiss her. 'It was a wonderful race, Judith. He looked as though he might catch you.'

'He did and should have passed me,' she said, 'but he misjudged the corner and had to pull back or he would have landed in a steep ditch. Elver warned me of it so I may have had the advantage—but his horses could have beaten mine over a longer test.'

'Well, that is as may be,' Lucy said. 'I did it in nineteen minutes and fifty-five seconds, you know.'

'As I expected, you have flair. I have been driving much longer. When you have more experience, I shall race you one day, Cousin. Elver will arrange it for us—but we shall not invite all these people to watch. I'm not sure I know half of them.'

'Well, I do think there must be some uninvited guests,' Lucy said, hearing some gentlemen laughing and jesting a little crudely. 'Shall we join Mama and Captain Ravenscar?'

'Yes, why not?' Judith replied and smiled. 'I did not drink before the race, but I should enjoy a glass of champagne now.'

'Oh, yes. You must be so pleased, dearest.'

'Yes, I am, for I knew my darlings were game,' Judith said. 'Carter's horses are good—but he is too rash and does not judge his corners well.'

She looked about her. The crowd was beginning to thin a little.

'Elver said we should go up to the house. He has arranged a light tea for a few of his closest friends…though I am not sure I could eat a thing, but it is what he wants.' She looked at Lucy, a smile on her lips. 'He has something to announce.'

Lucy arched her brows, but Judith merely laughed and shook her head. 'Is it what I think, Cousin?'

'You must just wait and see,' Judith told her, but she looked happy and her eyes danced with merriment.

The announcement of their engagement was duly made after the guests had assembled for tea, which consisted of delicious salmon-and-cucumber sandwiches, tiny chicken treats in flaky pastry with a cream-and-wine sauce, and a variety of dainty cakes. The gentlemen wolfed down the savoury treats while the ladies nibbled at a sweet cake with their dish of tea.

'I have the delightful duty of announcing that Lady Sparrow has done me the honour to accept my offer of marriage,' the marquis announced, looking at her proudly. 'Please, my dearest...'

Judith went to him and he slipped a magnificent diamond-and-emerald ring on the third finger of her left hand.

'I wish to thank you for making me the happiest of men—and for ensuring that my future life will not be in the least dull.'

Laughter and cheers greeted this sally and Judith looked at him gratefully. 'I fear I shall not make you a comfortable wife, sir,' she told him.

'I may land you in scrapes and lead you a merry dance—but you have my promise that I shall be a loving partner.'

More laughter followed this and more than one envious look was directed at the marquis. Lucy, who happened to look at Earl Daventry, was shocked by the expression in his eyes. He was staring at Elver as if he could cheerfully put a ball through his head. She felt a cold shiver at her nape as he turned and looked straight at her.

He was very angry, but she did not think he had a broken heart and guessed that whatever his true reason for wishing to provoke Judith, it was not love that motivated him. He might claim to have loved her once, but it was selfish displeasure that Lucy saw in his face and it made her glad that she had decided against him.

In a moment the menacing expression was gone and he smiled as he came to her.

'You drove well, Miss Lucy,' he said. 'I think with a little tuition you might handle your horses even better.'

'You flatter me, sir,' she replied. 'Captain Ravenscar says that he will teach me when we return home and I shall hope to improve—though I could not have expected to do so well. Had he wished, I am certain that Paul could have passed me. Besides, he loaned me his own horses and borrowed a team for himself.'

'Very probably he could have beaten you had he wished,' Daventry said in a cold voice. 'He is clearly quite the proper gentleman. Excuse me, I must speak to someone.'

Lucy felt a little shiver go down her spine. The earl was obviously irate—with her or with her cousin? Possibly both of them, for they had both rejected him in their various ways. She only knew that she had not liked the expression in his eyes when Judith had spoken of making Elver a loving wife.

Was he jealous? Lucy was puzzled. At Dawlish he had seemed to be courting her and even in Bath he had paid her very pleasing attention—until she made it clear that she had not made up her mind to marry him if he asked. Yet she had heard that argument between him and her cousin in the garden and she wondered if his attentions to her had been a cover for his true feelings.

Once he had courted Judith and stolen her heart, then he had deserted her. Did he now regret it? Was he jealous of the man she had agreed to marry? Or was it simply, as Judith more cynically said, because he admired her fortune? Lucy, too, was an heiress, though her fortune was not as large as her cousin's.

'So, Lucy, are you satisfied now?'

She turned to discover Paul at her side and smiled up at him. 'I am very grateful to you and the marquis,' she said. 'My cousin owes the fact that she still has a reputation to you both.'

'She has come off very well,' Paul said. 'Now we may all forget this nonsense and enjoy ourselves.'

There was at that moment such a look of promise in his eyes that she wished she might melt into his body and regretted that she had not lost to him, for then he would have demanded his forfeit. Her mouth tingled at the thought of what that kiss might be like, for he had never kissed her other than a brief touch of his lips. To be held and kissed until she could scarcely breathe… Her pulses raced at the thought of it and she was forced to look away lest he saw her longing.

Lucy smiled and agreed. Now was not the time to tell him that she still had doubts about her cousin's future.

## Chapter Ten

'I must go to town to buy my bride clothes,' Judith told Lucy when they were home again. 'London will be thin of company or I would beg you and my aunt to come with me, Lucy—but I shall write to my late mother's Aunt Susan and ask her to chaperon me. I dare say your mama is wishing me to the devil by now.'

'No, of course she isn't,' Lucy said. 'Mama never bears a grudge. Besides, how could she be angry when you have made such a brilliant match?'

'I have been lucky,' Judith agreed. 'You know that I was not sure whether I should take him, but when he did so much for me…it was as if a veil had been lifted from my eyes and I saw him for the first time.'

'Then you do truly care for him?'

'Yes, I do.'

'I am glad you are happy. I wondered for a time if you still cared for the Earl of Daventry?'

Judith laughed. 'I wondered myself, Lucy. I was so desperately in love with him when I was seventeen. He made love to me… I will confess that I was fortunate to escape with my virtue intact, for had he chosen to seduce me I should have allowed it. When he left me, I was forced to marry an older man my father had chosen and…' She shook her head, as if she had put an end to something in her mind. 'I shall not dwell on that, for I came to care for my husband. Suffice it to say my heart was broken, but it has mended.'

'Would you have wed Daventry now if he had asked?'

Judith's cheeks flushed. 'I must tell you that he did ask me one afternoon at your house. I was so angry with him, for it was after your dance and everyone expected that he would offer for you. I told him that he was a despicable rogue and… well, you know the rest. Just think—if I had taken him—what it must have been like for you, Lucy. Everyone would have thought ill of him…and me. I believe that it was at that moment I began to see him for the selfish, ruthless man he is. He used us both, Cousin—and I cannot forgive him for that.'

'Oh, I see. So that was why you quarrelled.'

'Yes. I was distressed and it made me feel uncomfortable with you for a time, though I tried to hide it—I shall admit, however, that for a moment I was tempted. I did love him once, you see. When he left Bath we had argued again—just before we left for the theatre. After he had gone, I was angry that he had allowed you to think he intended marriage for I thought it would hurt you if you discovered what a shallow fellow he truly is— but then you told me you did not care for him...'

'Is that why you were so reckless that night at the assembly, because he had made you unhappy by leaving?'

'Yes, and, no,' Judith said, half-shamed by her admittance. 'A part of me could not forget what he had once been to me, but it was not just that. Elver had made it plain that he admired me and I felt...desperate...for I did not know what to do. I knew that it would be a good marriage and yet a part of me still hankered for...' She shook her head, clearly annoyed with herself. 'It was mere irritation of the nerves, Lucy dearest. I did not know my own heart. I assure you that I have made my decision and shall not waver again.'

'Even if Daventry makes it plain he cares for you?'

Pride glittered in Judith's eyes. 'I think he is at heart a selfish man who will never truly care for anyone but himself.'

'Well, I am glad that you have chosen Elver,' Lucy said. 'I have become fond of you, Cousin, and wish you happy. I shall ask Mama if she will take us to London to buy your bride clothes, if you wish it?'

'I should not wish to put my aunt to so much trouble. My mother's aunt will do the pretty by me, I dare say—and Elver intends to escort me. I know you are fixed in Bath for another week and I shall stay with you until you leave. Then Elver will escort me to London to stay with Great-Aunt Susan.'

Lucy gave way, for if her cousin's mind was made up there was no more to say. Judith asked her if she would be a bridesmaid at her wedding and she agreed. On this cordial note the cousins parted to dress for the evening. They were to attend a card party at Lady Milton's house and, since she had a long gallery, some of the young ladies and gentlemen would be able to dance if they chose.

Lucy wore a gown of primrose silk, caught with a white sash under her breast to which she had fastened a posy of white roses. She had not used the gold pin that Daventry had given her, but instead a small pearl pin of her mother's. She wore a simple string of pearls about her throat and some diamond-and-pearl earrings.

Judith wore a gown of emerald green and a pendant of emeralds and diamonds, her hair swept up high on her head with one ringlet over her shoulder.

'Elver regrets he will not be able to join us this evening,' she said before they left, 'for he had made prior arrangements, which he cannot break. Tomorrow evening he has promised to escort us to Lady Norton's ball.'

'A pity he cannot come this evening,' Lucy said, but she could not help smiling. 'However, Captain Ravenscar will be present, for he knows Lady Milton's son well and has been invited.'

Judith smiled at her in a knowing way. 'You are

well suited, you know,' she said. 'I wish I'd realised you cared for him earlier, for I fear I may
have caused you pain.'

'A little, but it was not your fault. Paul seemed
changed, distant, when he returned from Vienna.
I thought he had forgot me, but now...' A little
smile touched her mouth. 'He was more like his
old self this morning and I think...' Her smile
faded as she recalled that Paul had something to
tell her about Mark. 'Perhaps this evening we shall
have a chance to talk properly.'

'Does one ever have time at a social affair?'
Judith asked. 'If you wish to be private with him,
you should arrange to go driving with him tomorrow.'

Lucy agreed, but yet hoped that she might have
a little private time with Paul that evening.

The party had barely begun when Lucy saw
Paul walking towards her. She smiled as he bowed
to her and asked if she meant to dance that evening.

'It is but an informal affair,' Lucy replied. 'But,
yes, I shall dance if you ask me, sir.'

'I shall engage for the first set of country

dances, the first waltz and the supper dance,' he said promptly and a flush came to her cheeks, for he was making it clear that he intended to stake his claim to her. 'I came early for the purpose. I remember that I came to *your* dance too late to secure even one dance.'

'I should have kept some later in the evening,' Lucy said, 'but I was not sure... I thought that perhaps...'

'I believe we were at cross purposes,' Paul said and smiled. 'Much as I like and admire your cousin, Lucy, I do not think I should care to be married to her. I fancy she will lead Elver a merry dance.'

'Perhaps...' Lucy wrinkled her brow. 'Yet I believe that she likes him very well—indeed, I think her fond of him. I do not see that she will be a trouble to him.'

'Ladies such as Lady Sparrow cannot help themselves,' Paul replied wryly. 'I do not say that she will be unfaithful—but she is wilful and must have her own way.'

Lucy knew that he was right in her heart, but she did not like to hear him speak so of her cousin.

'Fie on you, sir,' she said. 'I think you are unkind. Judith may be a little headstrong—…'

'More than a little,' Paul said and then cursed softly. 'Damn it, I did not think that fellow would be here tonight.'

Lucy glanced in the direction of his gaze and saw that the Earl of Daventry had entered the room. 'No, I wish he had not returned to Bath. I know he promised to escort us back to Dawlish, but that was… I mean, Mama thinks him charming, but I do not like him.'

'I thought you rather partial to his company?' Paul's eyes narrowed as he looked at her. 'At one time I thought you might marry him, Lucy?'

'I did not then know all I know now.' Her cheeks were warm as she looked up at him. 'I considered it when…because I thought…' She was flustered and could not continue. 'Judith warned me at the start that he was a rake, but I did not believe her. I did not know then that he once broke her heart.'

'Then you are not in love with him?'

'No, not at all,' Lucy assured him. 'How could I be when…?' Once again she faltered and could not go on. 'Oh, I think they are going into the gallery to dance. Shall we go…?'

Paul inclined his head, offering her his arm. She glanced at Daventry, but saw that he was not looking at her, his eyes intent on Judith who was speaking to some ladies and gentlemen. From the air of excitement about them, she guessed they were talking of the race and her cousin was enjoying herself.

Perhaps Paul was right, she thought, Judith seemed to attract attention without even trying. She would have thought it better to forget that infamous race, but perhaps her cousin had no choice. Besides, it would be forgotten within a few days, for there was sure to be some other amusing scandal to divert the minds of the society gossips before long.

Lucy had forgot her cousin as she allowed Paul to lead her into the small but merry group of dancers. They went through the first set of country dances together and then became part of a little group of young people who exchanged partners between dances and kept themselves amused.

Once or twice Lucy had looked for her cousin to join them, but she did not come into the gallery and she thought that perhaps Judith did not care to dance since her fiancé was not present that evening. After the supper dance, Paul took her into the room where a delicious buffet was laid out for the guests. She saw Judith with Lady Dawlish and they went up to them as they chose their meal from the various trays and dishes.

'You do not dance this evening?' Lucy asked, spearing a tiny morsel of chicken. 'Those peas look nice—shall you try them?'

'No, just this lobster tart,' Judith said, 'and perhaps a syllabub.'

'Oh, yes, they are very good.' Lucy took one of the tarts herself. 'Why don't you join us for supper, dearest?'

'I should like that, but I am promised to some friends. I have been playing piquet and must continue after supper.'

Judith looked a little distracted and Lucy sensed that something was bothering her. 'Is anything the matter?'

'No…at least…' Judith shook her head. 'No, I am sure he did not mean it.'

Lucy saw an anxious look in her eyes. 'Did Daventry say something to upset you earlier? I saw him come in.'

'Yes, it was most unpleasant,' Judith replied. 'He threatened me, Lucy…but I told him that I would not be cowed by him and left him standing. I joined the friends I told you of and have been with them since. I have not seen him since so I believe he left.'

'What did he say to you?' Lucy asked indignantly, but her cousin gave a little shake of her head.

'I cannot tell you here, dearest, but I shall tell you when we are home. I am so glad that you did not care for him…you would have been very unhappy—'

She broke off as Lady Dawlish came up to them. 'Dear Captain Ravenscar has arranged for a waiter to bring champagne to our table—that one by the window,' she said. 'Do you have all you want, Lucy? Judith, you are joining us?'

'I am engaged to friends.' Judith smiled regretfully. 'I shall see you both later.'

She went off to join a little group of ladies and gentlemen. Lucy and her mother sat down at the table by the window and were soon joined by Paul, who had prevailed upon a waiter to bring them not only champagne, but more of the delicious food.

'It is always so comfortable to have a gentleman looking after one,' Lady Dawlish said. 'The Earl of Daventry was here earlier, but he did not stay. I think he came only to speak to Judith, for he went off after she spoke to him. I thought it a little odd in him, for he did not even come to greet me. Do you imagine something has happened to upset him? He did not even nod to me.'

'Did he not, Mama?' Lucy sipped her champagne. 'I should not be surprised if we were all mistaken in him. He has charming manners, to be sure, but I am not certain he is to be trusted.'

'Why, what can you mean?' her mother asked, looking shocked.

'Oh, nothing, just that I have discovered I do not think him quite the man we all believed him.'

'Well, perhaps you may be right,' Lady Dawlish said. 'It was certainly not polite of him to go away without at least speaking to me. If he continues in this way, I may have to write to your papa and ask him to escort us home at the end of the week.'

'There is not the least need,' Paul said. 'Please do not put Lord Dawlish to the trouble when I am here to escort you anywhere you need to go. I know there is a ball tomorrow evening, but I had thought we might take a box at the theatre the following evening.'

'Yes, that would be nice,' Lady Dawlish said. 'It is our only free evening, for we hold a small dinner the following day and there is another card party the following…and then of course we leave for home at the end of the week.'

'Shall you be pleased to be home, Miss Lucy?' Paul asked.

'Yes, I think I shall, though I have enjoyed my stay here. Judith will not return with us, for Elver is to escort her to London to buy her bride clothes. She is writing to her mother's Aunt Susan and expects to stay with her until the wedding…which I believe will be held at Elver in six weeks' time. She has asked me to be her bridesmaid, which I should like very much, and so I think we shall all come down for the wedding—Papa, too, would you not think, Mama?'

'Certainly we shall all come for your cousin's wedding,' Lady Dawlish replied. 'Are you certain you are able to stay until the end of the week, Captain Ravenscar? What of your dear father?'

'Father is as well as he can be for the moment. He insisted that I stay as long as I wished.'

'Well, I dare say we might cut our stay short… though we could not leave until after our dinner, of course.'

'I should not dream of asking you to cut short your stay,' Paul said and smiled. 'I believe they are dancing again, Lucy. Do you care to dance again?'

'Oh, I think not,' Lady Dawlish said and smiled at him graciously. 'We have monopolised your time too much this evening, Captain. Lucy may bear me company in a rubber of whist, if she will, and perhaps you would care to join us. Mr Henderson will make our fourth. Here he comes now.'

Lucy made a little face behind her mama's back as she got up to greet her friend. She would have liked to go on dancing with Paul all night, but they had already danced three times, which, she knew, was enough to start the tabbies gossiping.

'Mama is only trying to protect me,' she whispered to Paul as they followed her mother to the card room. 'I do not wish to dance if I may not dance with you.'

Paul laughed softly and took her hand to press

it. 'I shall call for you in the morning,' he said. 'You will allow me to take you driving?'

'Yes, if you will let me drive for a little,' she said, giving him a sparkling look.

'Of course...'

They had entered the card room. Lucy saw that there were ten tables set up, and once they sat down all the tables were fully occupied. However, she could not see Judith anywhere. She continued to look for her until the first hand was played, then spoke directly to her mama.

'Judith said she would not dance because she was engaged to play piquet with friends, but she is not here—and there are no empty seats.'

'Perhaps she is still in the supper room,' Lady Dawlish said. 'Pay attention to your cards, my dear. Your cousin is well able to take care of herself.'

Lucy glanced down at her cards and played a small club. However, she could not concentrate on her cards and she and Paul lost the next few tricks because she did not follow the trumps. Her mother remonstrated with her and she forced herself to concentrate on her cards, succeeding in taking the next two tricks.

'That is better, Lucy,' her mother said and placed a ten on the table, which Lucy trumped with her Jack.

She looked about the room constantly, hoping to see Judith, but grew anxious as the evening drew to a close and spoke to Paul as they rose from the tables.

'I am concerned for Judith,' she said in a low voice. 'She told me that Daventry threatened her earlier. She said she intended to play cards and I think something has happened to her.'

'Surely not?' he said, arching his left eyebrow. 'He could not snatch her from under the noses of so many people.'

'No, I suppose not,' Lucy replied. 'Yet where is she?'

'She was perhaps tempted to dance or caught up with some friends…'

They walked through into the main salon, which was by now thin of company. Everyone was taking their leave of the hostess and Lucy's feeling of foreboding had begun to grow. Her cousin could not simply have disappeared—so where was she?

'Where is that girl?' Lady Dawlish asked, a note

of irritation in her voice. 'She must know that we are ready to leave.'

'I shall look in the gallery.' Lucy walked swiftly from the room before her mother could stop her. She looked inside the long gallery, which had been cleared of furniture for the evening; it was empty apart from a little group of four, who were still talking and laughing.

'Have you seen Lady Sparrow?' Lucy asked and was met with shakes of the head and denials. They had not seen her since supper.

Lucy returned to her mother and Paul. She was feeling very anxious now. 'She is not here,' she said, her eyes flying to Paul's. 'No one has seen her. I am frightened. I think she has been abducted.'

'Do not be foolish, Lucy,' her mama told her. 'How could she be abducted?'

'She is not here. I've asked and no one has seen her since supper.'

'Then she must have called for a cab and gone home. I am sure it was most impolite of her to leave without telling us, but she is a law unto herself.'

'No, Mama, I am sure she would not,' Lucy

said, beginning to feel very anxious. 'My cousin is independent, but not thoughtless.'

'Are you looking for Lady Sparrow?' a voice asked and she whirled round to see a young woman looking at her. 'I saw her go out to the garden after supper, but I did not see her return.'

'Was she wearing her cloak?' Lucy asked, her fear for Judith mounting.

'No, merely a light stole, which she had worn all evening,' Miss Lemon said. 'I thought it odd that she did not return, for she was promised to us for cards. When she did not join us we found another to take her place.'

'Now will you believe me, Mama?' Lucy asked.

'I dare say she called for a cab and went home,' Lady Dawlish said, but she was frowning, a little cross. 'She is a thoughtless girl to cause you so much worry, Lucy. Come along, I imagine she will be in her room resting, for I must suppose she felt unwell—after the excitement of the day I dare say she should never have come out this evening.'

Lucy turned to Paul, her look beseeching him. 'Will you come with us, sir? I do not believe Judith went off alone.'

'I shall follow you,' Paul replied with a slight

frown. 'I shall make some enquiries and discover what I can.'

Lucy was forced to follow her mother to their carriage. Once inside, Lady Dawlish began to complain bitterly.

'I cannot think why I agreed to have the girl to stay with us,' she said. 'She has been nothing but a trouble to us both…flirting with Captain Ravenscar the way she did. I know that hurt you, Lucy. I wonder you will stand up for her the way you do.'

'Judith did not mean to hurt me, Mama. I told her that I did not care for P—Captain Ravenscar. I thought he had forgot me and…' She caught her breath in her throat. 'Judith told me at supper—the earl threatened her earlier in the evening. She told him to leave her alone and that is why he went off in a temper.'

'Threatened her?' Lady Dawlish looked uncertain for the first time. 'In what way did he threaten her?'

'She promised to tell me later, Mama. It was something serious, for she could not speak of it in company for fear of being overheard. I think he was angry because she became engaged to Elver this morning. I think he wants her for himself.'

'Then why did he dance attendance on you?' Lady Dawlish demanded. 'Oh, it is all of a piece, I dare say. If the wretched girl wanted him, why did she flirt so with Captain Ravenscar? I cannot understand the ways of the young these days.'

'I am not sure, Mama, but I think at first she flirted with Paul Ravenscar to punish him for scolding us for driving on the road, and then… then I think she was not sure how she felt about the earl. You see…they were once in love.'

'Then you may depend upon it that the wretched girl has gone off with him.'

'No, she would not,' Lucy said. 'She told me she cared for Elver and was happy with her engagement. She had thought she might care for the earl, but his behaviour towards me gave her a disgust of him.'

'Then she will be at home,' Lady Dawlish said. 'Do not look so anxious, my love. I am sure your cousin is laid down on her bed with a headache.'

Lucy followed her mother into the house and ran upstairs without waiting to take off her velvet evening cloak. She burst into her cousin's bedroom, hoping that perhaps her mother was right, but the room was empty. Judith had not returned to the house. Lucy was checking her cousin's clothes and possessions when Lady Dawlish entered the room.

'She has taken nothing with her, Mama,' Lucy said, her face pale. 'Had she planned to leave us, she would have had her maid pack her things...' Judith's maid, Anna, entered the room at that moment. 'You have not seen Lady Sparrow since we left this evening?'

'No, Miss Dawlish,' the girl said, clearly puzzled. 'She went to a party with you.'

'This is beyond me,' Lady Dawlish said, finally struck with anxiety. 'What can have happened to her? My brother would never forgive me if anything should happen to her while she was in my care.'

'She has been abducted,' Lucy said and the maid gave a little scream. 'No, do not cry, Anna. I am sure he means her no harm... At least. I think he means to compromise her so that she is forced to wed him.'

'Surely not?' Lady Dawlish was now truly concerned. 'He is a wicked rogue. He must not be allowed to get away with this—but what can we do?'

Lucy heard the knocker downstairs. 'That

will be Paul,' she cried. 'He will tell us what we must do.'

She ran out of the room, leaving her mother to deal with the maid and to warn her to be discreet. Reaching the hall just as Paul was admitted, she went to him at once. He raised his brows and she shook her head at him, holding out her hand.

'Please come into the parlour, sir. We must talk.'

Paul followed her inside. As soon as the door was closed, Lucy turned to him, taking urgent hold of his arm. She gazed up at him imploringly.

'It is as I thought, she is not here. Her room has not been touched—all her clothes are still here.'

'So she did not plan to run off with him.'

'No, indeed, she did not,' Lucy said. 'I knew it from the start. Judith opened her heart to me earlier this evening. She was happy, looking forward to buying her bride clothes and to her marriage. I do not say that she is head over heels in love with Elver, but she respects him and she likes him very well. She had got over any feelings she'd had for Daventry. I think because he did not behave well to me, the scales fell from her eyes and she saw him for what he truly is—a heartless flirt who cares not how many hearts he breaks.'

'Yes, I think you are correct in your estimation of Daventry,' Paul said, looking thoughtful. 'He is a rake. I know something to his discredit, for it happened in Vienna, and it was whispered that he had behaved shamefully to a young widow. The scandal was hushed up for her sake, but he was asked to leave. I ought to have spoken out before, and indeed, I did try to warn you, but your cousin seemed in no danger. What can have made him abduct Lady Sparrow from beneath our very noses?'

'She thinks he wants her fortune,' Lucy said. 'He was angry when she became engaged to Elver. I can see no other reason for it.'

'There are men who like to make mischief for the sake of it,' Paul said thoughtfully. 'He might have felt himself ill used if she had encouraged him to think... You will admit that your cousin has a wayward streak in her. I think she cannot resist making men fall a little in love with her.'

'I know she has a mischievous manner at times,' Lucy said. 'She is headstrong and cannot bear to be told what she must or must not do—but she is not heartless. I do not think she encouraged the earl. Indeed, I heard her quarrelling with him once.'

'Then perhaps he means to force her into marriage…'

'She would be so miserable. It must not be.'

'I am not sure what we can do about it. It may already be too late. Her disappearance this evening will already be talked off in Bath—she has been careless of her reputation, Lucy, and people will be quick to censure.'

'It is so unfair. She is merely a little thoughtless and does not deserve this. We have to find her, Paul. We have to get her back before he…' She caught back a sob. 'Can you not try to find her… before Elver knows what has happened?'

'I think that would be useless, Lucy,' he said gravely. 'My best course would be to ride to Elver at once and ask him to assist me in the search.'

'It will be the end of her hopes.' Lucy felt tears trickle down her cheeks. 'Could we not search for her ourselves? I could come with you.'

'You will stay here, Lucy. Do you hear me?' There was a note of authority in his voice, his gaze serious. 'If Daventry has her, he is a dangerous man and I will not have you risk yourself. I shall do what I can to find and rescue her—and Elver will wish to do the same. If he rejects her out of hand for something that is not of her making, he is not the man I think him.'

Lucy stared at him, tears on her face. He was so stubborn and sure of himself, and she wanted to shout or scream at him. Could he not see that it was urgent to find her cousin before she was forced into a terrible situation?

'Paul, I cannot stay here while my cousin is—' She got no further, for Paul dragged her into his arms and kissed her soundly on the mouth. She felt her senses swooning and clung to him when she perhaps ought to have pulled away. This was no time to be making love, yet all she wanted was to stay in his strong arms and to feel this wonderful sensation of drowning in love. 'Paul...' she began, but ceased as her mother entered the room.

'What is going on here?' Lady Dawlish demanded on seeing their embrace. 'Sir, have you forgot yourself? My daughter is not to be treated in this manner, no matter what her cousin has done.'

'Madam, you misjudge her and me,' Paul replied with an odd smile. 'Lucy has this moment done me the honour of agreeing to be my wife. I wish that I might stop to explain, but I must go, for every moment Lady Sparrow remains undiscovered, the more she is in danger.'

He turned to Lucy and smiled, touching her cheek with his fingers. 'Do not worry, my love. Elver and I will find your cousin and bring her back to you.'

Then he was striding from the room and they heard the front door shut with a snap after him. For a moment Lucy stared at her mother in silence, then Lady Dawlish smiled.

'Well, of course, my dearest, I always knew this would happen. You were made for each other. It is a happy end to the whole sorry business…or it would be if your wretched cousin had not got herself into another tangle.'

'Mama, you must not blame Judith,' Lucy said. She was feeling shocked and bewildered, both by the suddenness of Paul's kiss and the way he had announced their engagement to her mother without one word to her. How dare he behave in such an outrageous manner? Yet she had clung to him so readily that he must naturally believe her willing—otherwise she would be a wanton wretch.

She could feel a little tingle of happiness inside, but the doubts soon followed. Would Paul have offered for her if her mother had not discovered them kissing? These past two days she had felt that they were on a better footing, but something told her that Paul had not been ready to propose marriage to her just yet. He had been forced into it because he'd kissed her on impulse.

Lucy's mind worked furiously.

He had asked her to drive out because he wished to tell her something about Mark. What was it and why did he consider it important? How frustrating it all was, for it might be some time before Paul was able to take her somewhere they could talk privately. And he had not even told her that he loved her.

Her thoughts were whirling in confusion.

Oh, how could she even think of her own happiness when Judith was in trouble? What a selfish girl she was to be sure! Her own future must be put on hold until her cousin was safe.

'Paul is going to Elver, Mama,' Lucy said, taking a hold on herself. 'I am so very distressed, for I know that my cousin must be in terrible trouble…and I think this might be the ruin of her hopes.'

'You must not worry too much,' her mother advised her with a smile, obviously more interested in Lucy's news than her niece's disappearance. 'Well, well, your papa will be surprised when I tell him. No, do not look like that, Lucy. We can do nothing but wait after all. We must leave it to the gentlemen to settle.'

'But, Mama…how can you be so calm? I wish that I were a man. I would be out there searching for my cousin now.'

'Well, you are not, so you must go to bed and try to sleep, for the morning will not come any faster if you lie awake all night. Captain Ravenscar and the marquis will manage this awkward business between them.'

Lucy was in no position to disagree, for there was nothing she could do to help her cousin. Had there been a chance of finding her, Lucy would have risked censure to do what she could, but she had no idea where to start. Paul and the marquis would garner what information they could and try to rescue Judith…but Lucy was very much afraid that by the time they found her it would be too late.

# Chapter Eleven

'Miss Dawlish is certain she was abducted?' Elver looked at Paul, his expression giving little away. 'Forgive me, I must ask…there is no possibility that she went willingly?'

'I am told Lady Sparrow took nothing with her. We cannot know the circumstances, but we have been informed that she went out to the terrace for some air during the supper period last night and has not been seen since.'

'If only I had been there.' Elver swore softly. 'She was not missed until the end of the evening, which means that he has a head start on us.'

'Where do you imagine he has taken her?'

'If he intends marriage, he will be heading towards Gretna Green,' Elver said. 'We must hope he stole her out of a desperate love for her—if not...' His expression became grim. 'I fear what may have already happened.'

'But surely he must love her to desperation,' Paul said, puzzled. 'Why else would he snatch her on the very day she became engaged to you?'

Elver's gaze narrowed, becoming cold as ice. 'What I am about to tell you must go no further, Ravenscar. That devil once tried to persuade my sister to elope with him. I do not know what mischief he intended, though she is a considerable heiress. Fortunately, my sister is a minx, and while she allowed him to believe that she would meet him, she came instead to me. It was I who met Daventry that night and we fought. I do not mean to boast, but it was I who won—and he received a beating he will not forget. I imagine that his plan was hastily formed when he discovered that Judith had consented to be my wife.'

'That makes me fear for her safety,' Paul said, his mouth thinning. 'For it can hardly matter to Daventry whether he marries her or merely ruins her—either way he has dealt you a heavy blow.'

'Yes, I imagine this must be his aim. From what I know he had been merely amusing himself with her cousin prior to this—I believe he was expected to make Miss Dawlish an offer at one time?'

'We all thought it might happen, but you see… Lucy had too much good sense and she told him that she could not give him an answer, because she had not made any decision about her feelings for him. Realising that she would not have him, he went away. When he returned, he discovered that Lady Sparrow had a new admirer…'

'A man he disliked intensely,' Elver said, looking grim. 'I shall set out for Scotland immediately, Ravenscar. I shall take two of my grooms with me, men I can trust to use their fists or a gun if necessary. However, I may be wrong and he may have chosen somewhere nearer to take his captive. I would beg you to make discreet enquiries in the district—whether he has property or was seen driving in a direction other than north.'

'Yes, of course,' Paul said. 'I shall hope that you discover them on the way to Scotland, but in the meantime I shall leave no stone unturned here. We must find them, for Lucy is distressed and she will not forgive us easily if we neglect the least thing in our search.'

Elver nodded. 'I believe you have an interest there?'

'Yes, I hope that Miss Dawlish will accept an offer from me—but I know she would not dream of it until her cousin is found.'

The two men shook hands and parted. Paul rode back to Bath. It was too late to make enquiries at this hour, for most of the inns and hostelries would have closed their doors against the night. He would do better to get some rest, if he could, for the next day would be busy.

Lucy slept, but dreamed and woke several times, rising before the dawn had quickened and sitting by her window to watch the sun rise in the sky. Where had Daventry taken Judith? If only she could think of something that might help in the search.

Had they gone to Scotland or somewhere nearer? Lucy could not believe that Judith would agree to marry him after this. Had he behaved like a gentleman and spoken to her of his feelings at Dawlish, before Lucy's dance and instead of paying her so much attention, her cousin might have forgiven him for deserting her in the past.

Had Judith not been so open with her, Lucy might not have raised the alarm; she might have believed her cousin had gone willingly, for the earl was handsome and had charming manners when he chose…but she sensed there was also a ruthless side to him, a side he kept hidden. She could only be grateful that her own heart had remained untouched, for even though she had considered marriage with the earl for a time, she had always known he was not the man she truly wanted.

Where would he have taken Judith? Lucy cudgelled her brains as she tried to think where they might have gone. She knew his own estates were some distance away and thought he would have wanted something closer to hand—unless he had headed straight for the border?

Why had he suddenly decided to abduct Judith? At Dawlish there had been far easier opportunities, because the open countryside around Lucy's home offered plenty of chances to snatch a young woman driving out only with a female cousin or her groom. To take her from the garden of a house in Bath and from under the noses of her friends and relatives, was far more risky and might be called reckless. The earl must have had a strong reason for doing so.

Lucy recalled the look in his eyes when Judith's engagement to the Marquis of Elver was announced—he had not looked upset or hurt, merely angry. It could be no coincidence that he had decided to strike that very night. If he meant to punish Judith...or Elver...then it made his actions more sinister and Lucy trembled for her.

She was afraid that her cousin might be in more danger than she'd previously thought.

What could she do? She felt frustrated by her inability to help her cousin, and when her mother suggested that they should attend the Pump Room, she could only agree.

There was surely no point in staying here, for she was unlikely to receive news so soon...and they must do what they could to squash any suggestion that Judith had eloped with another man on the day of her betrothal to Elver.

Judith opened her eyes and looked about her. The light was dim inside the coach, for the blinds had been drawn at the windows and she judged it to be still early in the morning. She could feel tenderness at the back of her head and the vomit rushed suddenly up her throat and poured out as she turned her head towards the man sitting next to her in the fast-moving carriage. As the foul-smelling brown liquid poured out of her mouth, splashing over his boots and breeches, he gave an exclamation of disgust.

'You stupid woman,' Daventry said. 'What a foul stench! Could you not have turned your head the other way?'

'Why should I do anything to oblige you?' Judith asked icily. 'You hit me on the head, dragged me into this coach and made off with me—and then, when I first woke, you poured some vile drug down my throat. You might have expected I should be ill.'

'Had you come with me willingly none of this would have been necessary,' Daventry said, scowling at her. He dabbed ineffectually at his breeches with a large handkerchief, but there was no way of removing either the stench or the stain. 'For goodness' sake, Judith. You were angry because I deserted you, but I tried to explain. I had no fortune and your father would have none of me as a husband for you. He sent me off and told me that if I married you out of hand I would not get a penny from him.'

'And I was not enough for you without a dowry?' she said scornfully.

'You forget that I had not inherited the title then and had no hope of it—had a fever not carried off my cousins I never should have much to offer. I could only leave and hope to find some other heiress who was not so well guarded.'

'Why did you not tell me? I would have gone with you willingly then.'

'We should neither of us have had a feather to fly with…but it is not too late for us to be happy.'

'It was too late when I saw the way you led my cousin on,' Judith said. 'Oh, for a time your despicable plan worked and I was jealous—and thought I still cared, but then I realised you were worthless.' Her eyes were scornful. 'I do not think you ever loved me. It was always money with you, was it not? I was merely a flirtation to pass the time, but then you discovered I was now wealthy and thought you could trick me into marriage.'

'So now you want to play happy families with Elver,' Daventry sneered. 'Well, he won't have you now, Judith. Everyone will think you've run off with me. You are known to be flighty and care-less of your reputation. You'll take me or no one, my love.'

'Then I shall take no one,' Judith said, turning a look of disdain on him. 'I would rather die than marry you, Daventry.'

His eyes narrowed unpleasantly. 'I dare say that could be arranged,' he said, 'but I intend to have my fun with you first… I'll have you crawling at my knees, my proud beauty.'

Judith felt the pace of the horses slowing. 'Why are we stopping?' she asked. 'I thought we were headed for the border. Where are we?'

'Oh, just a little place I bought recently,' Daven-try said. 'They will look for us on the road to Scot-land and I have no intention of receiving another beating at the hands of your fiancé and his bully boys. No, I have a little hideaway much closer to Bath than the border. Let them search the high roads for us as long as they wish. Once I have you safe, I shall enjoy teaching you to mind your manners, my love.'

'I am not your love and never shall be again,' Judith said defiantly. 'If you try to make love to me, I shall be ill over you again. In fact…'

She felt the vomit in her throat once more and smiled wryly as he jerked back out of reach. Although she was feeling wretched, she had the wit to realise that her illness might keep her safe from him for a time—and in the meanwhile, she must find some way of escaping him.

'Miss Dawlish.' Captain James Havers came up to Lucy as she sat in the Pump Room looking about her. Her mother was talking with friends, trying to explain that Judith had been called away urgently to the bedside of a sick aunt and that her message had somehow gone astray. Whether or not the story would be believed was doubtful, but Lady Dawlish had felt it her duty to try. 'I am so sorry for this scandal. You must be distressed by it?'

Lucy did her best to smile. 'I fear it was my fault for making such a fuss last night. My cousin was called away to her aunt...'

'I hope the story may help to cool the scandal,' Mr Havers said. 'I must tell you in confidence that I saw a coach leaving Bath by the London road last night. It was moving fast and I caught sight of a face at the window...Daventry's face. I could not swear to it but…I happen to know that he recently purchased a small hunting box not more than thirty miles from here.'

'A hunting box?' Lucy stared at him in surprise. 'What are you saying, sir?'

'If your cousin was abducted…I suggest that you try looking in the direction of Throckmorton…which is a small village in—' Havers broke off as he saw Captain Ravenscar striding towards them. 'You will wish me to the devil…but I wanted to tell you what I knew.'

'Please wait, sir,' Lucy said and caught at his coat sleeve. 'I wish you will tell Captain Ravenscar what you have just told me.'

'As you wish…' he said, and as Paul came up to them, drew him aside to a window where they might speak without fear of being overheard. Mr Havers then took his leave with a nod for Lucy and Paul came up to her.

'Havers has told me of a hunting box just outside Throckmorton. I have been asking for information of anyone I thought might know something, but this is the first real clue to come my way. You have heard nothing from her, I suppose?'

'Nothing. Mama is telling people that she was

called to a sick aunt, but I do not think people will believe her.'

'I have no other leads,' Paul said, looking anxious. 'I am glad to have seen you, for I shall drive out to Throckmorton and see if I can find this place. He may not have taken her there, of course—but it is all I can do, Lucy. Elver and his men have gone to Scotland, but I have a feeling that Daventry will not be that easy to find.'

'Why has he done this?' Lucy asked, a break in her voice. 'Is it merely to spite Judith for giving her promise to another?'

'I rather think it is Elver he wants to punish—there is history between them. Who knows what happens in the mind of such a man?' Paul said. 'Forgive me, I must go, for I have wasted enough time.'

'Please take me with you,' Lucy begged. 'I feel so helpless sitting here when Judith is in trouble.'

'Forgive me, Lucy, but I must refuse you,' Paul said. 'It is too dangerous—and you would only hinder me. I should be anxious for you, because Daventry is spiteful and, if he cannot harm Judith, he is not above taking his spite out on you, my dearest.'

Lucy was honest enough to know that he spoke the truth and inclined her head. 'Go then,' she said. 'I shall pray that you find her before…it is too late.'

'I promise you that I shall keep looking for her,' Paul said and then he was gone.

Lucy felt the sting of tears, but was forced to blink them away as some ladies came up to her. She did her best to reassure them that it was all a mistake and that Judith's message had gone astray, but she was sure they did not believe her.

She wished that she might have taken some part in the search, but she knew that Paul was right; she would have hindered him, for he must be free to act as he saw fit. If she had insisted on going with him, she might have been more trouble than help.

It was frustrating, but for the moment all she could do was to wait patiently and pray that either Paul or the marquis found Judith before… she suffered harm at the hands of the rogue who had abducted her.

Judith shuddered as she opened her eyes. Her head ached shockingly, though she thought she must have slept for some hours after she was brought to this house. It had been still early in the day when they arrived, having driven throughout the night with only one stop to change horses. She vaguely recalled that, for Daventry had held a pistol on her and told her that if she screamed he would shoot. She'd been feeling very ill again and any thought of resistance had been far from her mind at that moment. She had only been half-awake when she was carried from the coach into the house and up some stairs, receiving only a dim impression of her surroundings.

It was not, she imagined, a large house, for it was used only occasionally, by gentlemen for hunting. She wondered if Daventry had bought it for the purpose of hiding her, but dismissed it because she was certain that he would not have been so reckless had the idea of her marriage to Elver not angered him so much. Why had he suddenly decided that she must marry him or no one when she could swear he had not thought of her for years—until he'd seen her at Dawlish?

Was it Judith he wanted to destroy in truth or the man she'd promised to marry? Something he'd said to her in the carriage seemed to imply that he had a score to settle with Elver…and that meant that he might not care whether she became his wife or not. He might even prefer to seduce her and then return her to her fiancé, rejoicing in the pain he had caused.

Only a cruel, fiendish mind could dream up such a scheme. If any lingering doubts had survived in her mind concerning the earl, they were banished now. She was angry, disgusted with him for venting his spite on her—a woman he had already harmed. His tale of her father sending him away might indeed have been true, but had he loved her he would have taken her without a penny. Had he done so, her father would have relented in time, for he loved her. Daventry had not cared enough—and that stung her, made her anger burn and grow inside her.

She would never submit to him. She would prefer to die rather than let him touch her intimately; the very thought made her sick to her stomach.

Looking about her, Judith saw that the room had not been cleaned in an age and Daventry must have thought up this abduction without much of a plan. There were chests, a bed, an armoire and a chair, also heavy brass candlesticks…which would make a weapon to defend herself, though only in an emergency. She was not sure she could strike a heavy enough blow to knock him out and to stun him would merely make him angrier than he already was.

What else might she find if she looked? She got up from the bed where she had been lying and began to walk across the room. Opening first some drawers and then the door of the armoire, she saw that the room had previously been occupied by a sporting gentleman. There were clothes, boots, whips and various items of sporting paraphernalia, but nothing that would make an effective weapon. Turning round in a circle, she saw the oak hutch and walked towards it. She lifted the lid and then smiled as she saw exactly what she needed.

Lying on top of a velvet cloak was a box, which she was sure contained a pair of duelling pistols. Her father had a box just like it with the word 'Manton' embossed on the mahogany lid. She reached for it, opened it and took out one of the pistols just as she heard the door being unlocked behind her.

'So you are awake,' a voice said. 'Good. I think

it is time for your lessons in obedience to begin…
Good grief, what have you there?'

'A pistol,' Judith replied coolly. 'Come one step
closer and I shall fire.'

'You little fool,' Daventry said and moved towards her.

Judith fired. She was a little surprised when the
sound of a shot exploded, for she had not known if
it was loaded, and even more shocked that her ball
hit Daventry in his right shoulder. He lay groan-
ing as she approached him, then she stepped over
his body and walked out of the room without a
backward glance.

All she could think of was that she must escape
before one of Daventry's servants came to investigate.

Paul had been driving at breakneck speed for
most of the day. He'd stopped once to change his
horses and to snatch a glass of ale and a pork pie,
which he ate while the grooms saw to the horses.
Then he was off again, having been told of a
route through narrow country lanes that would
cut several miles off his journey to the village of
Throckmorton. He had been told that he would

come to a gentleman's hunting box just a mile outside the village.

'Have you seen a coach pass this way in a hurry—either last night or this morning?' Paul asked the man who had directed him.

'There was a coach passed by in the early hours,' one of the ostlers ventured, 'but they didn't stop to change their horses, sir.'

Thanking the ostler, Paul took up the reins of his curricle again and set out. His groom was sitting beside him, keeping an eye out for signposts to Throckmorton, and it was he who cried out when he saw the woman walking down the country lane towards them some twenty minutes later.

'Look, Captain,' said the former trooper. 'Damn my eyes if it ain't the lady you're lookin' for. I'll swear she's got away from the rogues.'

Paul gentled his horses to a walk as he saw the rather bedraggled young woman walking slowly towards them. She was weaving oddly from side to side, clearly in a state of distress. Her evening gown was torn and stained, her feet bare and a long-barrelled duelling pistol dangled from one hand. From the look of her face he could see that she had been crying and her cheeks were smeared with mud, her hair straggling about her shoulders.

Paul gave the reins to his groom and jumped down, running towards her in relief. 'Lady Sparrow,' he said, feeling pity as he saw that she was close to exhaustion. 'How glad I am to have found you. Lucy was sure that rogue had abducted you and—'

'I shot him,' Judith said, dropped the duelling pistol at his feet and then swooned into his arms.

Paul caught her and carried her to his curricle, taking care to set cushions beneath her head and to cover her with the blankets he had brought for the purpose.

'Did she say she had shot him, Captain?' Paul's groom asked. 'She's a game 'un, by George.'

'Yes, very brave,' Paul said. 'I hope that she may have killed him, Ned, though it may cause us some trouble to sort out.'

'He don't deserve to live and that's a fact,' Ned replied. 'Anyways, he ain't goin' ter complain ter the magistrate, is he?'

'No,' Paul said grimly. 'He certainly is not. We had better get her home, Ned. We can't stop to investigate now—happily, it will be dark by the time we reach Bath and so we may avoid more scandal if we are fortunate.'

'I reckon as Fortune was on our side right enough, Captain,' Ned said. 'If you hadn't come across country instead of sticking to the high road, we might never have found her.'

Paul nodded, his mouth tight. 'She could not have got much further in her state and might have lain out here all night. I think the shock could have killed her. We have been very lucky, Ned. Very lucky indeed.'

'You always was lucky, Captain,' Ned said with a grin. 'That's why the men was glad to serve under you.'

It was late and Lucy was on the verge of going to bed when the door knocker sounded. They had sat at home all night, cancelling their engagements, for neither Lucy nor Lady Dawlish had the heart for an evening of pleasure at Lady Norton's ball. Lady Dawlish had retired to her bed with a headache, but Lucy had sat up, hoping that something would happen.

She ran to the door as it was opened and gave

a strangled gasp as Paul entered carrying an unconscious Judith in his arms.

'Is she hurt badly?' Lucy cried. 'Oh, that devil has harmed her.'

'If he did, he received just punishment,' Paul said. 'She told me she had shot him before she passed out.'

'Was she at the hunting box Mr Havers told you of?'

'She must have been at one point, I think, for it was not far from Throckmorton that we found her. It was by sheer chance that we took the country roads rather than the high road. Had we not done so, we must have missed her.'

'Oh, thank God you did not,' Lucy said, tears starting to her eyes. 'Will you carry her up to her room, sir?'

'Yes, of course. I have sent my groom for a doctor, for she must certainly be seen. As soon as he returns I must ride over to Elver, for her fiancé must be in despair.'

'Yes, I am certain of it…' Lucy caught her breath. 'Will he stand by her if…if she is ruined?'

'I believe he would, he cares for her very much, Lucy.'

Lucy went ahead, leading the way to her cousin's room. Anna had come out to see what was going on and gave a little cry of relief mixed with anguish as she saw her mistress carried in Captain Ravenscar's arms.

'Look at the state of her,' she cried. 'Her pretty gown…and her feet. She has cut her poor feet.'

'Captain Ravenscar rescued her,' Lucy said. 'Put her down on the bed, Paul. Anna and I will tend to her now.'

'I shall wait for the doctor downstairs,' he said after placing his burden carefully on the bed. 'I shall not return this evening, Lucy, but perhaps tomorrow…'

'Yes, thank you,' she said, a little distracted. 'Thank you. I must help Anna look after her now.'

'Yes, of course, Lucy.'

She glanced his way and smiled, hardly noticing as he left the room and went downstairs. Together she and Judith's maid undressed her and Anna fetched water to wash the blood and mud from her feet.

'She must have cut herself on stones,' Anna said. 'I wonder what made her take off her shoes?'

'I dare say she needed to run,' Lucy replied. 'I

think she is not badly hurt otherwise, so why does she not stir?'

Anna shook her head and looked worried. 'I do not know…what can have happened to her?'

Lucy wished that she'd asked for more details, but she'd been too concerned for her cousin.

They had just settled the sheets about Judith when they heard the doctor arrive. He was shown up by the housekeeper, who tutted as she saw Judith's pale face.

'Here's a pretty thing,' she said. 'When a decent young woman cannot go into a private garden without being abducted.'

'Please,' Lucy said. 'We do not know what happened yet. We must try to keep the details quiet.'

'Yes, of course, Miss Dawlish. I shall not breathe a word.'

Lucy forced a smile. If the servants knew it all, how soon before the whole of Bath was talking of Judith's abduction? She feared that her cousin might be ruined, especially if Elver withdrew his offer.

However, she had little time to think of such things, for the doctor was examining his patient and looking grave. After a while he turned and looked at Lucy.

'Has she been like this ever since she was brought back?'

'Yes, I think so, sir,' Lucy said. 'Do you think she suffered a blow to the head?'

'I have found no sign of it. I think she has fallen into a state of exhaustion and may just be deeply asleep. There is little I can do for her, because she has no physical injury...but let me know if she does not wake by morning.'

'What is wrong with her?' Lucy asked anxiously.

'I cannot say, Miss Dawlish...unless she has suffered an unpleasant shock, which has temporarily robbed her of her senses.'

'She will recover?'

'Oh, yes, I believe she will...but she may be unlike herself for a while.'

'Yes, I see,' Lucy said, though she wished she did understand. Why could he not be more certain of his diagnosis?

'Lucy, what is wrong?' a very tired and slightly irritable voice asked from the doorway.

Lucy turned her head to see her mother standing there in a pale-ink satin wrap, her hair tucked into a lace nightcap.

'Judith is back, Mama,' she said. 'Paul found her…but she is not well.'

Lady Dawlish gave a little scream and rushed towards the bed. She stared down at her niece's pale face and moaned, twisting a scented kerchief in restless fingers.

'Oh, the poor child. What has that wicked man done to her? My brother will never forgive me. I should have taken more care of her…' She looked on the verge of hysterics.

'None of this was your fault, Mama,' Lucy assured her quickly. 'I believe it relates to the past… some quarrel between—'

Lady Dawlish gave another cry of despair and fainted, falling to the floor in a crumpled heap.

'Mama!' Lucy cried and rushed to her. 'Oh, Mama, please do not upset yourself. We have Judith back…'

The doctor knelt and felt for a pulse. 'Do not distress yourself, Miss Dawlish,' he said. 'The poor lady has merely fainted.' He took a little silver vinaigrette from his coat pocket and waved it under Lady Dawlish's nose. She moaned and opened her eyes, and he beckoned to Anna. 'Help me get your mistress to her room, girl.'

'Yes, sir,' Anna said, though she was Judith's personal maid.

She and the doctor helped Lady Dawlish to her feet. Still moaning and weeping, she was helped along the landing to her own bedchamber. Lucy was about to follow when she heard a faint noise from the bed. She went quickly to Judith's side and looked down at her. Her eyelashes flickered, then she opened her eyes and stared up at Lucy.

'Where am I?' she asked. 'Lucy...how did I get here?'

Lucy sat down on the edge of the bed and reached for her hand. 'You are safe now, dearest Cousin. Paul found you wandering. He told me that you had escaped somehow.'

A look of pain passed across Judith's face. 'It was horrible,' she whispered, her voice hoarse. 'I went out for a little air on the terrace because it was hot and I wanted to be alone for a moment. Daventry had threatened me earlier and...' She shook her head in distress. 'I never dreamed he would do anything so wicked. They threw a blanket over me and carried me to a coach. I struggled, but I could not fight them…'

'Oh, my poor cousin,' Lucy said. 'You must have been frightened and in such distress.'

'At first I was so shocked I did not know what to do, but when he had me in the coach he took the blanket away and told me I would marry him rather than Elver or suffer the consequences. Naturally, I refused and started to fight him. He gave me a foul drug and I slept for some hours. When I woke I was sick over him, which did not please him…'

'It was no less than he deserved. Did he take you to his hunting box near Throckmorton? Mr Havers told us he had recently purchased it.'

'Yes, he did,' Judith said. 'I dare say he had never looked at it—possibly bought it through an agent. The last owner had left the contents untouched…perhaps he died… Whatever the situation, his possessions had been left intact and it was that that saved me.'

'What can you mean?' Lucy asked and then, as her cousin moaned and closed her eyes, 'I do not mean to tease you, Judith. I dare say you would rather rest?'

'My head aches and I feel strange...faint,' Judith said. 'I dare say it was the foul drug he gave me... but I was telling you. I searched the room they locked me in and found a pair of pistols in a box.'

'Did you use one of them to shoot Daventry?'

'Yes, I did. He came into the room just after I'd taken one out to examine it. I did not even know if it was loaded, but he spoke of—of forcing himself on me and I fired in desperation.'

'Did you kill him?'

'I do not know,' Judith said and shuddered. 'He was hit in the shoulder, I think, and in pain... I did not bother to see how badly he was hurt, but ran from the house before his men could discover what had happened. I thought they might try to stop me or come after me, so I kept the pistol to threaten them, but I saw no one. Perhaps they were in the stables, tending the horses, and did not hear the shot. I believe I heard a cry after I left the house, but by that time I was running so hard that I cannot be sure.'

'You must be exhausted. We were anxious because you did not wake, but after what you have told me...'

Judith's forehead wrinkled. 'I thought I heard a scream?'

'Oh…it was nothing,' Lucy said. 'Mama was a little upset to see you looking so pale.'

'I have been such a nuisance to you all,' Judith said. 'But it was not my fault, truly it was not. I could not have known that Daventry would be in the gardens, waiting on the chance that I would go out for some air.'

'He must have come in the hope of somehow capturing you,' Lucy said. 'You must not blame yourself. If you had not gone out for some air, it would have happened somewhere else. He was determined to hurt you…and I think the marquis.'

'Yes, he said as much.' Judith closed her eyes and a tear slid down her cheek. 'I do not see how I can marry Elver now. There will be such a scandal…'

'I dare say he will not care for that,' Lucy said. 'Paul has gone to tell him, but I do not think they will return this night. You should rest now, Judith.'

'Yes, I think I should,' her cousin said. 'Thank Paul for helping me. I had lost my shoes somehow and I do not think I could have walked much further. My feet were painful…'

'Paul told me that you managed to tell him that you had shot Daventry and then fainted. It was good fortune that he found you then or you might have been very ill. Rest now, my dearest. You will feel better in the morning.'

Lucy left her to sleep. Anna had settled Lady Dawlish. She met Lucy as she returned and stopped to tell her that her mother had requested her presence when she felt able to leave Judith.

'My cousin is resting. She woke and now feels sleepy. I think she is just very tired, but if you would look in on her now and then, Anna—to make sure that she does not take a turn for the worse.'

'I shall go into her now, Miss Dawlish. I can sit with her if you think it advisable?'

'I think she will sleep, but if you will go in again later? And you must call me if she should take a fever.'

'Yes, of course, miss.'

They parted and Lucy went along the hall to her mother's room. Lady Dawlish was sitting up against a pile of soft pillows, a glass of cordial in her hand. She looked at Lucy as she entered, anxiety in her eyes.

'How is she? My poor niece?'

'She woke and told me her story, Mama. I think she was simply exhausted, for she has suffered a terrible ordeal…' Lady Dawlish gasped and looked distressed. 'No, I do not believe she was harmed in the way you fear, Mama. She was fortunate in finding a pistol, which was loaded, and brave enough to use it when she was threatened. Had she not been enterprising enough to search for a weapon, she might have suffered far worse, for I do not think Paul could have reached her in time. Too many hours were lost before he set out in pursuit. Judith escaped because she is brave and she refused to give in to the rogue's bullying.'

'It was my fault so much time was lost,' Lady Dawlish said, looking sorrowful. 'Had I listened to you, Lucy…'

'No one could be certain of what had happened,' Lucy said. 'Just be glad that we have her back not too badly harmed.'

Lady Dawlish dabbed at her eyes with a lace kerchief that smelled strongly of lavender. 'If only the marquis will stand by her…'

'If he loves her, he will do so,' Lucy said. 'If he does not, then we must, Mama. I shall not allow the gossips to influence me. Judith is my cousin and I do not care what people say, I shall always be her friend. You must do the same.'

Lady Dawlish looked at her in silence, then inclined her head. 'You have grown up, Lucy. I am proud of you for standing by your cousin and I must do the same, as you rightly say. She may have been a little reckless in the matter of that wager, but she did not deserve to be treated so harshly.'

'No, she did not. He was a wicked man for all his charming manners and I thank God I did not agree to marry him,' Lucy said. 'Go to sleep now, Mama dearest. Anna will look after Judith—and in the morning we shall see what happens.'

'Yes, I shall sleep now,' Lady Dawlish said and looked brighter. 'We have something to look forward to, Lucy dearest. You will be engaged soon and we must hold another dance for you—and prepare for your wedding. Your papa will be so delighted, for Lord Ravenscar was always his dearest friend.'

Lucy smiled, inclined her head and left her mother to sleep. Lady Dawlish was anticipating her wedding with a great deal of pleasure, but

Lucy was very much afraid that Paul might have been forced into something that was not truly of his choosing.

She did not wish to be married merely because her mother had seen her in Paul's arms, but the noose had grown tighter and she could not think of a way to extricate both her and Paul.

Yet she would not be happy knowing that he was marrying her out of a sense of honour...if that was the case.

## Chapter Twelve

The loud, insistent knocking at the door the next morning woke Lucy. She yawned, sitting up in bed and glancing at the little watch that lay on the table beside her bed. It was almost noon and well past the hour she normally rose.

Throwing off the bedclothes, she pulled on a pretty white-silk wrapper and went out into the hall to hear a loud voice demanding to see Lady Sparrow.

'But, sir,' the housekeeper's voice said, 'she is still in bed and feeling poorly. I do not think you can see her today.'

Lucy went to the head of the stairs. 'Please ask Lord Elver to wait in the parlour, Mrs Hickson. I shall go into my cousin and ask if she feels able to receive the marquis.'

'But, Miss Dawlish…'

The marquis looked up at her and smiled. 'Thank you, Miss Dawlish—and forgive me for calling so early, but I could not rest without seeing her.'

'I believe she will be glad that you have called,' Lucy said. 'I do not know if she is well enough to see you, but if you care to wait I shall enquire.'

Ignoring the housekeeper's scandalised look, she went along the hall to her cousin's room, knocked and entered. Judith was sitting up in bed, wearing a pretty pink-silk jacket over her nightgown and sipping a cup of hot chocolate.

'The Marquis of Elver has called and is anxious to see you,' Lucy told her. 'Are you feeling well enough to receive him for a few minutes, Judith? I think he is in some distress, for he went chasing off to Scotland, thinking that to be Daventry's destination, and must feel that he let you down.'

Judith glanced in the silver hand mirror that lay on her bed, checking her reflection, and then smiled. 'It was good of him to come so early,' she said. 'Please tell Mrs Hickson to bring him up—and, Anna, you may make yourself busy with my clothes or something, but stay in the room for my modesty's sake.'

'I'm glad to see you better, Cousin,' Lucy said and went out into the hall.

She ran downstairs to the parlour and told the man, pacing the floor anxiously there, that he might go up. He thanked her and went past her, taking the stairs two at a time.

Lucy returned to her room and found that her maid had brought warm water and a tray of hot chocolate.

'I shall not bother with that yet,' Lucy said. 'I shall wash and dress—and then I shall eat something downstairs.'

'Lady Dawlish thought you might like breakfast in bed, miss?'

'No, thank you, I shall change and visit my cousin and then my mother, then I will take breakfast in the parlour.'

Lucy washed and put on a pretty green-striped morning gown, then went along the hall to Judith's room and knocked. She was invited to enter and discovered that Elver had brought a chair up to the bed and was sitting by his fiancée's side, holding her hand.

'Is everything settled?' she asked, feeling relieved as she saw Judith's happy smile. 'I am so glad. I was afraid you might blame Judith, sir, and indeed, it was never her fault.'

'I should be a fool if I thought it,' Elver said, his eyes warm with love as he looked at Judith. 'Daventry had a score to settle with me, damn him! I wish he had challenged me to a duel rather than take his spite out on Judith—for I should have killed him.'

'Is it known whether he is alive or dead?' Lucy asked.

'He has disappeared,' Elver replied, a look of anger in his eyes. 'We took some trusted men last night and made a search for him, but it was seven of the clock before we reached the house—and it was deserted.'

'Deserted?' Lucy stared in surprise. 'But Judith shot him…'

'We found evidence of that, for there was blood on the stairs and in one of the bedrooms. His men must have found him and carried him away before we could get there.'

'That is a pity,' Lucy said. 'It would have been better if we knew exactly what has happened. If he is alive, as seems probable, he might—' She broke off with a little gasp.

'Yes, it is possible that he might try something of the sort again,' Elver said. 'We shall have a search made for him, of course, but we do not know where he may go…perhaps abroad.'

'Yes, perhaps he will go away and we shall not hear of him again.'

'I wish I might believe it, but a man like that…' Elver shook his head. 'I have told Judith that she must forget buying her bride clothes in London. She must come to Elver, where I can protect her—and we may send for anything she needs, but her trousseau can be bought in Paris when we are married.'

'I've told you, I shall take more care in future,' Judith said and frowned. 'I do not see why I should not—'

'I think Lord Elver is right,' Lucy said at once. Her cousin was too stubborn for her own good! 'You must be careful, Judith. When you are married, Daventry can no longer hope to cause harm between you. I think you would be safe at Elver.'

'Oh, well, I suppose…but will you come with me?' Judith begged. 'Please, Lucy. We can send for a local seamstress and have our gowns made for the wedding at Elver. I would like you to stay with me…and you were coming down again for the wedding. It makes sense if you stay, especially as Elver is to purchase a special licence and bring the wedding forward…'

'Yes, if Mama will allow it,' Lucy said. 'I think she may wish to return home, for she has had enough of Bath and has cancelled all her engagements, including our own dinner.'

'Your mama is welcome to stay at Elver with you,' the marquis said and stood up. 'I believe I should go, for your housekeeper already thinks I have ruined you both by calling before either of you were up.'

'I got up three times in the night to see if my cousin was resting,' Lucy explained. 'I should otherwise have been dressed.'

'If you will excuse me, ladies,' Elver said and bowed to each of them. 'I shall call again later this afternoon, Judith.'

'I shall be dressed by then.' Judith shook her head at his motion of protest. 'Indeed, I am perfectly refreshed now that I have slept—and I cannot abide to be an invalid.'

Lucy laughed and looked at Elver. 'Shall I show you out, sir?'

'I think I can find my way,' he said. 'I am eternally grateful to both of you and to Captain Ravenscar for rendering me a service I shall never forget.'

'It was Paul who found her and brought her home to us, sir, and we are all grateful for it.'

'Judith has told me how kind you have been to her,' he said. 'I can never thank you enough.'

Lucy shook her head, but when she sat on her cousin's bed and sought her hand, Judith squeezed it and smiled at her.

'Elver is right, you know. I have been a trial to your mama and to you, Lucy—but you've stood by me and I am grateful. Had you not brought me to Bath I might never have met Elver and I should never have known what it was to be truly happy. He blames himself for my abduction and does not care what happened, for he says the moment Daventry laid a hand on me he was dead. He truly loves me and cares only that I should be well and happy.'

Her eyes sparkled with happiness, and it was plain to see that she had at last put the past behind her.

'I can see that you are happy, Judith. Last night

I feared the worst, but we should have known a little thing like an abduction would not overset you for long,' Lucy said on a teasing note and was rewarded with laughter from her cousin.

'Exactly what I told Elver. I wish it could all be forgot as if it had never happened, but he is determined to pursue Daventry and to punish him... if he still lives.'

'I think he must. If he were dead, his men would have run off and left him there. I dare say it was merely a flesh wound, which makes him a dangerous enemy, Judith. He may return seeking revenge.'

'If he does, he will rue the day,' Judith replied. 'Elver intends to have his estate patrolled day and night—and I shall carry my pistol with me always. Had it been in my power, I would have shot him in the first place rather than let them take me.'

'You could not take a pistol to a party, Judith.'

'No...' She smiled at Lucy. 'Of course I could not, but you know what I mean. If I walk out on the estate, I shall do so...though I think Daventry must have learned his lesson. He will not think me a weak woman that he can bend to his will in future.'

'I am certain he never did, but he was too angry to think what he did,' Lucy said, and then listened as she heard the door. 'I think we have a visitor. I wonder...'

'My aunt is keeping to her room today,' Judith said. 'She has cancelled all her engagements, as you know, for she means to tell everyone that she has an indisposition as a reason why we do not venture into company.'

'Then I shall go down and see who has called.'

Lucy went to the head of the stairs and looked down. Seeing that the caller was a gentleman bearing flowers, she hesitated, then went down to greet him.

'Mr Havers,' Lucy said. 'How good of you to call, sir. Are those flowers for my cousin?'

'Yes. I heard...there was a tale that she had been rescued and brought home. I wanted to call to ask how she did—and to reassure you that for once the gossips are all on her side. If it was Daventry that abducted her, as the tale goes, he will not be welcome in Bath for many a day.'

'If the Marquis of Elver has his way, he will pay a heavy price for what he did to my cousin, sir,' Lucy said. 'Would you care to step into the parlour for a moment? I should like to explain to you how things stand so that you know the truth.'

'There are so many stories circulating,' he said and, after handing the flowers to Mrs Hickson, he followed Lucy into the parlour.

'Well, we were right in thinking that Daventry had snatched her when she went out for a breath of air—he threw a blanket over her and then drugged her.'

'The devil he did,' Mr Havers said. 'He deserves to hang. Has a magistrate been informed?'

'I dare say Captain Ravenscar and the marquis have it in hand,' Lucy said, 'though they will do their best to keep things as quiet as possible, for my cousin's sake.'

'I fear it will not be possible to quell the gossip entirely,' he said. 'I wish it might be so. Elver will stand by her?'

'Certainly. He is very much in love with her and has called already to see how she goes on.'

'Then she will brush through,' Mr Havers replied. 'No blame can attach to your cousin, Miss Dawlish—and certainly none to your family.'

'Oh, I should not care for that,' Lucy said at

once. 'I told Mama that I intended to stand by her whatever anyone said of her.'

'Just as I expected,' he replied with a warm smile. 'It is not the time to be thinking of myself, Miss Dawlish, but…once you are home again, I should like to call on your father for his permission to address you…if you would be pleased to see me.'

Lucy drew a deep breath, for he had been so kind to her that she did not wish to answer him harshly. She placed a hand on his sleeve. 'Sir, I—' She broke off as she heard a sound from the doorway and, as her startled gaze flew to the man that stood there, she felt her cheeks heat. 'Paul… Captain Ravenscar, I did not hear you come in.'

'Miss Dawlish,' he said and there was a questioning look in his eyes. 'Your housekeeper opened the door to look out as I was about to sound the knocker. Forgive me for intruding. She told me you were in the parlour. I did not know you had company. Shall I go away again?'

'No, no, of course not,' Havers said before Lucy had her breath back. 'I merely called to ask how Lady Sparrow went on. I shall call another day, Miss Dawlish.'

'I believe we leave tomorrow. Lord Elver is to escort us to his home and we shall stay there until the wedding…'

'Then I may call on you there,' Havers said and went out.

There was silence as they heard him speak to someone in the hall and then the front door was opened and closed. Paul looked puzzled as he regarded Lucy.

'Forgive me, did I interrupt something? I believed we had an understanding, Lucy…or was I mistaken?'

'You were not mistaken, of course you were not.' She felt a flow of relief as she saw he was not angry, but merely uncertain. 'Mr Havers spoke of approaching my father and I meant only to refuse—in the kindest way I could—but you came before I had time to explain.'

'Then it was my fault. I am sorry to have embarrassed you.' His eyes were thoughtful as they went over her. 'Did I rush you the other evening, Lucy? I believed you felt as I do.'

'Yes, of course…you must know…' She faltered and her eyes fell before his gaze. 'Mama wished me to marry and I did not know…there were several gentlemen who seemed to—to take an interest, though Mr Havers was one of the most persistent. I had not encouraged him in particular,' Lucy ended a little stiffly.

'I only wish you to be certain, Lucy,' Paul said softly. 'I would not wish to push you into something you might regret.'

'How could you think it?' she cried. 'I should not even have thought…but you were so reserved when you first came home, so distant and cold to me. I hardly knew you and then I thought you liked my cousin…and I was so miserable. Is it any wonder that I should think of perhaps…but it was all your fault. How could you have used me so when you knew—you always knew that it was you I loved? I know I was to have married Mark, but he was a hero and…and I could not hurt him…hurt everyone by withdrawing and then…' She blinked hard, tears hovering. 'You must have known how it was.'

'Lucy,' he said and now there was confidence in his eyes. 'Yes, I admit that I was a little reserved when I first returned, but you will admit that I had much on my mind?'

'Yes, of course I will—but you seemed to like Judith better than you liked me.'

'No, surely…what can have given you that idea?' Paul looked at her. 'I do like your cousin, but never better…surely you did not think it? Is that why you kept me at a distance and flirted with Daventry?'

'I did no such thing!'

'He danced with you several times at Dawlish while you had none for me.'

'He did not come late to the party—besides, you ignored me. You paid attention to Judith and I thought…I must marry one day, and I thought he might do as well as any other if I could not have…'

'You foolish little goose, how could you?' Paul's voice held tenderness, but Lucy did not notice.

She stared at him, the tears very close. How could he speak to her so? How could he look at her as if he thought her a foolish child? Her head went up proudly and she gave him a fierce look.

'Daventry seemed charming. I did not know what a rogue he was…' She faltered. 'If you had… but you did nothing. I thought you had forgotten me…that you never cared for me at all…oh, I cannot bear this.'

'Lucy…' Paul took a step towards her, reached out to draw her into his arms, but she would not allow it. She avoided his grasp, ran past him and up the stairs to her room, closing and locking the door after her. Then she flung herself down on the bed and gave vent to her emotions.

Downstairs in the parlour, Paul hesitated. Lucy was suffering a fit of sensibility and it would have been better if he could have gone after her and made her understand just how much he cared. He realised now that he had been much at fault by keeping his distance when he returned home from Vienna. He should have declared himself at once, but it had not been until he discovered his brother's secret that his guilt had finally left him. Since then he'd been waiting for the right moment, which was surely now—but to race upstairs and hammer at the bedroom door of a young unmarried lady would cause censure—from the servants and from her mother.

Damn it! He was a clumsy idiot and it was no wonder that Lucy had lost patience with him. He had come here to ask her formally to marry him and ended by distressing the girl he wanted for his wife. Yet her outburst had told him that it was not too late. Had her affections not been engaged she would never have reacted in such a way. The tension left him and he smiled, sure now that his love was returned. It was merely a matter of making amends—and the fault was his entirely.

He'd known what the situation must be and might have avoided this distress had he simply ignored what he'd seen, but he'd wanted to be sure. He'd always known that he wanted Lucy for his wife and he was certain now that she loved him. They had always been meant for each other—but both of them had adored Mark. Lucy had mistaken hero-worship for love, but at that ball, she, like Paul himself, had realised the truth—yet she'd been too young and too nervous to break off her engagement.

When Paul followed his brother to fight against the French, Lucy had still been too young to even think of asking her to save herself for him. She was still a schoolroom miss, he a year and a half older and unready to commit to marriage, though he'd known that one day she would be the woman he wanted to wed. By the time he'd returned from his duty it was too late. Mark had got there before him…she was promised to him and their engagement was to be announced after Lucy's Season.

Paul had been devastated, but once Mark had proposed, there was nothing he could do. He had tried not to show that he was angry and jealous, but when dancing with Lucy he had almost been undone. It had been in his mind to have it out with Mark, because he'd been certain that his brother was not truly in love with Lucy. Yet he'd hesitated at breakfast when he might have raised the subject for he was unsure of Lucy's feelings…and then it had been too late.

Mark's murder had ruined everything. Paul was struck with guilt and grief for the brother he'd truly loved. So deep was his pain that he could hardly bear to look at Lucy. To think of her as free from her promise was to betray Mark and he could not bear it—and so he'd run away, leaving everyone else to bear their sorrow as best they could.

What a fool he had been! Paul's disgust of his own behaviour had added to his feelings of guilt at inheriting everything that should have been his brother's. By working hard in Vienna he had managed to find a new path for himself, to accept that he owed it to his father and his people to take up the duties that came with an estate of the size of Ravenscar.

It had taken him longer to bring himself to a position where he could think of Lucy as a possible bride—the only one he truly wanted. Any other would be a compromise and that was hardly fair to his future wife or to himself. Yet he'd hesitated, unsure whether she still felt as she once had towards him.

Now, he had distressed Lucy again. Paul left the house and began to walk towards his lodgings. Cursing himself for a clumsy fool, Paul knew that he must find some way of convincing Lucy that he loved her—and of persuading her to forgive him for hurting her.

He had been selfish, thinking of his own pain. Lucy must have suffered terribly...especially if she had not truly wished to marry his brother. Paul realised that she, too, had been guilty—grieving, but guilty—because she had not loved Mark as a girl should love the man she intended to wed.

Paul wanted to sweep her into his arms and carry her off to his home. He would spend the rest of his life making her happy—but he must be patient. Lucy had been hurt by his reserve and she did not quite trust him. How could he blame her after the way he'd behaved? The blame was entirely his. He must show her that he was to be trusted, show her that he loved her more than life itself—and give her a reason to love him and put her life in his hands.

She was going to stay with Elver for her cousin's sake. Paul knew he must return to his home and make sure that his father was well and his cousins prepared to stay with Lord Ravenscar for a little longer…and then he would return to Bath. He had promised to escort Lady Dawlish to her home so he must call and ask her when she wished to travel, for if she was not ready he might have to return for her…and he would hope to find that Lucy had forgiven him.

'How are you now, Mama?' Lucy asked as she went into her mother's bedchamber and found her still in bed. 'Are you truly unwell?'

Lucy had cried for a short time, then washed her

face and used a little powder to cover the ravages of her tears. She had then looked in on Judith, who had decided to get up and was dressing behind a lacquered screen. Now she had come to try to encourage her mama to leave her bed.

'No, I was just a little tired,' Lady Dawlish said. 'I have been thinking that I shall return to Dawlish tomorrow if Captain Ravenscar will escort me.'

'Shall you not come to Elver, Mama? You know that Judith has begged me to keep her company and I think I ought.'

'Yes, I know. I'm not sure I like that, Lucy. It might be dangerous.'

'Daventry is not interested in me,' Lucy said. 'He paid court to me while it suited him, but I had decided against him, even had he offered. You know that, Mama.'

'Yes, and I am very glad of it,' her mother said, forgetting that she'd once considered it a good match for her daughter. 'Has Paul called this morning?'

'Yes, he called to see how Judith was…' Lucy swallowed hard, wishing that her mother would not question her too carefully. 'I told him you were feeling unwell and he did not stay.'

'Very proper of him,' her mother said with a nod of her head. She smiled at Lucy. 'I think I shall get up now—and then I shall send a note to Paul. If he will escort me home in the morning, I shall ask him to do so.'

'Yes, Mama, of course.'

'Well, run away then, my love,' Lady Dawlish said. 'There are some books that need returning to the lending library on the table by the window. Pray give them to the footman and ask him to take them for me.'

'Yes, of course,' Lucy said, picked up the books and took them downstairs.

She handed them to the footman, who promised to take them later that afternoon. Normally, Lucy would have preferred to visit the lending library herself, but she did not feel like walking out in Bath at the moment. It was not that she feared the earl, for as she'd told her mother, he was not interested in her. Besides, he would surely not have recovered from being shot, for even if it was not a serious wound it must be painful.

Lucy's avoidance of the Bath streets was more

to do with the questions that she was sure to be asked, so she sat quietly with a book in the parlour until Judith came down to join her, followed half an hour later by Lady Dawlish. All three ladies were seated in the parlour and about to send for tea when the knocker sounded.

Judith was immediately alert, but when their visitor entered it was discovered that they had two and not one. Elver and Paul had met at the door, it seemed, and in the flurry of greetings, Lucy was able to compose herself enough to greet them both politely.

'I am delighted to see you both,' Lady Dawlish said. 'Lucy, ring the bell for tea, my dear. Please be seated, gentlemen.' She turned to Paul with an enquiring air. 'Would it trouble you to escort me to Dawlish tomorrow, Captain Ravenscar? I should like to leave about noon—if that would not inconvenience you?'

'It would suit me perfectly, for I must go home soon to see my father,' Paul replied, smiling. He glanced at Lucy, arching his brows, but she neither smiled nor spoke, looking at him uncertainly. He smiled at her and was rewarded by a flicker of response in her eyes. 'I understand that Lucy is to visit Elver with her cousin?'

'Yes,' Judith replied. 'I cannot spare her before my wedding and she has been kind enough to give me her promise. I hope both my aunt and uncle will come down for the wedding—and you, sir, if you can? I owe you a debt I shall never repay.'

'Not at all,' Paul replied politely. 'Lucy was in distress and I promised her I would do all I could. I was fortunate enough to be given accurate information…and even more fortunate to find you when I did.'

'I do not know what I should have done had you not discovered me,' Judith said, 'for I was suffering from the after-effects of that evil drug and felt very ill. Had I passed out, I might have lain all night in the lane.'

'Fortunately for all of us, Ravenscar was there,' Elver said. 'I wish it might have been me, my dearest, but I thought he had taken you to Scotland.'

'He knew you would, of course,' she said and gave a little shudder of disgust. 'I suppose he has not been found?'

'As yet I have heard nothing. I have sent to London for a Bow Street Runner,' Elver told her. 'Such men are skilled in tracking others and I must hope Daventry can be found soon—but within a few days we shall be in Paris, my love. I am certain that by the time we return this matter will all be settled. Abduction is a serious crime and Daventry is going to pay for what he did to you, I give you my word. If he is not killed trying to resist arrest, he shall hang.'

Judith nodded, but added no more to the conversation as the tea tray was brought in. Lady Dawlish proceeded to dispense it and Lucy helped to pass cups and little sandwiches and cakes. After the maids had gone, leaving them to serve themselves, as they preferred when the company was intimate, Lady Dawlish spoke of her niece's wedding.

'It will be such a happy occasion, for I dare say you may not have heard, Lord Elver—my daughter is to marry Captain Ravenscar. Their engagement cannot be announced until Lord Dawlish has been consulted, but I am sure he will be only too happy to agree. To have our daughter living so close to us can only be the best of arrangements.'

'Mama…' Lucy caught her breath as both Judith and Elver congratulated them. She glanced at Paul and saw that he was smiling and nodding at her and her cheeks burned.

'Yes, I am very happy that Lucy has agreed to be my wife,' Paul said, as if nothing had occurred that morning. 'Our other reason for saying nothing was that we did not wish to steal your thunder, Elver. Our marriage will not be for another couple of months, I dare say.'

Lucy sent him an agonised glance, but he ignored it.

'Papa has not given his permission yet...'

'Lucy is right,' her mother said approvingly. 'However, I know you will not spread it abroad—and I am so pleased that I could not keep it to myself a moment longer.'

Lucy inhaled deeply, but said nothing. Her mother was making it harder and harder for them to escape the bonds that seemed to be tightening about them. Paul was behaving like the perfect gentleman, but there was no reason why he should have been forced into this situation. He had done nothing but kiss her once—a passionate kiss, it was true, but surely he could not feel it bound him to marriage?

Yet her mother had drawn the net tighter, and if Paul walked away now he would be damned for jilting her—and that could only reflect badly on her. People would be bound to remember her dance and tongues would wag, making something out of nothing.

Lucy felt her insides curling with shame. She did not wish to trap Paul into marriage if he did not want it…and how could he after their stupid quarrel that morning?

If only Mr Havers had not tried to propose to her at the very moment Paul chose to call. He had jumped to conclusions and now thought of her as shallow and a confirmed flirt.

Lucy could feel the heat in her cheeks and would not look at Paul, even though he tried to attract her attention more than once.

When the gentlemen finally took their leave, Paul glanced at her as if to ask if she would go to the door with him, but she merely smiled and wished him a safe journey.

'I shall not be here when you call for Mama in the morning,' she said. 'I shall see you at the wedding, sir.'

'Yes, of course,' Paul said and came to kiss her

hand. Lucy rose to her feet, looking at him uncertainly as he took her hand in his. 'It will be all right,' he spoke softly so that the others could not hear. 'Do not worry, Lucy. I am very happy to marry you. I'll be back soon and then we shall talk, my love.'

She was unable to answer, giving him a pleading look and regretting that she had not found an excuse to have a few moments alone with him, as Judith had when she saw her fiancé to the door.

The touch of Paul's lips on her hand sent a little flutter of pleasure winging through Lucy and in that moment she wished herself in his arms. She would have given anything to be alone with him, to have heard from his own lips just why he was happy to wed her—when surely he could not be.

She was very confused, unable to trust her own feelings or to gauge his properly.

Her eyes met his, trying to read the message he was sending her. Her heart was racing and as he smiled she felt a flicker of hope—of belief that he truly cared for her.

Then, before she could recover her wits, he was gone and she was left to wonder and to regret. How could Paul be happy to wed her? He had never told her that he loved her…or was he simply marrying her because he wanted to make up for all she'd lost when his brother was murdered?

## Chapter Thirteen

Lucy spent a restless night, hardly sleeping. Every time she thought about her mother's unwelcome announcement of her engagement she felt a squirming sensation inside. Paul had spoken reassuringly to her before he left, but how could he do otherwise? He was, after all, a gentleman and had been placed in an impossible situation. Lucy wished with all her heart that it had not happened. She could see no way of escaping the marriage and did not truly wish to—except that the thought of a future spent with a man who had married her from a sense of duty was appalling. Especially as she loved him so very much.

Would Paul do that? Would he marry her out of a sense of misplaced duty? She was very much afraid that he might. After all, she knew that he needed to marry to provide heirs for Ravenscar.

She believed it would please his father, because they had formed a bond during his recent illness.

The thought kept her tossing all night long and it was the early hours before she finally slept.

However, in the morning Lucy took a fond farewell of her mama and went off to stay with her friends with a smile on her face. She must not allow herself to be gloomy, though inside she was fretting, unsure whether she wanted Paul to hurry back or not.

Elver's house was extremely pleasant, a large, light and airy building with several long windows that gave it an agreeable aspect and wonderful views of the gardens. There was a lake to be seen from the west wing and beyond it a huge stretch of beech, ash and oak trees.

Lucy thought it would be pleasant to walk to the lake sometimes, for the weather continued fine and warm. The room she was given looked out towards the lake and was only three doors away from her cousin's so that they were able to go in and out whenever they pleased.

Judith had driven them here in her phaeton and asked Lucy if she would like to continue her driving lessons now that they had many fine roads to choose about the large estate.

'It depends on what else you want to do,' Lucy replied with a smile. 'There are some pleasant walks in the gardens, Judith—and I dare say you will be busy with fittings for your new gowns.'

Judith agreed that she would, but thought there would be plenty of time for other activities because she was to have only her wedding gown made for the moment.

'I shall have most of my new gowns made in Paris and I have a new carriage gown for travelling after the wedding.'

Lucy agreed that it was sensible to buy most of her trousseau in Paris. They could simply enjoy the fine weather.

Since her cousin wished to discover all she could of her husband's estate, she rode out with Elver in the mornings and took Lucy driving in the afternoons.

Lucy had discovered Elver's well-stocked library, and what with walks in the garden, her driving lessons and evenings spent in the company of friends invited to dine with them, she discovered the time passed more quickly than she had expected.

At night in her bed, she allowed herself to think about Paul and to dream of what it might be like to marry him. He had changed from the young man she'd fallen in love with years before, becoming more authoritative…and sometimes prone to dark moods. Yet there were moments when he looked at her and she felt her knees weaken, as if she could swoon for pleasure if he took her into his arms.

The day of her cousin's wedding had been drawing closer and before she really knew where the time had gone it was only two days to the wedding. The seamstress was coming that morning to fit Judith, Elver's sister and Lucy for their gowns. The maids of honour were to wear pale-blue gowns with white sashes and satin bonnets trimmed with ribbons and fresh roses from the gardens. Judith was to wear a gown of ivory silk trimmed with silver, a garland of fresh roses twined with ribbons and silver threads in her hair.

As soon as the news of the wedding had got abroad, presents had begun to arrive. Judith unwrapped each gift, showed them to everyone and then gave them to the servants to arrange on a long table where they could be displayed to the wedding guests. She spent an hour or so before dinner every evening writing letters to thank all those who had sent gifts. It was as Lucy joined her in the parlour that morning, three days before the wedding, that a parcel wrapped in silver tissue was delivered to her.

Judith thanked the footman and asked who had sent it, for a footman or a servant delivered most gifts and it was usual to say who had sent the present.

'I do not know, my lady,' he replied. 'It was discovered on the doorstep this morning quite early.'

'Oh, that is a little odd...' Judith looked at the parcel doubtfully.

She began to untie the ribbon, but, finding a wooden casket inside hesitated before lifting the lid.

'What is wrong?' Lucy asked. 'Do you think...?'

'I can smell something unpleasant...' She put the box on the table and rang the bell. A footman answered and she motioned towards the box. 'Please open that for me, Frederick.'

'Yes, my lady,' he said, looking puzzled, but as he half-lifted the lid he hesitated and glanced at her. 'I think this is a hoax, my lady. I believe I should take this to his lordship.'

'Yes, please do. I think it might be some kind of a dead animal.'

'Yes, it has the smell of decay,' he said, bowed to her and took it away.

Lucy saw that Judith was looking pale. 'What a disgusting thing to do, Judith.'

'It can only be him...Daventry,' she said. 'No one else would wish to upset me two days before my wedding. It is a warning that he has not forgot me, Lucy.'

'Do not allow him to disturb you, dearest. It is a foolish prank, no more.'

'Yes...but don't you see? If he could have that delivered...what more could he do?'

'It was a spiteful trick. Elver will double the guards patrolling the grounds. He will not allow Daventry to come near you, Judith.'

'No, of course not,' she agreed, recovering her spirits and her colour. 'As you say, Lucy, it was just a nasty prank.'

Lucy changed the subject and in a few moments

the seamstress joined them and the unpleasant gift was forgotten as they examined silks and ribbons and tried on their new gowns.

Lucy was thoughtful as she changed her gown for lunch a little later that morning. She had brushed over the incident to Judith, but it was unpleasant to think that either Daventry or one of his servants had managed to get so close to the house.

What could have been his reason for sending her something so sinister two days before her wedding?

'Lucy, my love.' Lady Dawlish kissed her on the cheek. 'I am so glad to be here. At the last moment your father had some urgent business and I began to think we should never get here.'

'Your mama is always in the fidgets when we travel,' her father said and laughed as he embraced her. 'So my little girl is to marry, then—and we shall not lose you altogether for you will be living near at hand. I could not be more pleased, Lucy.'

'I am glad you are pleased, Papa.'

Lucy's cheeks were warm, but she had made up

her mind she must accept her fate, for it would upset everyone if she were to break it off now.

'Ravenscar is delighted. He sent you his best wishes and says you must visit him as soon as you return. We dined with him yesterday and he gave me a gift for you. It is packed in my trunk and you shall have it later.'

Lucy thanked him. 'Paul did not come down with you?'

'He is an hour or so behind us, I think,' her father said. 'He had some business to attend to and, no matter what your mother thinks, these things are important.'

'Yes, of course, Papa,' Lucy said and smiled at him.

She was trembling inside, for although she could see no way that either of them could withdraw, she was still concerned that Paul must feel he had been trapped into a marriage he did not want.

Lucy sat with her parents after nuncheon, talking with them, Judith, Elver and his sister. After tea, her mother went up to rest before dinner and her father went off with Elver to look at some rare books in the library. Judith suggested to Lucy that they should take a little drive in her phaeton.

'Is it not a little late to go driving?' Lucy asked.

'It is so pleasant and we have two hours before we dine. Let us walk down to the lake. If you do not feel we should take the horses out at this hour, there can be no harm in a walk.'

Lucy could only agree. She sensed that Judith was feeling uneasy and wanted to talk away from the house. Having sat indoors all day waiting for her parents, she, too, would enjoy a breath of air.

'I needed to get out for a while,' Judith told her as they began their walk. 'It was a dead rat in that box yesterday, Lucy…and something else was delivered today…'

'Another dead animal wrapped up as a gift?'

'It was worse…' Judith looked at her. 'A wreath of dead flowers was delivered this morning…and Elver had instructed the guards to keep a twenty-four-hour watch. How can he have evaded the guards?' She shivered and there was a look of unease in her eyes. 'It can only be Daventry, do you not agree?'

'Yes, I think it must be,' Lucy said and glanced over her shoulder. She saw a man carrying a shotgun over his shoulder walking a few paces behind them. 'We are being chaperoned, Cousin.'

'Yes, of course,' she replied with a smile. 'Elver told me I was at liberty to go where I wished, but a keeper or a couple of grooms would accompany us wherever we go. I should not have dared to come out otherwise.'

'I am glad of it,' Lucy said, 'for I should be anxious for your safety otherwise, Judith.'

'I do not go out unarmed,' she said and a grim smile touched her lips. 'I have a pistol in my purse, Lucy and should not hesitate to use it if we were attacked. He will not again take me so easily.'

Lucy could see that she was more angry than frightened and felt pleased. Daventry was trying to intimidate her with his cruel tricks, but it was only making her angry and that banished her fear...though it had thrown a shadow over her wedding.

'He is a cruel and thoughtless man,' Lucy said. 'I hope they will soon catch him, for he deserves to be punished for what he did to you, Cousin. He is trying to spoil your wedding for he cannot truly think to capture you again.'

'Oh, let us forget him,' Judith said and tossed

her head defiantly. 'The day after tomorrow I shall be married. He will surely cease his tricks then, for what can it avail him after I am Elver's bride?'

Lucy did not immediately answer. She was thoughtful because it seemed to her that the earl might not care whether she was Elver's bride. He was not so much interested in making her his bride as in wreaking revenge on her bridegroom. It could not matter to him how he did it as long as he caused the marquis pain…her death might do as well, for he was already outlawed from society.

Judith continued to chatter as they walked and Lucy laughed and answered, though she had been feeling uneasy for a while. She glanced over her shoulder and saw the keeper walking a short distance behind them and that reassured her…and yet she had a feeling that someone else was watching them.

They had reached the lake now. Lucy looked about her. She could see no one other than a man she took to be another keeper at the far left of the lake. Shadowing the far bank was the wood of beautiful trees. Lucy's gaze was drawn towards the wood. She put up a hand to shade her eyes as something glinted amongst the trees, and then she saw it—a long-barrelled gun pointing at Judith.

'He's going to shoot!' she cried and thrust Judith aside just as the sound of a rifle cracked and she felt the wind as it passed her cheek and then a second shot that caught her arm. She gave a cry of pain and sank to her knees beside Judith. Vaguely, she heard a flurry of shots and screams, but her arm was hurting and she passed into an unconscious state as she heard Judith cry out, 'My cousin has been shot. Help us…we must get her back to the house…'

Lucy was not aware of being carried back towards the house, or that someone came striding to take her from the keeper's arms and carry her up the stairs to her room, Judith running ahead to pull back the covers. She knew nothing until some minutes later when she opened her eyes to discover that her arm was being bound by sure gentle hands.

'Paul…?' she whispered as she looked up into his eyes. 'What happened? When did you arrive?'

'Just a few minutes ago,' he said. 'I was about to come in search of you, my foolish little love.

Judith told me what you did. You saved her life, for those shots were meant for her. Daventry was bent on his wicked revenge and would have killed her had you not pushed her down.'

Lucy's eyes filled with tears. 'I could not let that wicked man have his way,' she said. 'He was bent on revenge—and wanted to kill or injure her to break Elver's heart.'

'Yes, my darling, we know,' Paul said and finished binding her arm. 'That will hold it until the doctor comes. Will you have a sip of laudanum for the pain?'

'No, not yet,' Lucy begged. 'It stings, but I can bear it. Is Judith all right? He did not harm her? I heard more shots…'

'That was the keepers,' Paul said. 'Apparently, they knew he was in the wood and had been tracking him. Elver wanted him taken alive so that he might stand his trial…but when he fired two shots at you and Judith, they killed him before he could reload his rifle.'

'Oh, thank God,' Lucy whispered and a tear trickled down her cheek. 'You cannot imagine what dreadful things he has done to her, Paul.'

'None as bad as he has done to you,' Paul said

fiercely. 'I wish to goodness I had been here sooner. I should have been there to protect you, my sweet, loyal darling.'

'You could not have foreseen what would happen. There were keepers everywhere and we thought we were safe—but then I felt something, a tingling at my nape. I looked towards the woods and I saw the sunlight reflect on the barrel of his gun. Instinctively, I knew it wasn't one of the keepers and I pushed Judith out of the way. His first shot missed me, but I think he fired at me the second time…he did not care who he hurt and I dare say I had angered him.'

'Hush, my love, you must not try to talk.' Paul sent and bent to kiss her softly on the lips. 'I should leave you to rest.'

'Please do not leave me…' Lucy began. The words caught in her throat as she heard her mother's voice and then Lady Dawlish entered the room.

'My poor, poor child,' she cried in distress. 'That evil man might have killed you. Where were Elver's keepers? He assured me that you would be safe or I should not have—'

'Please do not upset Lucy,' Paul said as she

threatened to become hysterical. 'She is in pain, Lady Dawlish, and must be allowed to rest. Lucy saved her cousin's life and unfortunately was caught in the firing line.'

'You brought her home,' Lady Dawlish said. 'Thank goodness you have come. We shall go home to Dawlish as soon as we can.'

'Lucy cannot travel so far yet,' Paul said firmly. 'Besides, she will want to attend the wedding—'

'She is too ill—'

'No, Mama,' Lucy said. 'Paul is right. The wedding is not until the day after tomorrow. If I can get up, I shall want to do my duty as a bridesmaid. Please, do not make a fuss. I should just like to rest…if everyone would go away.' She looked at Paul imploringly, hoping that he knew she wanted him to return.

'Take a sip of this, dearest,' Paul said and held a little glass to her lips. 'Just a sip and it will ease you. If you sleep, perhaps you will be able to attend the wedding, but you must rest until after the doctor has been.'

Lucy slept until the early hours of the morning and woke to find that Judith was sitting by her bed. She opened her eyes and smiled at her, but when she tried to sit up, her arm pained her and she gave a little cry, falling back against the pillows.

'Are you in much pain, dearest Lucy?'

'My arm is very sore,' Lucy said and sighed. 'I thought it might be better when I woke, but I think it is worse.'

'You saved my life.' Judith's voice was emotional, her eyes caught with tears. 'I thought we were safe. I did not see the rifle.'

'It was the merest chance that I did, but something made me uneasy… I suspected he must be hiding somewhere on the estate, because of the wreath. Paul told me that the keepers hoped to capture him alive?'

'Elver sends his apologies. Those were his instructions, but he did not dream that Daventry would simply try to kill one of us—he thought another kidnap attempt might be possible.'

'Daventry must have been evil indeed, otherwise he could not have done what he did to you, Judith.'

'I do not think he ever cared for me, but it is you who has suffered the most,' Judith said. 'I know your mama and papa are angry. They want to take you away…' She hesitated, then, 'I could postpone the wedding. There is no need for haste now. I shall be perfectly safe to buy my bride clothes in London.'

'You must not postpone on my account,' Lucy told her. 'If I am able, I shall be your bridesmaid, as we hoped—if not, I shall rest here, but come down to wish you happy afterwards.'

Judith bent down to kiss her. 'Paul went to rest for a time. He sat with you for most of the night. Do you wish me to wake him?'

'No, let him rest,' Lucy said. 'Go to bed now, Cousin. You must not have dark shadows under your eyes for your wedding.'

'There would have been no wedding had you not pushed me out of the way,' Judith said and bent to kiss her. 'I shall let you rest now, my love.'

Lucy yawned as she left the room and closed her eyes again. She was very tired and soon drifted into sleep.

It was morning and the sun was pouring into the room when Lucy woke once more. A maid had brought warm water and some soft cloths, which she set upon the washstand before coming to greet Lucy.

'Several people wish to see you, Miss Dawlish,' she said. 'Captain Ravenscar thought you might like me to wash your face for you, miss?'

'How thoughtful of him,' Lucy said. 'I feel warm and sticky. If you can bring the bowl closer and hold it, I shall try to wash myself.'

The maid obliged her and Lucy struggled to make herself more comfortable, then fell back against the pillows, feeling exhausted.

A short time later the maid brought up first the doctor, then her father and her mother, who was still a little weepy, but there was no mention of the person she most wanted to see.

'Will you ask Paul to come and see me, please?' she said to Judith when she followed Lucy's parents into the bedchamber a little later.

'He and Elver have gone to see the magistrate,' Judith said. 'He looked on you first thing when you were still sleeping. What did the doctor say to you—will he allow you to get up?'

'Not today. He has given me a mixture to help the pain, but he was pleased there was no fever and says that was due to whoever bound my wound. I wanted to thank Paul, for I should have felt much worse had I taken a fever.'

'I think he has had much experience of tending wounds in France and Spain,' Judith said. 'He will be pleased to see you looking better, Lucy.'

'I shall get up tomorrow,' Lucy told her. 'But it may be best if I simply attend the reception for a little while. I am sorry to miss the ceremony, but it might be too much for me to stand in the church.'

'Yes, I understand,' Judith said. 'I feel wretched that this has happened to you, Cousin.'

'It is better than seeing you dead,' Lucy said.

A maid entered with a tray of tea and what appeared to be some thin soup, and Judith stood up.

'I shall let you have your meal in peace and return later,' she said and went out.

Lucy looked at the thin soup doubtfully, but tasting it, she discovered it was pleasant and drank half of it. She was sipping a cup of tea when Paul came in.

He was wearing pale breeches, riding boots and an open-necked shirt, and Lucy's heart leaped at the sight of him. He looked so strong and handsome and she wished that he would take her in his arms and kiss her. His eyes swept over her and then he smiled.

'I see you are a little better, Lucy. You have been so brave throughout…but I wish it had not happened. This is not what I planned. I had hoped to dance with you, take you driving and make love to you…we have our own wedding to plan soon.'

'Are you sure you wish to marry me?' Lucy asked the question that had been burning inside her since the night her mother had discovered her in Paul's arms. 'I do not think you were sure when you returned from Vienna.'

'I was still feeling uncomfortable with the situation, Lucy,' Paul said. 'You should have been Mark's bride had he not been murdered.'

'Yes…though had he lived…forgive me, I might not have been.'

'Were you ever in love with him?' Paul's eyes were intent on her face.

'No, I do not think I was ever in love before…' She faltered. 'I loved Mark as a friend, worshipped him as a hero and—and thought that was enough…until…'

'Until what, Lucy?'

'Why are you happy to marry me?' she asked,

unwilling to confess all without some statement of his feelings. 'I thought you felt guilty because of Mark?'

'I did for a long time,' Paul said and frowned. 'Then a letter came and what I discovered made me realise...' He drew in his breath. 'I hope it will not hurt you or change your opinion of my brother... Mark was a hero, Lucy—but he should not have asked you to marry him, for he had a lover and she bore him a child.'

Lucy stared at him. 'I thought there was something... Did he love her? Was she—was she a lady?'

'Her father was a younger son with no fortune. Rosalind tells me that they were in love. She says he had promised to wed her, though she was not his equal. She was the daughter of a regimental parson and followed the drum with us in Spain.'

Paul stood up and paced the floor, then turned to look at her. 'When we marched into France she was left behind because she was heavy with child. I knew that she had been Mark's lover, but I did not know his intentions towards her. When I asked, he told me it was not my affair.'

'I see…' Lucy said doubtfully. 'Do you believe her when she says he promised to wed her?'

'She was not of his class, but she was not a woman of the street,' Paul said. 'I can only think she believed it to be the case…and I cannot understand why he came home after the victory in France and proposed to you, Lucy.'

'It was not well done…if he had promised to wed her. Does your father know of her and her child?'

'Yes, I thought it best to tell him he had a granddaughter, for I have no reason to disbelieve her.'

'Was he pleased or angry?'

'At first he was a little angry, but then he asked to see her…that was the reason I was delayed coming here. Now that he has seen the child he believes she is Mark's, and he means to do something for them.'

'I am glad. I cannot understand why he behaved in a way that seems dishonourable.'

'Nor could I until I came across a letter in his things,' Paul said. 'I think that he believed she had died in childbed and the babe with her…soon after we crossed into France.'

'So he proposed to me believing his lover was dead...'

'Yes—and then he received a letter from France, where she had gone looking for him.'

'I noticed a change in him just before we were due to have our engagement ball.' Lucy was thoughtful. 'He could not in all honour jilt me— and yet it was she whom he loved.'

'I am so sorry,' Paul said. 'I hope this does not hurt you terribly—but I thought you should know the truth.'

'I am glad you have told me,' Lucy said, but she was looking up at him, searching his face. 'Is that why you feel obliged to marry me, Paul? I thought it might be because Mama had pushed you into it, but—'

'No, of course it isn't my reason for asking you to marry me...which I do not believe I actually did, Lucy. So much seems to have happened and I never made you an offer...did I?'

There was humour in his eyes as he came to the bed and sat on the edge. She looked up at him shyly as he took her hand.

'I thought you were angry with me, because of Mr Havers. He intended to make me an offer,

Paul, but…I did not give him hope. I know you must think me a terrible flirt.'

'Have I said as much?' He laughed as she opened her eyes at him. 'I was surprised to walk in on you like that, because I thought I might have misjudged the situation. I believed we had an agreement when I left you the previous night, Lucy.'

'Yes, so did I,' she agreed. 'But I could hardly tell him and he seemed to be so earnest. I did not wish to hurt…but I should have refused him had he asked. He was merely preparing the way.'

'And I upset you by questioning you? Can you ever forgive me, my love?'

'Yes, I was distressed,' Lucy said, her cheeks warm as she looked up at him. 'I thought I had given you a disgust of me…and Mama told Elver and Judith that we were engaged…putting you in an insidious position. How could you withdraw after that without causing more scandal? I knew you could not.'

'Lucy, my foolish little love,' Paul said and captured her restless hand as it moved on the bedclothes. 'Surely you must know that I—'

'Captain Ravenscar…' Lady Dawlish interrupted from the doorway. 'While I understand your feelings, I must remind you that you are not yet married. Your being here alone in my daughter's bedchamber is not quite proper. Last night when she was so unwell I overlooked it, but I do not think you should make a habit of it.'

'Please, Mama,' Lucy begged. 'Do not send him away. We have had so little time to talk—and I need him here. If he cannot stay, I shall get up and come down.'

'No, you will not,' Paul said and gave her a firm look. 'You will rest today or you will not be fit to attend the wedding tomorrow. I shall go away now and perhaps Judith will visit with me next time.'

'Oh, you need not go away if Lucy is distressed,' her mother said. 'It is not quite proper, but with everything that has happened of late, I shall be glad to see her happy again. Your wedding cannot come soon enough for me.'

'Mama,' Lucy cried. 'Paul has not been able to propose to me properly yet. If you would go away and stop fussing, perhaps he could do so. If I *have* a reputation to guard, I assure you that Paul will do nothing to besmirch it.'

'Oh, I see.' Lady Dawlish laughed. 'In that case,

I must oblige you both. I shall return later and I shall expect to see you wearing a ring.'

She went to the door and looked back with an arch smile. Lucy shook her head as she closed the door behind her.

'Forgive her, Paul. She is very anxious for me to be married and happy, because of what happened before.'

'That is only natural,' he said and returned to his place on the side of her bed. 'This is not the most romantic of settings…but I hope that you will do me the honour of becoming my wife…and I very much hope that will make you as happy as I shall be, if you say yes.'

Lucy laughed, looking up at him with her heart in her eyes. 'Of course I shall say yes—what else could I do?'

'But will it make you happy?' he asked as he took her hand once more.

'Very happy,' Lucy replied.

'Then I hope this ring will please you,' he said and slid a diamond ring with several large stones in the form of a daisy on to the third finger of her left hand. 'I thought it was pretty—and there are so many heirlooms waiting for you, my love—but

I wanted you to have something different, something just for you.'

'It is beautiful,' Lucy said as she looked at the lovely ring sparkling on her finger. 'I love it and I shall wear it with pride.'

'How soon will you marry me, dearest? My father hopes it will be soon, but if you wish for a longer engagement...'

'I would marry you tomorrow if I could be sure of walking down the aisle without fainting,' Lucy said. 'We must let Judith have her wedding first and then...we shall go back to Ravenscar and make the arrangements. Do you think we might have the ceremony at your home so that your father may witness it?'

'He tells me that he will come to the church if need be,' Paul said. 'But I see no reason why we should not use the old chapel. It has not been used for a wedding for years, but we still worship there sometimes—when a visiting chaplain will oblige. It is just like you to think of it, Lucy—and it will please my father no end...'

'Then that is what we shall do.'

Lucy lay back against her pillows with a sigh. 'I

am satisfied, but now I really think I should rest if I am to attend Judith's wedding tomorrow.'

'Yes, my love, you should certainly rest. I shall visit you again later if your mama will permit me—and if she will not, I shall come after she is in bed.'

Paul bent his head to kiss her lightly on the lips and then left her to sleep.

# Chapter Fourteen

'Judith made a very pretty bride, did she not?' Lucy said to Paul as they walked in the cool of the gardens later that evening, when most of the guests had gone. 'Elver is taking her to Paris to buy her bride clothes, for he would not allow her to visit London before the wedding.'

'Well, she need have no fear now,' Paul replied and looked down at her. 'Your cousin is safe and happily married—and we can move on. We should begin to think about our own wedding, Lucy. In the morning we shall all return to our homes. Father will wish to speak with you. I think he hopes we shall make our home with him.'

'Yes, of course. Where else would we wish to be?' Lucy asked. 'I am very fond of your papa and should wish to see him comfortable and happy.'

'You do not long for a house of your own? I

do have other estates, where we might reside for some of the time.'

'Ravenscar is a beautiful house. I have always felt at home there, Paul. I visited so often as a child; if I was not at your house, you were at mine. Mama will enjoy having me close enough to visit when she chooses.'

'Then I am satisfied. I did not wish you to think that you had no choice.'

They had stopped walking. Paul gazed down into her face, drawing her close to kiss her softly on the lips; he stroked her cheek with the tips of his fingers.

'As far as I am concerned, our marriage cannot be soon enough,' he murmured and held her pressed so tight against him that she felt the urgent need in him. 'When shall we be wed, Lucy my love?'

'As soon as the banns may be called,' she replied, her eyes warm and tender as she returned his urgent look. 'It seems such a long time since I first realised that I cared for you in this way, Paul. I think because we were always friends, I saw you almost as a brother—and then, quite suddenly, it all changed.'

'When we danced at that ball?' Paul asked, his fingers caressing her nape. 'Before that I knew you were special to me, that you were the girl I wanted for my wife, but I did not know until that moment how much I loved you.'

'So much time wasted,' Lucy said on a sigh. 'We must not waste another moment, Paul. You must set the banns as soon as we return home.'

'You look so lovely, my darling,' Lady Dawlish said when she entered Lucy's bedchamber that morning in August and saw her dressed in her gown of white-silk tulle, which sparkled with silver embroidery and tiny diamonds. 'Such a beautiful bride…'

Lucy laughed softly as she saw her mama sniff into the pretty lace kerchief she carried. The mother of the bride was dressed in shades of lilac and looked very attractive herself, a spray of pale-pink roses pinned to her bodice.

'Thank you, Mama,' Lucy said. 'Did you see this wonderful string of pearls Lord Ravenscar sent me? It has a diamond clasp that you can wear at the front if you wish. Paul sent me these earrings and a bracelet to match. Was that not thoughtful of them both?'

'I expected no less,' her mama said and nodded in a satisfied way. 'I am convinced that they will spoil you, my love. Lord Ravenscar told me how pleased he was that you would be his daughter-in-law.'

'Yes, I dare say they may spoil me, for already I dare not say I like something or it is instantly mine,' Lucy replied with a laugh. 'I was a little anxious lest Paul's father should become ill again, but the prospect of our wedding seems to have revived him. The doctor has warned us that he will be up and down for the rest of his life, but our wedding has given him such happiness. I believe he means to live until we have given him an heir.'

'Yes, I imagine it might.' Lady Dawlish frowned. 'Do you mind that he has asked *that* woman to live on the estate with her daughter?'

'You mean Rosalind Fullerton and little Lizzie?' Lucy shook her head serenely. 'Mark did not marry her when they were in Spain, which was remiss of him. If he promised her marriage, he should have kept his word. It was not well done of him, Mama—and he should not have asked me to marry him.'

'What I do not understand is why he proposed to you if—if he loved this woman.'

'I am sure he intended to marry her, but she was left behind when the army made a push into France. She was close to giving birth and they thought she would be better resting in a house they had hired. We are not sure what happened, but we believe that Mark must have been told that both she and her child had died of a fever. I believe it was in an effort to forget her and to put the past behind him that he proposed to me.'

'Well, really, it was too bad of him,' Lady Dawlish said. 'If he had not been so thoughtless, he might have spared you so much pain.'

'Yes,' Lucy agreed. 'I sensed a change in him just before he died, Mama—and I believe he'd learned that Rosalind was still alive. He did not know how to tell me, for a gentleman cannot withdraw—but if I had told him of my doubts, he would have spoken I am sure. If only he had not been murdered, all might have been settled years since.'

'Well, I suppose it hardly matters now,' her

mama said. 'You are happy now, my love—and that is all that matters to me.'

'Thank you, Mama,' Lucy said and looked towards the door as someone knocked and then entered. 'Judith, you have arrived in time. I was afraid that you might not.'

'We were not sure we could get a passage in time,' Judith said and came to embrace her. 'But, as I told Elver, I must get here somehow. We came over on a merchant ship, which was not particularly comfortable, but the crossing was fair and here we are.'

Lucy hugged her. 'I am so pleased you are here, Cousin. Tell me, are you happy?'

'I shall leave you to talk,' Lady Dawlish said, looking from one to the other. 'You must both be ready in half an hour so do not forget.'

Lucy looked at Judith's face as the door closed behind her mother. 'Tell me truly, my love—is all well with you?'

'Very much so,' Judith replied. 'Elver is determined to spoil me, but I do not mind it, because I love him…Yes, truly, it is so, Lucy. Even when I took him I was not sure, but I know now that I could not have chosen better. I feel so lucky to be alive—and much of that is due to you, Cousin.'

'I did very little…it was just a push…'

'But that was not all. You saved my life twice. If you had not realised something was wrong the night I was abducted, I might have died before anyone found me.'

'Well, you did not,' Lucy said. 'We shall not think of it again, Judith. Your gown is waiting in your room; you must change, while my maid finishes putting up my hair, for I do not wish to keep Paul waiting.'

Paul turned to look as the music started. The bride was fashionably late, but only by a few minutes, and to his mind she was worth every second he had waited…including the years of desperate longing when he had thought she was beyond his reach.

He smiled as she came to stand beside him, the delicate scent of her perfume arousing his senses so that he longed to take her in his arms and kiss her. Lucy's face was visible through the fine veil she wore over her pale-pink satin bonnet. The veil had threads of silver and was trimmed with deep-pink roses, which matched the posy of roses that she carried. They were tied with silver ribbons, the pink of her bonnet the only touch of colour about her.

She looked young and innocent, which he knew her to be, and the thought of teaching his lovely young wife the pleasures of love were uppermost in his mind as he thought of the coming night.

How often he had lain in a lonely bed and wished that she were by his side. For a long time he had believed that his desires were foolish and forced himself to forget the need she had aroused in him, but now his dream was about to be re-alised and the love swelled in his breast as he looked at her with pride.

She was the woman he had loved all his life, for years as a playmate and a friend, and she would continue to be his friend throughout their lives because they had always thought so much alike.

The vicar had begun to intone the marriage service. Paul gave his answers in a clear voice that carried, as did she. Then he lifted the veil and looked down at her sweet face, kissing her softly on the mouth.

'I now pronounce you man and wife...'

Taking his lady by the hand, Paul led her first to the high altar and then to the vestry to sign the register. Then they were arm in arm and walking from the chapel to the sound of bells ringing out joyously. In the distance the church bells had also begun, a tribute from the village to the marriage of a popular young couple.

Outside in the sunshine, Paul glanced down at his wife, his right eyebrow arching. 'Good morning, Mrs Ravenscar,' he said, a teasing smile on his lips. 'I trust you are happy, for it is too late to change your mind now—what is mine is mine.'

Lucy laughed, for she knew he was teasing her in his old way—the way he had teased her all their lives. Sometimes she had been cross with him when they were children playing; she would strike his chest and he would pull her hair, but the bond between them had always been there as they followed their leader and basked in his glory.

Now Lucy knew that she had always been his. Her foolish heart had betrayed her for a short time, but she had soon come to realise that it was Paul she loved.

'It is all I wish to be,' she said and took his hand.

Together, they ran laughing to the carriage as

they were showered with rose petals and rice. Once inside, Paul picked some petals from her bonnet, his eyes sparkling with love and laughter. He reached out to untie the strings of her very fetching bonnet, removing it so that he could kiss her thoroughly.

'Just in case I haven't told you, Mrs Ravenscar, I love you so much that I have no words to tell you what I feel.'

Lucy sighed with contentment and kissed him back.

They were staying one night at one of Paul's smaller estates, before making a trip to Paris. It had been arranged that Jenny and Adam should stay with Lord Ravenscar while they were away on their wedding trip, though it was to be only of ten days' duration.

'You must go for as long as you wish,' Lord Ravenscar had told Lucy when he kissed her goodbye after the reception. 'I shall be perfectly all right with my nephew and Jenny—and I have my little granddaughter now to keep me company.'

'She is a little darling and you can see something of Mark in her,' Lucy had told him. 'But if it pleases you, sir, I should like to make a start on refurbishing our apartments. It will give me great pleasure to choose materials and furniture.'

It was Lord Ravenscar's gift to them. The west wing had some large and beautiful rooms, but the décor was in need of refreshment and the furniture heavy and outdated. Lucy had already planned her colours for their apartments and she thought they might purchase some fine French furniture while in Paris.

Now, as she sat before the dressing mirror brushing her long hair, having dismissed her maid for the night, she heard the door open behind her and turned to greet her husband with a smile.

'Paul, my love,' she said and stood up, holding out both hands to him. 'This is a pretty house. Is it where you would have lived had you not become the heir to Ravenscar?'

'Yes. My maternal grandfather left it to me,' he said. 'I usually stay here once or twice a year.'

'Then we shall do so,' Lucy told him as she lifted her face for his kiss. 'I like it very well and should have been happy to make it my home had we not Ravenscar.'

'I am glad,' he said and bent his head to kiss her on the lips.

Light at first, his kiss deepened as her lips parted to allow the delicate intrusion of his tongue. She sighed and pressed herself closer, feeling the arousal of his desire though the thin silk of her night chemise and his dressing robe.

Sweeping her up in his arms, Paul carried her to their bed, which smelled of lavender and roses. He placed her carefully on the linen sheets and then removed his robe. He was naked beneath it and Lucy saw at once how urgent was his need.

He was so tall and strong, his limbs well formed and lean—all muscle and no fat was the thought that came to her mind—and she shivered in delight as he lay beside her, kissing her until she, too, raged with desire.

Her nightgown was removed as she lay without moving, because he wanted to look at her. So long did he gaze down at her that she wriggled and reached up to touch him.

'Is something wrong?'

'No. You are perfect. You always look lovely, Lucy, but I have wanted to see you this way for so long...'

And then he kissed her again, not stopping at her lips, but covering her face, throat and breasts with little feathery kisses that made her gasp and wriggle as she felt sensation sweep through her— heat and need, a tingling between her thighs.

Paul kissed all the way down her navel, to the soft curls that covered her mound of Venus, and then between her thighs, to her very toes. Lucy sighed and wriggled in the sheets, her body arching as if it begged—for what she hardly knew.

His hand was gently parting her legs, stroking her soft flesh before moving to the part of her that craved attention. His fingers stroked her there and she felt the moisture begin to trickle down her thigh and she moaned, arching her head back and her hips forward as he lavished attention on that part of her that had never been touched by a man before this night.

She was aflame with passion, panting, her body reaching out to his in urgent need as he slid his body up hers and she felt the heat of his pulsing manhood against her thigh. She whispered his name and he slid into her, her wetness welcoming him until his hardness pressed against her hymen and then he broke through. She stilled and whimpered a little, for it hurt her, but then his lips were on hers and he begged for forgiveness. She told him none was needed and pressed her body to his, begging him to continue what he had begun.

At first a little sore, she was swept on a tide of passion, panting, her body moving with his in perfect harmony until he gave a cry and emptied his seed inside her.

'My darling…' he murmured as he clasped her to him. 'My perfect little love.'

Lucy lay within the circle of his arms. Although his loving had hurt her a little at first, she knew instinctively that it must always be so the first time. She had received so much pleasure from his gentle loving that she anticipated further happiness in the future and the tears that trickled down her cheeks were those of happiness.

'Have I hurt you too much?' Paul whispered. She shook her head, snuggling against his naked shoulder. 'It should not hurt next time, my darling.'

'I know,' she said and kissed him. 'I am happy, Paul. I have wondered what loving truly was and now I know. It is all I could have hoped and more…'

She burrowed into him like a little trusting kitten as he held her, and after a while they slept.

At some period in the night she became aware that he was awake, looking at her. She smiled and touched his cheek tentatively, wondering what he wanted of her.

When he knew that she was no longer sleeping, Paul kissed her again, making love to her slowly with his hands, his mouth and his tongue. He brought her gradually to such a climax that she screamed and clawed at his shoulder, her body shaking with the force of her pleasure as she was swept away on an avalanche of pleasure.

It was only afterwards that she realised he had not taken his own pleasure and shyly asked him why.

'You would be too sore,' he murmured against her ear. 'But do not think I had no pleasure from yours—it gave me a wonderful feeling to see you so lost to everything but the pleasure of love, Lucy. You must always be the same, my darling. Never lose what we have together.'

'How could I when all I want is to be with you like this?' she said. 'I love you, Paul. I love you so very much.'

'And I love you,' he said. 'I have waited for you and I almost lost you…but nothing shall ever part us again for the rest of our lives.'

\* \* \* \* \*

Discover more romance at

# www.millsandboon.co.uk

- ❤ WIN great prizes in our exclusive competitions

- ❤ BUY new titles before they hit the shops

- ❤ BROWSE new books and REVIEW your favourites

- ❤ SAVE on new books with the Mills & Boon® Bookclub™

- ❤ DISCOVER new authors

PLUS, to chat about your favourite reads, get the latest news and find special offers:

- ❤ Find us on facebook.com/millsandboon
- ❤ Follow us on twitter.com/millsandboonuk
- ❤ Sign up to our newsletter at millsandboon.co.uk